SOUL
STORM

SOUL STORM

Kate Harrison

Indigo

First published in Great Britain in 2013
by Indigo
a division of the Orion Publishing Group Ltd
Orion House
5 Upper St Martin's Lane
London WC2H 9EA
An Hachette UK company

1 3 5 7 9 10 8 6 4 2

A catalogue record for this book
is available from the British Library.

ISBN 978 1 78062 025 1

Typeset by Input Data Services Ltd, Bridgwater, Somerset

Printed and bound by CPI Group (UK) Ltd, Croydon, CRO 4YY

The Orion Publishing Group's policy is to use papers
that are natural, renewable and recyclable products made
from wood grown in sustainable forests. The logging and
manufacturing processes are expected to conform to the
environmental regulations of the country of origin.

www.orionbooks.co.uk

To Amber, for believing in the Beach and
helping to make it even stormier ...

Loneliness is worse than death.

It rots you from the inside out, making you disappear. I avoid mirrors, because I am afraid I will see a space where I should be. And when I accidentally catch a glimpse of my reflection in a window, I am surprised at how solid I look. How 'normal'.

All that keeps me going is the knowledge that, one day soon, the loneliness will end. When I confide in the right person, I know I will finally be understood.

Now, I think of what happened to Meggie as a dress rehearsal. I didn't remember my lines, or the right time to exit. It was a failure on my part that meant Meggie and I both suffered more than necessary.

Yet the lessons I learned from Meggie will benefit her sister – how bittersweet is that?

This time, I will get it right. I can only hope that Alice is intelligent enough to understand her role. To realise it is in her interests to be understanding.

1

I think she's following me. Again.

I check the mirror. Nothing. Signal. Move into the kerb, then pull the handbrake, hard.

Check the mirror once more. *Where is she hiding?*

My instructor is smiling. 'The test should be a doddle, Alice. You've good motor control, and your hazard awareness is excellent for someone of your age. When I taught your sister, she seemed oblivious to the rest of the world . . .'

He stops, blushing all the way across the dome of his bald head.

'It's OK,' I say. 'I don't mind it when people talk about her. We don't have to pretend she never existed.'

He takes a deep breath. 'Of course. I just meant – well, you have the makings of a very safe driver, Alice. Confident, but observant, too.'

I won't tell him that I love driving because it gives me eyes in the back of my head, and a hard shell of metal to protect me. And because the car lets me cover more ground than I could ever hope to on foot.

'Thanks, Mr Gregory. So – next Monday, eleven thirty. My date with fate.'

He nods. 'You've got some practice drives set up this weekend?'

'With friends, yes.'

'Don't pick up any bad habits between now and then. Hopefully you should be on the road on your own by Monday afternoon.'

'Thanks.' I'm about to climb out of the car when I see something in the rear-view mirror. It's hot, even for July, and the street is busy with sunburned shoppers, but I'm certain that *was* her.

Well, as certain as I can be.

'Alice? Time to let go of the reins now.' He taps the steering wheel and I release the seatbelt, bracing myself to leave the one place I feel in control. 'You can't wait to be in the driving seat full-time, can you?'

I fake a smile. When I step out, the pavement feels spongy under my feet, and goosebumps ripple across my skin, even though the sun is scorching hot.

Out here, I am completely exposed.

I look for her wiry body, straw-coloured hair, pale face. If she *was* following me, she's found a way to disappear. Town shouldn't be this busy on a Thursday afternoon, but the pavements are full of people shopping for their holidays.

Crowds are perfect cover.

'Watch it.'

A skateboarder misses me by millimetres after I step right in front of him.

'Sorry . . .'

He's already gone, the death-head design on his t-shirt getting smaller and smaller.

I try to slow my breathing, think straight. Why would she follow me? I'll be seeing her on Sunday; she's always got another visit planned, whether I want to see her or not. So there's no logical reason for her to snoop on me.

But logic can't explain that feeling of darkness. The same one I felt in my sister's old uni room, and on the smoky streets of Barcelona, and at Tim's inquest.

It's stronger than a feeling. It's instinct.

'. . . bridge o-ver tr-ou-u-bled water . . .'

Two girls I half recognise from school are busking on the

4

street corner. They smile at me, and I smile back. As I pass, they exchange glances with each other. I know what people think of me. Yeah, Meggie's death was a tragedy, but the word on the school corridor is that I should have got over it by now.

If only they knew how hard I've tried to move on. But the visit on Sunday isn't a *choice*. It's not like I *want* to hang out with someone I suspect of killing two people, and almost murdering a third.

Of course what I'm doing could be dangerous. Stupid. No one sane would willingly get close to a potential psychopath. But how else can I get justice for the people I've lost? First, my sister, murdered in a way that the entire world agreed was motivated by possessiveness or jealousy. Then her boyfriend, Tim, killed in a staged suicide attempt that had everyone fooled except me and his closest friend, Zoe. And where is Zoe now? She's in a coma, after an 'accident' in Barcelona that no one witnessed.

The world has accepted that everything was wrapped up by Tim's 'suicide'. That he was responsible for my sister's murder. So why can't I let it lie?

Because my gut tells me my stalker's guilty, just as it convinces me she's tracking me like prey right now, when she should be studying twenty miles away.

It wouldn't be the first time she's done it. Last week, as I ate my lunch alone on the far side of the playing field, that same icy sensation spread through me, the feeling of being watched. But I dismissed it as paranoia: till I walked straight into her outside the school gates, three hours later. She blushed, insisting she was 'just passing'.

Since then, I've realised I *must* listen to my instincts. And my instincts say that only one person knows the truth about my sister's death.

Sahara.

2

Warm rain starts the second the final bell goes, but that doesn't stop Cara racing out into the playground, throwing off her jumper and dancing like a banshee.

'Seven weeks of FREEDOM! Seven weeks of boys, beaches and . . .' she tries to think of a third 'b' and then a huge grin transforms her face, 'BOOZE!'

I laugh. 'Yeah. I reckon you'll come back from the Caribbean looking like a piña colada.'

'I hope I'll be browner than that. More like a rum punch.' Cara's mum has arranged a bonding holiday for the two of them at a health spa in Bermuda. I give it twelve hours before they're screaming at each other. 'You could still come, you know.'

'Mum and Dad aren't exactly keen on me leaving the country. Not after Barcelona.'

Cara stops dancing. Her blouse has gone transparent in the rain, and the lads from the boys' school opposite are pointing. 'But they're happy to let you hang out with Sahara and Ade, the gruesome twosome?'

'Er, four weeks ago you thought he was a sex god.'

'No, I didn't.'

'You should see a doctor about your memory, Cara.' Before we went to Spain, she drooled over his pale Scandinavian looks and planned to steal him from Sahara, even though he'd been dating her for years.

Cara smiles. 'OK. Maybe I did think he was averagely hot. But that was before I realised that he and Sahara deserve each other.'

Like everyone else, she believes what happened to Zoe in Barcelona was accidental. But now she associates Ade and Sahara with our ordeal at the hospital, and the police interrogation, and our awful encounter with Zoe's devastated parents.

Thank goodness. Avoiding Sahara and Ade will keep her safe. I couldn't forgive myself if something happened to *Cara* too.

'I'll give them your love when I see them on Sunday then, shall I?'

Cara groans. 'Jeez, Alice, why are *you* still hanging out with them?'

'I need the driving practice. And they've got a car.'

'*I've* got a car.'

'Yeah, and three points for speeding even though you've been driving less than a month. I don't think I should be taking lessons from you.'

She laughs, but only for a second. 'Promise me – once you pass your test, you'll stop seeing them?'

There's nothing I'd rather do than ignore their endless calls and texts, and consign the two of them to the past.

But I'm getting closer. Once I've made sure the world knows what Sahara did, it'll be over, for good.

It's what I want more than anything . . . though it will come at a price. Because if . . . no, *when* I've finally got justice for Meggie – and Tim and Zoe – I'm scared I'll lose the most precious thing in my life. Time on Soul Beach with my sister, and the boy I love.

'Alice?'

'It's nearly over,' I say. I long to confide in her, but the few times I've hinted at my suspicions, she's always got that worried look.

Even now, she is watching me closely, her brow furrowed. 'It's over already, hon. Tim's inquest made it absolutely clear.

He killed himself because he couldn't live with the guilt after killing your sister. But you've got your whole life ahead of you and you need to make the most of it. Especially after what happened to Zoe . . .'

I nod. 'I'll be ready to let go soon, honestly.'

She tuts, not believing me. I think she's about to say something else, but then she shakes her head and begins to run, heading for the river.

I run, too. Once we get as far as the bench that overlooks the lock, she reaches into her bag and pulls out two party bottles of champagne, shakes them and gives one to me.

'Three, two, one . . .' we chant, slightly out of breath. 'GO!'

When we pop the corks, most of the sticky fizz spills out onto the riverbank. She groans, but I'm relieved; I need to keep a clear head at the moment.

Cara knocks her bottle against mine, then swigs. 'Cheers, honey. Hey, when's Lewis back from San Francisco?'

'Tomorrow, I think.'

'Can't *he* give you driving lessons?'

'Not on the road. Can you imagine what he'd do if I scratched his car?'

She raises her eyebrows. 'Lewis would forgive you if you smashed it into a brick wall and wrote it off. He *lurves* you.'

I shake my head. 'Rubbish. He's the big brother I never had. He feels responsible for me.'

Cara sighs. 'If you say so. Though at least I know he'll be looking out for you while I'm away. If I thought you only had the ghouls for company, I'd cancel my bloody holiday.'

'And miss out on boys, beaches and booze?'

'OK. Maybe that would be a step too far.' She throws her arm round me. 'You know me too well, Alice. I'm just hoping that by the time I get back, you'll be the Alice I knew before. Fully licensed to drive and ready for a summer of fun and games.'

3

On Soul Beach, it's fun and games all year round.

Well, if you're a Guest, like Meggie and Danny, it is. If you're a Visitor, like me, things are more complicated.

When I log on, it's the middle of the day. Brunch time. I see azure skies. Green birds with orange wings. Calm turquoise water.

But it's the dead people who catch my eye, as they always do. Half a dozen beautiful kids jamming on the steps of the beach bar. Blissed-out couples leaning on rough-barked palms, smooching, staring into each other's eyes, knowing they have all the time in the world. Ice clinking against crystal as Guests carry jugs full of ruby and mint-green cocktails to their friends, to while away yet another perfect afternoon in a barely-there haze.

A flash of something fire-bright from a metal barrel, the smell of smoke, a silver bullet shining in bright sunlight as it speeds towards me—

Then darkness.

'Oops, sorry.'

I open my eyes to see the girl who's just brushed past me. She has an open face, a string of heavy-scented lilies around her neck and dark eyes.

Gunmetal grey.

She drifts off towards her boyfriend, leaving me with the chilling memory of her last moments. So she died in a shoot-out. Each Guest has his or her own tragedy, most of them bloody, all of them horribly unjust.

That's why the Beach is so beautiful: to help them forget.

But these days I'm never allowed to forget. As a Visitor I'm part-confessor, part-detective. The Guests tell me their secrets and beg me for help in making things right in my world. They want me to seek justice or warn the loved ones they left behind. And when I succeed – as I have, twice – I am granted new powers: first, the sense of touch and now . . .

Since I helped my friend Javier, I've been able to experience what a Guest went through in their last moments of consciousness. If I touch them, it's almost as though I *become* them, see what they saw and feel what they felt before they died.

Maybe this brand new power is designed to make me seek justice for even more Guests. But this latest 'gift' is more like a curse.

'Florrie!' My sister is striding across the sand, calling out the silly nickname she has for me, the one no one else is allowed to use. Her long fair hair trails behind her in the sea breeze like a silk scarf. She's wearing a bronze bikini which emphasises how pale her skin is compared to the other Guests': white-gold, instead of deep tan.

I flinch before she throws her arms around me, bracing myself for *her* last vision. At least it's weaker every time, as though the effect is wearing off. Maybe even the Management realise an endless replay of death would be enough to drive a Visitor crazy.

Assuming I'm not crazy already and this whole virtual reality is not a figment of my grieving imagination.

I take a step back, buying time. 'Meggie! You smell of pineapples.'

'It's the cocktail of the day. Vodka, fresh fruit, honey. The Soul Beach Sweetie.'

She hugs me.

Gloved hands bear down on me, and a pillow covers my eyes, turning light to dark.

This is Meggie's memory, yet it feels as though it happened to me. It makes no sense, but nothing here does – like the fact that I can talk to my big sister.

Or the way I've fallen in love with a boy who died almost two years ago.

That boy is running across the bar towards me, smiling with relief, as though he never thought he'd see me again. Neither of us can ever be *quite* sure.

'Alice, you're early today,' Danny calls out.

'Because school's out!' I laugh.

His moss-green eyes shine. Every time I see him, I wonder what he sees in *me*. He's incredibly handsome, but in a crumpled way that doesn't hint at the privileged life he lived before the Beach.

As we touch, I feel the jolt as an image forms in my mind. However hard I try to focus on the warmth of his lips, the chill of his last moments passes through me. Burnt orange earth speeds towards me at a thousand miles an hour. Every time I hope it might be different, that the plane will recover its stability before it smashes into the desert.

But it never does.

Tim hovers in the background, with Meggie. We should make the perfect foursome: me and Danny, plus my sister and *her* first love. But even though the Beach has smoothed Tim's frown lines, made his hair more strawberry-blond than copper, he still keeps his distance. Maybe there's something about his final moments he doesn't want me to see.

No. Tim was innocent, whatever the police said. Otherwise, my sister would surely sense it, keep away.

Danny kisses me again, and the red earth is fuzzier, less menacing this time.

'What news, Alice?' Danny asks me.

'Summer's here. Cara's going to the Caribbean. I'm staying at home.'

Here, I stick to the meaningless trivia that makes up my boring routine. Guests love to hear about school, and music, and especially the seasons: the smoky smell of autumn, the chill of winter, the first flowers of spring.

So as I read Danny's face, I'm surprised at how bored he looks by the idea of summer.

Then I realise: why would he be interested when every day is summer on the Beach?

'Why aren't you going on vacation?' He's trying to hide his relief, but he's hopeless at lying to me.

I shrug. 'Dad's busy with work. They're talking about a big holiday at Christmas. Australia, New Zealand.'

'Wow. I always wanted to go there.' He'd have made the perfect Bondi surfer dude, with his soft blond curls and hard, muscular legs.

'I'll make sure I tell you every detail.' Except Christmas is almost half a year away. Who knows what'll happen between now and then?

'What will you do with your spare time? Aside from spend it with me?'

'If I pass my driving test next week, I'll have . . .' I'm about to say 'freedom', but it seems too cruel, '. . . wheels. Mum's, of course. Not my own. Plus I might get a holiday job.'

'Oh, get a room, you two!' my sister says, then beckons us towards the sea. Tim has grabbed a bucket of cold beers and a few bowls of ice cream from the beach bar, so I pull away from Danny and the four of us head for the water's edge.

As I sit down, the sand under my body is slightly damp. It cools me. I try not to analyse the sensations too much, because it's hard not to doubt my own sanity . . .

Too late. The doubts accelerate; my real surroundings

close in on me again, in lurid focus. The duvet cover with its retro tulips pattern. The pile of schoolbooks in the corner that I don't intend to look at again till September. The driving test paperwork.

The Beach is a website. *Nothing I feel can be real.*

'Florrie, don't zone out on us, babe.'

My sister touches me on the arm. The image of the killer's black leather gloves lasts less than a fraction of a second this time, but it's enough to remind me of my responsibilities to her.

I focus on Meggie's swimming-pool-blue eyes, on the kinked white streak in her blonde hair that I've never noticed before. After she was killed, the murderer combed her hair, fanned it out against the pillow so that Zoe – who found her – said she looked like an angel.

'Florrie!'

'Sorry. I was thinking of something else.'

'Right.' Her eyes have darkened. She looks at Tim, who nods, slowly. 'Maybe this is a good time to talk.'

'About what?'

She sighs. 'About this. Here. It's wrong, me expecting you to be with me the whole time.'

I shake my head. 'No. It's cool. I want to be here too. We're sisters.'

But Meggie's still frowning. 'Just because we *want* to be together, doesn't mean we should be. This isn't a good place. Tim thinks—'

'What are you talking about?' I break in.

'The sun and the sea are just disguising the reality. This is a dark place.'

A breaker crashes, spraying me with foam. I turn to Tim. 'What have you been saying? I don't need you babying me. We got along just fine before you showed up.'

He steps back, as though he's been slapped.

13

'Don't blame him, Alice,' Meggie says, softly. 'He's got your best interests at heart. I've been too selfish to see that the time you spend here . . . it's like being in a cemetery, or a ward full of the dying. It's not what a sixteen-year-old should be doing.'

'Seventeen,' I correct her.

Meggie blushes. 'Sorry. I lose track here, which is the whole point I guess. But that's part of the problem. You can't move on.' She takes a deep breath. 'Neither of us can.'

At first I don't understand what she means. Then it hits me. 'This isn't for my benefit at all, is it? You just want more time alone with *him.*' I point at Tim.

'Alice. NO!' The shock on her face makes me realise I've got it wrong. 'I'd love you to be here all the time, but we're bad for you.'

'In case you've forgotten, I'm your only hope of getting justice, Meggie. Or doesn't that matter to you any more?'

Her eyes are locked onto mine. 'It matters, oh, God, it matters. This place is a prison and there is nothing I want more than to leave the Beach behind. To find peace. To know the right person has been punished, whoever that person is. But there is one thing that matters more: your future.'

The waves – the first thing I heard on the Beach – are getting louder, and the heat of the sun makes my head throb. I'm losing any sense of what she really wants. I reach out for Danny, ignore the brief vertigo as I 'fall' yet again. 'Are you in on all this?'

He squirms. 'It's a horrible situation. I don't want to lose you. I love you more than anything. But I don't have anything to offer you except this,' he waves at the Beach, 'and *this* is not enough. I won't ask you to sacrifice yourself for an afterlife of limbo.'

Why does he look guilty? Then I realise. 'Have you talked

about this behind my back? Decided it's time for little Alice to get on with her little life in the normal world, leaving you to live your *special* lives without me?'

Meggie steps towards me. 'You've got it wrong. You're the one with the power here, the power to get away, live your life.'

'But you *have* talked about me?'

Meggie's eyes are cloudy again. 'Of course. Endlessly. And I've lain awake, night after night, wondering what to do. God knows I didn't care about being selfish when I was alive, but this is too serious to get wrong.'

I want to tell her she's not selfish, that I'm sorry for shouting. But there's something I need to ask first. 'What do you want more, Meggie? For me to leave . . . or to escape yourself?'

The longer she stays silent, the more afraid I become.

Everything I've done since I first visited the Beach – trying to work out its secret rules, helping Javier and Triti get away, staying close to Sahara even though she makes my skin crawl – I've done for Meggie.

I can't bear it if all I've managed to do is make her even more unhappy.

'I want everything to be the same as it was, Florrie. To be alive. For all this to be a bad dream we're going to wake up from any moment now. But it can't happen.'

'Come here, Meggie.' I hold out my arms, bracing myself for the familiar vision of the pillow and the gloves. But it's so faint now that it's no more than a cloud across the sun as she falls into my arms. 'I can't turn back time, but I can put things right. Help you get away.'

I don't spell it out – once, I was banned from the Beach for saying too much. But she knows that justice is the key to her escape from 'paradise'.

'I'm afraid of that too, little sis.'

No one knows what comes next: somewhere even more

beautiful, or nothingness? By the end Triti and Javier both craved oblivion, a final resting place.

'It might be wonderful,' I tell her.

My sister's face changes. 'No, I'm not afraid of that. What terrifies me is that it might go wrong.'

'How could things be any worse for you, Meggie?'

'You really don't know?' She laughs bitterly. 'The killer could get you too, Florrie. Then we'd *both* be stuck here forever. And it would be my fault.'

I shake my head. It's not that I think I'm immortal, or protected. How could I? Two people I know have died in twelve months. Another is technically alive, but beyond help. Life is cheap.

'I understand the risks, Meggie, but I can't stop now.'

She shakes her head. 'Believe me, it's nothing like you think. The bleakness is the worst. And it's not just you. It's our parents, too.'

I step backwards, stumbling on the sand. We never talk about them. What could I say? Tell the truth: how her murder blew our family to pieces like a grenade? How Mum's still going to counselling with that creep Olav? How Dad has whole weeks where the only place he can sleep is slumped over his desk at work?

'Meggie, let's not go there.'

'I will if it's the only way to make you realise what you're risking.'

Tim and Danny are keeping their distance; this is about family.

'Are you saying you don't want me to come? Or that you want me to stop going after . . .' I just stop myself mentioning Sahara's name, 'the person who killed you?'

Meggie reaches for my hand again, and I let her take it. 'I'm not talking about you leaving right *now*. I couldn't bear it. But this can't go on forever.'

'I think I'm getting closer, Meggie,' I whisper.

'To what?'

'To knowing for certain. To finding the proof we need.'

She gulps. 'I *do* still want to know who murdered me. And I want the world to know, too. But that has to come second to your safety. When I was alive, I thought the world revolved around me but now I know better. I'm the past. A reality TV star-to-be that never was.'

'You *still* are a star. So many people remember your music. And you deserve justice.'

She says nothing for a moment. 'Sometimes I forget how much you've grown up, how strong you are. But that doesn't mean you're indestructible. Promise me you'll never put yourself at risk.'

I hesitate. 'I promise I won't do anything crazy.'

'I suppose I'll have to settle for that.' And she does the strangest thing: lifts my hand to her lips and kisses it, like I'm royalty. Tim whispers something in her ear, and she smiles and turns, walking away from me slowly but purposefully, towards the jetty. 'Time to leave you two lovebirds in peace.'

Danny's behind me: puts his arms around my waist and turns me round.

Red earth speeding towards me. Weightlessness.

'You were wrong, Danny,' I say, when the image fades. 'What you said before. I'm not sacrificing anything to be with you.'

But he's still frowning. 'You might not always feel that way. I'm scared you'll throw away your future on us. On me.'

'It's my future to throw away.'

'Sure, I know. I know. Don't hate me for wanting what's best for you.'

'I don't *hate* you, Danny. But I wish everyone round here would stop treating me like a kid.' I try to break away but he holds on to my hand.

'Don't go. Let's forget all that. Hang out. Watch the surfers. Listen to the birds. After all, it's vacation time!'

'I'd rather kiss than watch the surfers,' I say.

So we do.

4

'I'm not sure the world is ready for you behind the wheel, Ali.'

Maybe Lewis is joking. Then again, my reverse parking isn't up to its usual standards. For some reason, I keep getting flustered, even though we're the only people in the car park of a derelict warehouse. I can't get insurance to drive his fancy silver convertible on the road, plus I doubt he'd trust me with the super-shiny paintwork in traffic.

I'm not sure I'd trust me either.

'I'm normally better. You're making me nervous,' I say.

He runs his hand through his thick hair so it stands on end: always a sign he's under stress. 'You and me both. Can we take a break?'

I press a button to switch the engine off. *That's* how swanky his car is. He doesn't even have a normal ignition key.

'You've got me worried now. My driving instructor said I was ready, but—'

'I'm only teasing. You're great. Enviable control of your steering. Reversing is slow but sure. And that funny thing you do with your tongue – poking it out when you're changing gear – is a bloody winner!'

I punch him on the arm. 'Oi, you're meant to be encouraging me.'

'Seriously. It's cute. So long as your examiner is a bloke, you'll be laughing.'

I tut. 'Just because *you* passed first time.'

'Yeah, well, I had a *female* examiner. Worked the old

geeky charm on her. Not only did I change gear as smoothly as a racing driver, I kept up a running commentary on the workings of the engine, too. She gave me an A star. And then asked for my number.'

'Wow!' I say. 'I didn't realise they let people become driving instructors when they had eyesight that bad.'

But I've been noticing lately that women *do* seem to fancy Lewis. A particular kind of girl seems to like that long, lean body and the mad scientist hair and the designer glasses (which I know for a fact have clear glass in them, even though he insists they were prescribed to counteract the glare of all the computer stuff he does).

Luckily I have Danny, otherwise I might get a crush on Lewis myself. And that would *really* mess things up.

'So what's the first journey you'll take when you've passed, Ali?'

I shrug. 'Not sure.'

He gives me a sideways look. 'Really? Only I had it all planned out. I went to London, in the middle of the night, just because I could. Drove round the sights. Past Westminster. Along Buckingham Palace Road. The Embankment. Felt like James Bond.'

'Lucky you didn't get arrested as a potential terrorist.'

'I *did* get stopped by the police, actually. Even when I had my old car, they couldn't believe a kid like me could afford a decent set of wheels.'

'Show-off.'

Lewis blushes through his San Fran tan. He's not *really* a show-off. I honestly believe he bought this car because he appreciates its engineering, not to impress other people.

'Can't believe you haven't got a maiden voyage planned in your mum's Polo.'

I'm pretty good at lying these days but Lewis is the only one who can see through me. The truth is, I know *exactly* where I'll go if I pass. I also know he wouldn't approve. 'The seaside, maybe.'

'Ri-ight.' He's not buying that.

Neither of us says anything for a while.

'How—'

'What—'

We both talk at once.

'Ladies first,' he says.

'I was going to say, what about I take you out for the day when I pass? A magical mystery tour,' I say, 'as a thank-you for being so impatient with me.'

'That sounds very nice. But don't you mean patient?'

'No, no. I respond much better to threats. The idea that I'm about to be thrown out of the car and will have to walk home works very well for me.'

Lewis pulls a face. 'Yeah. You're right, I guess. My intolerance comes of spending so much time working for myself. I can be pretty impatient.'

'I wouldn't say that. The way you . . .' I stop.

He raises his eyebrows at me. 'The way I?'

'All of Zoe's photos. You were patient going through those. But I know we're trying not to mention that.'

'The elephant in the room. Or the car,' he says, running his hand through his hair again. 'I suppose it was too much to expect that we could get through an entire afternoon without death rearing its ugly head.'

'Perhaps.' I try not to sound hurt but I'm not sure I manage it.

'Sorry, Ali. That came out harsher than I intended. It's just sometimes I hope that maybe you might want more than . . .' he stops.

'I might want what?'

'Ah, nothing. You know I'm happy to talk about it anytime.'

Except, when I'm with Lewis, I think about 'it' less than

when I'm around other people. Plus, I don't feel that constant anxiety about being watched. This afternoon, I've looked in my rear-view mirror the *normal* number of times, i.e. not every millisecond. Sure, Sahara would be easy to spot in this deserted car park, but it's more than that.

Lewis makes me feel safe.

He knows more about me, and my fears, than anyone else. OK, I haven't told him about the Beach, because he's a scientist and he might think I'm mad. But he knows more about my campaign for justice than Cara or my parents.

'I still can't believe the photos revealed nothing new.'

'I might find something else. There are a few left.'

We both know he's just trying to make me feel better. We've pored over every pixel of the photos Zoe had on her computer. Freakish pictures we're certain must have been taken by the killer. Tim found them and left them in a safe place for Zoe to collect if anything happened to him.

Pictures of my sister alive. Pictures of my sister's hand, after she died. Her lips on a glass.

And one more photo – that single close-up of *my* eyes. The surest sign that I could be next.

But there's nothing we could take to the police to make them reopen the investigation. Sahara is as devious as she is deadly. I Googled 'psychopath' after we got home from Spain. The search results summed it up:

Grandiose sense of self-importance

Like believing the whole world is out to get her.

Pathological lying

Like insisting she was my sister's best friend, even though I know they fell out before she died.

Cunning/manipulative

Like fooling the world into thinking someone else killed Meggie.

'So. Shall we call it a day and try again tomorrow, Ali?' Lewis breaks into my thoughts.

'I'd love to, but I need real, on-road practice and I can't ask you to let me do that in your super-car. Ade and Sahara have offered.'

His upper lip curls. 'How nice of them to come all the way from Greenwich to help you.' Lewis isn't as obvious as Cara, but he thinks the same: that spending time with them is doing me no good at all. Even though he understands why I do it.

'It *is* nice, isn't it?' I say.

I choose to ignore the worry in his eyes. He knows I think my sister's killer is still out there and that it must have been someone close to her. He's begged me dozens of times to leave it be.

But he also knows me well enough to understand that there's nothing he can say to stop me pursuing it to the bitter end.

5

'Alice! Watch out! There's a bollard. You're going to hit it! Brake. Brake! God, that was close!'

'Sorry, Sahara. I did see it, it's just . . .' *It's just that my driving gets so much worse when I'm in the car with the woman I suspect of killing my sister.*

I try not to giggle. I know it isn't even a joke. Just a hyper feeling I get when she's around. I'm on red alert in case she says anything that might reveal the truth.

'Oh, don't worry, Alice,' Sahara trills, calmer now. 'Last-minute nerves, eh?'

I look in the mirror. Ade's in the back, nodding. 'Alice, relax. You're an excellent driver. We wouldn't take you out in our car otherwise.'

Our car. They bought it last month, traded in their motorbike for a heavy black Scandinavian estate. They were planning to take it round Europe over the summer. It's big enough to take surfboards on the roof, and a mattress with the back seats down, but they've travelled no further than Richmond-on-Thames.

'They only got it so they could give you lessons,' Cara said, when I told her. 'They have no intention of letting you escape their clutches.'

They're getting more serious about each other: there's the car, plus next week they're moving in together. Or, rather, Sahara's moving into the flat that Ade used to share with Tim.

The flat where Tim was found dead with a plastic bag over his face.

'Maybe that's enough driving for today,' Sahara says. 'Shall we get a drink and you can tell us what else you've been up to?'

'There's good coffee back at my house.' I feel safer on home territory.

'Great. Drive on then, Alice!' She hits the steering wheel, like a rider would kick a horse to make it gallop. 'You should know the way!'

Dad's out and Mum's sunbathing in the garden, so I leave my freaky driving instructors in the living room while I put the kettle on.

From the kitchen, I can see them whispering but I can't hear what they're saying. They're leaning in close, which emphasises how strange they look together. Ade's pale, with delicate features and fine blond hair. He's not my type but he's attractive: Cara would never have fancied him if he wasn't.

Sahara is all masculine edges, with serious arm muscles and a horsey face. Relationships aren't just about looks, I know that, but I can't imagine her intense personality is attractive either. I used to feel guilty about judging her so harshly. Not any more. But I wish I could understand why Ade puts up with her.

As I walk into the room with the drinks, they freeze. The expression on Ade's face is hard to read, but it could be *fear*. Maybe he's scared to leave her.

'Cheer up, it might never happen,' I say and they both gawp at me. It's not the kind of thing *I* say.

'No biscuits?' Ade says, and when I put the tray down and turn to go back into the kitchen, he follows me. 'Go easy on her, please, Alice.'

I turn round from where I'm rummaging through the cupboards. 'What do you mean?'

'Just that she's more vulnerable than you might think.'

But before I can ask him anything else, he's taken a packet of cookies from my hand and gone back to his girlfriend.

'Yummy,' says Sahara. Her smile looks forced.

Over coffee, conversation is stilted. They talk about moving in together – apparently Ade is a clean freak, while Sahara snores louder than a pig. *Nice*. Then Sahara gets uppity about the fact that Ade can't help her pack because he's going home to his parents for a few days, and she drops hints about me driving over to help, once I've passed my test. Hints which I ignore . . .

Finally she gets the message, and switches to interrogating me about my uni applications and my social life – though she doesn't mention Cara – but then she runs out of steam. It's not surprising. We don't have anything in common except my sister.

I want to scream at the top of my voice: 'Did you kill her?' But with Ade here, it's pointless. He never leaves her alone for a second.

'I need to go and freshen up,' she says eventually.

Now's my chance to ask Ade what he meant by her being *vulnerable*.

But he's already smiling. 'You know, you're a great driver, Alice. Much better than I was as a learner. If you don't pass, then there's no justice in the world.'

I stare at him. I know it's only a phrase, but it gives me a way in. 'Yeah, well, I'm not a big believer in justice, Ade.'

He looks down at his coffee cup. 'I can understand why.'

I take my chance. 'Do you . . . I mean, have you ever wondered about what happened in Spain?'

His face doesn't change. 'What about it?'

'Zoe's accident. Plus everything before.' I shake my head. 'Sorry, I'm not putting this very well. Do you think what happened to Zoe *and* Tim *and* my sister . . . that there could be a connection?'

Ade's eyes are fixed on mine. I've never noticed their colour before: a kind of violet. 'I see why you might think that, Alice. Really. It's no wonder. I've spent endless sleepless nights wondering what we've done to deserve coming so close to death three times.'

'I can tell there's a *but* coming.'

'No. I mean, who knows? Perhaps there was more to it,' he says.

'Really?' I lean forward. Apart from Lewis, Ade is the first person not to scoff when I suggest a link between the two deaths, and Zoe.

'The thing is, Alice, whatever was going on, we'll never know, will we? Any link died along with your sister, and with Tim, and with Zoe.'

'Zoe's not dead.'

He looks away. 'I haven't told you because I didn't want to upset you, but I wrote to them. Her parents. Hoping they'd have good news. But the tests they've done show very little brain activity. The doctors think that Zoe suffered oxygen deprivation in the accident.'

'Oxygen?'

'Perhaps in the crush.'

'So she . . . suffocated?' *Like my sister, and Tim.*

'Technically. But Alice, that doesn't mean there's a connection.'

'No?'

'Be careful. I've seen what becoming obsessed with death has done to poor Sahara. Wanting to contact you all the time. Turning up out of the blue, like she did after school the other week.'

So he knows about that too? 'Do you think there's something . . . the matter with her?'

He scowls. 'I wouldn't go that far. But I worry about her when you go off to uni – how she'll fill the gap in her life.'

I shiver. Will she leave me alone then, or . . . 'I'm not the same as Sahara.'

He smiles sadly. 'I never said you were. It's hard for all of us, in different ways. Remember, I was the one who found Tim's body. There was a time when everything was dark for me, too. You know how I pulled myself out? By knowing it's not what he would have wanted – what any of them would have wanted. You're wasting your life.'

I'm about to snap back that they would have wanted justice, but I see the impatience in his eyes and I realise there's no point. I thought Ade was different, but he's just pretending to care.

'Try to focus on the future, Alice. You should get your licence tomorrow. Then a place at uni. There's a big old world out there to be discovered.'

'And what does Sahara think—'

'What do I think about *what*?'

We spin around. I don't know what to say.

But Ade smiles. 'About Alice's chances tomorrow, of course.' He lies to her effortlessly. Perhaps it's a skill he's had to develop to keep her calm.

Sahara laughs. 'Not *that* again. You're going to walk it, Alice. Now, Adrian, I think it's time we get going. We need to buy some flowers for Meggie's grave. And then the traffic across to Greenwich on a Sunday is murd— I mean, bad.'

'I'll just use the bathroom, first,' Ade says.

He's leaving the two of us alone? I begin to form a question in my head: what is the most important thing I could ask Sahara?

'Must go and say bye to your mum before we head off, Alice,' Sahara's saying, and before I can stop her, she's heading for the garden. But not before I've caught a glimpse of her face.

The fake smile had faded completely. She looked anxious.

Does she know I suspect her?

And does that make me her next target?

6

It's raining, hard.

The windscreen wipers stay on through my whole test. I remember to indicate earlier, to brake sooner, to give pedestrians extra time to cross the road.

The rear window keeps steaming up so I can't see through it, but I *know* I'm being watched, and not just by the examiner. Though, however many times I check my mirror, I never catch a single glimpse of Sahara.

'Would you pull over, please?'

It takes me a second or two to realise that I've arrived back at the test centre. The examiner – a woman, perhaps the one who 'fancied' Lewis – is smiling. I can tell before she speaks that it's going to be good news.

My instructor drives me home – 'I've had more than a few of my candidates crash immediately after passing; it puts you in a funny state of mind.'

Mum opens the front door as soon as she spots the driving-school car turning into the close. When she notices I'm in the passenger seat, her face falls, but by the time I get out, she's wearing a sympathetic smile. 'Never mind, Alice, all the best drivers pass second time.'

I can't keep up the pretence. A grin is spreading across my face.

'Must make me a *terrible* driver, then, Mum, because I PASSED!'

'Oh, Alice, you're a star! Come here!'

She hugs me and I hug her harder, and Mr Gregory gives me a brief pat on the back.

'Come back to me for your free motorway-driving class, Alice. And happy driving. Safety first, safety always, right?'

I've rung Dad at work, and am about to text Cara and Lewis, when the doorbell goes.

Mum calls up from the hallway. 'Alice, I think this is for you.'

I feel dread, like ice down my spine. Visitors freak me out. Probably because most of our unscheduled visitors in the past year have been police officers bearing bad news.

Halfway down the flight of stairs, I realise who it is, or at least, what they're here for. I can't see the person, because of the big bouquet of flowers in the way.

It is *seriously* huge. Someone's entire back garden must have been chopped down to make it, and Mum's already sniffing from the pollen.

No one's ever bought me flowers before. These are worth the wait. Red roses, white lilies, lush tropical leaves in deep green.

The florist has to lower the bouquet to see over it. 'Alice Forster?'

It weighs so much I almost drop it. Meggie would have done this more elegantly; she was *always* being sent flowers.

'Well done on passing your test,' the florist says, and then turns to go. 'Oh, the card's buried in there somewhere.'

Mum closes the door, and takes the bouquet from me, heading into the kitchen. She sneezes. 'Wow. A five-hanky job, at least. *Someone* thinks a lot of you.'

I laugh. 'Someone, eh? Thanks, Mum. They're beautiful.'

She puts them down on the counter: there's a bag of water tied underneath which keeps them upright. 'No, they're not from us.'

'You sure Dad hasn't . . .'

Mum pulls a face. 'Come on, Alice. Your dad's a prince among men in many ways, but he's never seen the point of flowers, except for the supermarket variety, and these must have cost at least as much as my entire monthly supermarket shop.'

I stare at them. 'But . . .'

The smell of the lilies is more powerful now. Almost cloying.

'Look at the card, silly,' Mum says, grinning. 'Though I can think of one person who might think you're worth it.'

'No one else knows yet,' I whisper, more to myself than to Mum.

I push my hand into the bouquet. The stems are bound together tightly and I can't find the card.

'Ouch.'

I pull my hand out of the foliage. There's a spot of blood on my finger, growing as I watch.

'That's the trouble with roses,' Mum says, still smiling. She passes me some kitchen roll. The blood spreads through the white tissue, like an ink stain. 'Here, let me try to fish out the card.'

She rummages around. 'Bingo.'

The little envelope has *Alice* on the front, in curly handwriting. As I rush to tear it open, I leave smudged red fingerprints on the white paper. Mum leans in to look.

The card shows a tiny retro car driving along a country lane. The driver is throwing a torn L-plate up in the air. It's sweet.

Inside, the message is written in the same italics:

Congratulations, Alice! Stay safe!

But no name.

'Come on,' I say. 'Stop joking around, Mum. Only you two would send this. *Could* have sent this.'

Her smile is a little more strained. 'No. My money's still on Lewis. If only because . . . well, they're not the kind of flowers you'd buy for your daughter. I'd have chosen gerberas or freesias, something bright and young. These are . . .'

She stops herself.

I stare at the flowers. The scent is making me feel sick, and my finger hasn't stopped bleeding. For a tiny cut, it stings like hell. 'What were you going to say, Mum?'

She laughs. 'Oh, nothing, really. Just that when we were growing up, your grandma was superstitious about the meanings of flowers. You know, tulips mean love and carnations mean . . . I don't remember exactly. But she was very odd about red and white together.'

'Because?'

'I think it was from when she was a nurse. They didn't like that combination because,' she giggles, 'well, they called red and white flowers together "blood and bandages".'

It's supposed to be a joke. I know that. But my head throbs in time to the pulse of blood in my finger.

Only Mum and Dad know I've passed. Oh, and my instructor and my examiner, I suppose, but neither of those would send me flowers.

Unless I *was* being followed by the only person who might think anonymous flowers would be a good surprise, instead of something creepy. The only person who might ignore a florist's advice not to send *blood and bandages*. Sahara.

I don't want it to be true, but I'm struggling to find an alternative.

Could Lewis have sent them? I begin to make up a story in my head, about him hacking into the test centre's database to find out the second my pass was recorded, and then despatching those grown-up flowers to me.

But Lewis hates cut flowers. He likes huge parlour

palms, or tropical blooms that thrive in the little hothouse conservatory in his garden flat.

Outside, I hear a car rattling as it pulls up.

'Never mind your secret admirer. Shall we find out who's here?' Mum says, her voice oddly excited.

I follow her out, glad to leave the flowers behind. She opens the front door, and there's a silver car in the drive. One of those jelly-mould-shaped ones. A Ka.

I don't know anyone who drives a Ka.

Dad gets out of the driver's seat. He walks up the path, and hands me an ignition key.

'All yours, darling Alice.'

I take the key, not quite understanding. Dad hasn't noticed the bloody kitchen roll wrapped around my finger.

When I don't say anything, Mum puts her arm around me. 'I know it's not the flashiest car around, but it's in really good condition. And the airbags are fully tested, *and* the brakes. Your dad was waiting at the dealer's when you got home. Obviously we had to make sure you passed before we signed on the dotted line.'

'It's *mine*?' I whisper, unable to believe it.

'One hundred per cent yours.' Dad grins, and puts his arm around me too.

'Oh my God. I don't know what to say.'

'Don't say anything. Go and sit in the driver's seat,' Mum says. There are tears in her eyes.

'Sorry. Thank you. I should have said that straight away. Just . . . I really wasn't expecting it.' I hug and kiss Mum, then Dad. 'But how much . . . I mean, how did you afford . . .'

And then I realise. There's no way they could have afforded it if they still had a daughter in university. Meggie never got a car as a present when she passed *her* driving test.

But with my sister gone, they have a little cash to spare.

I know she'd be pleased for me. I try to focus on that as

34

I walk towards the car, climb inside, work out where the ignition is and then rummage around under the seat to find the lever so my feet reach the pedals.

My pedals. *My* steering wheel. *My* gear stick. *My* seats.

Mum's walking to the end of the bonnet. She's got her phone out, ready to take a picture.

I put on the seatbelt – *my* seatbelt – for the picture. But I'm not planning to go anywhere right now. I feel too dizzy and shaky.

This isn't just a car. This is my independence. The first step in growing up, moving away, getting on with my life. That's why they've bought it for me. Why they're *both* trying hard not to cry.

'Thank you,' I call out. Only they can't hear me because I don't know how to open the electric windows. 'Thank you so much.'

The rear-view mirror's all wrong, I can't see anything but the back seats. So I reach up and tilt it, until the whole of the road behind me comes into view.

It's empty. My finger throbs, reminding me of the flowers. Sahara's making her presence felt. The iciness travels down my back again, even though it's warm in the car.

What gives her the right to invade every part of my life, even a moment like this, which should be all about celebration? The flowers are the final straw.

And that's when I decide.

We've been playing the game your way for too long, Sahara. This is where I start to fight back.

7

I log on to Soul Beach to forget Sahara for a while. But Sam's sitting alone in the bar, which is not a good sign. To the Guests, she dishes out nachos and delicious cocktails. I get lectures and tellings off.

She waves me over. As usual, there's a cigarette between her stained fingers, but the shadows under her eyes are darker, the same faded blue-black as her tattoos.

'Hey, Alice, tell me something shiny and good.' Her voice is weary.

I sit down. 'I passed my driving test.'

She leans over and kisses me on the cheek, her dreadlocks rough against my neck. She's never done that before. The smell of nicotine is strong, and her lip ring is cold where it touches my skin.

But there's something missing . . .

Then I realise. When we touched, I saw no flash of memory, no vision of the moment just before she died.

Sam is different to the Guests. Older, sharper. She's the Beach agony aunt, as well as the girl who mixes the drinks and clears away the empties when the dead, cool kids decide to call it a night.

But she's also part of the Management, or at least she carries out their orders.

'Brilliant news, mate,' she's saying. 'Made up for you. Got wheels yet?'

'Yeah. My folks bought me a car. I'm really lucky.'

'You're growing up, eh?'

36

I nod. 'Sam, is there something wrong?'

She looks down, pulls at the skin around her nails. Sam doesn't have the gloss of the Guests. She seems real. 'Why do you say that, Alice?'

'Well, apart from anything else, I've never seen you not working before. You're always busy.'

'Ah, bless you, mate. You're pretty much the only one here who actually notices how I am. Or treats me as a human being.' She laughs, then coughs, a hacking sound that sounds wrong above the gentle whoosh of the breeze through the palm roof. 'If that's what I am.'

'*Is* it what you are?'

'Eh?'

'When you touched me just then, well, you know how since Javier went, I've seen . . . no, *felt,* a Guest's last moments whenever I make contact?'

'Uh huh. Your latest reward, right?'

Sam's the one who helped me see that whenever I help a Guest escape, the Beach experience intensifies, like a game. 'Yeah. Only with you, I saw . . . nothing at all.'

Sam looks at me. Her brown eyes are the only part of her that don't show exhaustion. 'No, well. Maybe I'm different.'

'Are you?'

'You know robots, right? They've been designed to be as smart as humans, but they're hollow inside. Like, in movies, they learn, but they don't have memories or feel joy – which is why they always end up smashing stuff up. Out of frustration at being, like, empty vessels. Soul-less.' She takes a puff, then breathes a long stream of smoke out of the side of her mouth, to avoid blowing it into my eyes. 'Like me.'

'Come on. You've got a soul. A good one.'

'What, you can see mine, can you? Souls aren't like that, Alice; they're not solid like a nose or a big toe.'

I gaze through the open side of the bar, towards the shore,

where the Guests are basking in the sun. Some of them while away the hours talking about this kind of deep and meaningful question. Whether they're really here. What's the difference between body and soul? It makes me dizzy, especially as no one ever finds the answers.

'I can't see it. But I know you're not empty.' I try to think of a way to convince her. 'Like, if you really don't have memories, how could you know about the movies where robots try to take over?'

Sam winks at me. 'Hey, good point. Though I could have heard the Guests talking about them. Or maybe I come pre-programmed, loaded with teenage facts so I can relate to the kids, but with no memories of my own.'

There's always been a darkness around Sam, but I hadn't noticed sadness before. 'You must have had a life, Sam. Honestly. Because you're wise. All the advice you've given me, and the tough love. You're too kind-hearted to be a robot.'

She laughs more warmly this time. 'I'll miss you when you're gone.' She puts her hand to her mouth. 'Don't panic. I don't have insider information about your departure date. It's just, well, you *will* leave, won't you? That's what Visitors do. I don't keep count but you've already stayed longer than any of the others.'

'A lot longer?'

Sam nods. 'Loads. I won't slag them off, but the few we have had didn't have the staying power. But it's obvious that you love the bones of your sister. And she's the same about you.'

Something about the way she says it makes me wonder. 'Has she been talking to you?'

'Maybe.'

'So you know she wants me to leave?'

'It's not that clear-cut, mate. She's just having her own

little crisis. They all go through it, sooner or later. Hers has been delayed, first by you arriving, then Tim. But now all the excitement's worn off, she's feeling blue.'

'Is there anything I could do?'

'Apart from the obvious thing?'

She doesn't have to spell it out: she means resolving the killing, ending my sister's unfinished business. 'I'm working on it, Sam.'

'Yeah, Meggie said. She's scared for both of you. Scared of the unknown if you do send her on her way. Scared of what's gonna happen to you if you don't.'

'I won't take any unnecessary risks.'

'Alice, *I* get that. So does she, deep down. But to be honest, I don't see the biggest threat as coming from whoever killed your sister.'

'No? Who does it come from?'

She stubs out her cigarette. 'Ah, take no notice of me. It's just unsettling, the way you've set this record as the longest-serving Visitor. The place feels weird, lately. Like we're all heading for a shake-up.'

'How—'

'I've got no crystal ball, but it's not a good feeling.'

The Beach looks exactly the same: turquoise waves lapping against sand that reflects the sunlight through a billion tiny crystals. I can't see any sign of trouble brewing.

'So what do I do?'

'You know what, Alice? My hunch is it's already happening, whether we like it or not. Not a thing we can do. Except live – or die – one day at a time.'

She stands up, walks towards the bar and fills a silver bucket with ice. Then she takes a bottle of champagne and four glasses, and places them carefully in the bucket.

'Compliments of the bar, of course, mate.' She hands it over. 'I know *you* can't drink it, but the others will want to toast your driving licence. Not often we have something to celebrate on the Beach.'

And she gives me a little push on the back, and I pad down the steps towards the shore. I can see my sister, Danny and Tim waiting. Am I doing them more harm than good, with my stories of outside, of things they can never do? I love Meggie and Danny so much. But maybe that's exactly the reason I should let them go.

No. I can't. *Not yet.*

Danny's seen me now and he's waving. His strong bronzed arm as defined as an athlete's. All of them are so beautiful. They shimmer in the heat haze, like spectral supermodels.

Maybe *that's* what souls look like.

8

The florist laughs when I call the next day.

'Sorry. We'd never reveal the name of the person who sent the flowers. Well, except to the police, I guess. You know how priests take an oath of silence? We do too.'

Would she change her mind if I told her why it matters, who my sister was, what happened to her and her boyfriend, why I need to know.

Instead, I say, 'I wouldn't ask if it wasn't important. *Really* important.'

But the girl on the end – she sounds my age – is still in la-la florist land, where the worst that can happen in life is that your lilies droop or your roses get greenfly. 'Ha, ha, that's what they all say. Valentine's Day is the pits. Husbands and boyfriends calling up because their other halves got flowers they never sent them.'

I ring off. It *had* to be Sahara, didn't it? Except why not put her name to the flowers? It's not like her not to want the attention, my undying gratitude.

Could I have got it wrong? Her guilt is such a certainty for me now that maybe I'm overlooking something – or someone. Ade knew my sister, but only through Sahara. And Lewis recognised her because they both grew up around here, but he never actually talked to her.

The only other possibility is some random stalker who fell for my sister after seeing her on TV. Which makes no sense, either. It was Zoe who told me that indifference doesn't turn people into killers – that I should be afraid of the people who adored Meggie.

And the one thing I know for sure is that Sahara adored my sister. Maybe I'll find out how much this morning.

Everyone knows I passed now. Cara texted congratulations from Bermuda, and Lewis called an hour after my test. 'I don't like to say I told you so, but I did, didn't I, Ali?'

I promised to take him out soon, if his street cred would survive a trip in a Ka.

'It's OK, I'll put on a ski mask. Have you decided where your maiden voyage will take you yet?'

I have, of course. But I didn't tell him.

Mum takes a photo of me as I leave the house and get into my car – *my* car – for my first drive, because 'it's one of those landmark moments, sweetheart. Don't get lost. Or drive too fast. Or too slowly. Just . . .'

I put my hand through the open window. 'Be careful? Don't worry, Mum. I won't get lost with your satnav to guide me. And the instructor says I am *very* safe.'

I reverse out of the driveway and take the corner out of our close, turning to the passenger seat to check whether my instructor is happy.

I jump when I realise I don't have an instructor any more, because I've PASSED MY TEST!

The thrill is soon replaced by nerves. The satnav is programmed to take me further than I've driven before, way beyond home territory. I'm trying to get used to the unfamiliar controls, the slight creak as the car goes over speed bumps, the ticker-ticker-ticker sound of the indicator. I don't turn on the radio, because it's taking all my concentration not to crash.

I catch sight of myself in the mirror. My jaw is tight. I unclench it, but the rest of me is still wired. This is the first time I've driven on my own and I'm about to hit central London for the first time, too. It's not what my driving instructor would have recommended. Even Cara didn't take such a mad journey so soon after taking her test.

But I can't wait any longer.

I'm going to Greenwich, to ask Sahara the questions I should have asked months ago. It's too good a chance to miss. She said Ade was going to his parents – probably to avoid helping her move. But with him out of the way, she's lost her bodyguard, and I might stand a better chance of getting some answers.

Mirror. Signal. Manoeuvre.

I drive perfectly all the way to the dual carriageway. It's muggy today, and as I see the elevated road looming above me, and the cars zooming past, the temperature in the car seems to rise by ten degrees.

It's now or never.

I put my foot down, and the engine growls and the speedo needle heads further and further to the right.

Forty.

To my right, cars and lorries are an intimidating blur.

Fifty.

Stop hesitating. Go!

Sixty.

A lorry with foreign lettering down the side races past and I know I must go after it. *Now.* I steer right so sharply I almost veer into the middle lane. But the car – *my* car – responds quicker than the tank-like driving-school one, and I correct myself with a light touch to the wheel.

I did it. And now no one can tell that I've never done this before.

The satnav tells me it's five miles to Clapham, fourteen to Peckham. Busy, unfamiliar places. But the thought of what I have to do when I reach my destination is scaring me more than the journey.

The entrance door to the halls of residence is propped open with a box full of text books.

I lean down to check, sweat from the long drive making my t-shirt cling to the clammy skin on my back.

History text books. That's not Sahara's subject, which means there must be other people moving out today. Knowing I won't be alone inside with her makes me feel slightly less breathless.

Though, of course, there were dozens of other students asleep in this building the night Meggie was smothered and none of them heard her. Or helped her.

I step inside. It was here that I first understood that evil had a presence, when Sahara took me up to my sister's old room. She'd kept Meggie's spare key after the forensics team had left. The tiny bedroom had been stripped of everything – carpets, furniture, even the washbasin fittings – but what remained was a darkness that overwhelmed me. Except now I realise it wasn't the room, was it? It was Sahara herself.

So much has changed since. Tim's died. Zoe is trapped in a living death. Perhaps that's what the darkness was trying to tell me back then: that Sahara killed my sister. If I'd realised, I might have saved the others.

'You're not supposed to be here, are you?'

A girl is coming out of the lift with another box of books.

I smile at her. I already have my story straight. 'Oh. Well, not till next term, anyway. This is where I'm going to be living. When *I* start.'

She frowns. 'What, have they already allocated you your hall? Weird. Didn't happen to me till after I got my results.'

'Ah. But I . . . had a gap year. So my place is confirmed.'

The girl sighs. 'God. I thought you knew you were old when the *policemen* started looking younger, not the freshers. Ah, well, enjoy it. It's a good halls. Sociable. Decent rooms.

Oh, and take no notice of all the bullshit about the place being haunted.'

'Haunted?'

She pulls a face. 'I shouldn't have said anything.'

'A bit late now, though.'

'That girl. The singer from the telly. She was killed here. They left the whole of the third floor empty this year as a mark of respect, but . . . they're opening it up again for the new academic year. So many students need accommodation.'

I say nothing.

'But, seriously, don't worry about it,' the girl says, her voice high-pitched. 'Even if they put you on that floor.'

'People think they have actually seen a . . . a ghost, though?'

The box looks heavy and I think she's losing patience with me. 'Only one girl and she's the dead girl's best mate. Poor thing. She shouldn't have stayed on. Imagine that! So sad to have all those memories. Me, I'd have left.'

'What floor's the friend on?'

'First. If you see her, don't mention it, eh? Nice girl, but I'm not sure she ever got over it.' She sighs. 'The place is fine, right? I've never heard or seen anything creepy. What happened was sad but, you know, people move on.'

She heads past me towards the front entrance, and I try to smile. I can't imagine ever being ready to move on.

I skip the lift and walk up the stairwell to the first floor.

Even though I've prepared myself, the sight of the landing makes me dizzy. The layout's identical to the third floor, where my sister died: there are four security doors with glass panels, leading to the bedrooms which share a kitchen. Through one door, a couple of girls are leaning against the wall, chatting over mugs of tea.

That could have been Meggie and me. I used to love

visiting. Yet, to those girls, her death is ancient history.

But there is one person here who remembers. I must focus on *her*.

Each security door has a buzzer, with a list of names stuck next to it. I check the lists in turn. I've never been inside Sahara's new room; she was too keen to show me inside my sister's old room the last time.

I shiver at the memory.

At the third door, I see her surname: *Du Lacy.*

I look around me. No security cameras, even now. CCTV might have helped to bring Meggie's killer to justice.

Could Sahara get away with killing me too?

Maybe I have the question the wrong way round: why would she *stop* now? The driving kept me distracted on the way here, but now . . .

There's a tightrope I have to walk between seeking the truth and accusing Sahara directly. I daren't fall off.

I push the buzzer, holding my breath.

A shape appears through the glass. I breathe again; it's too petite to be Sahara.

A girl comes to the door, opens it. 'Who are you after?'

'Sahara?'

She opens the door. 'Oh. OK. I think she's packing up.' And she points to her right.

I step through the door, and the girl disappears into the kitchen. Not just a girl, I realise. A potential *witness.*

For a moment, it makes me feel safer. She'll remember me, won't she? And so will that girl I met downstairs. Then again, Zoe wasn't involved until she saw my sister's body. It's not a good thing, to be a witness.

I hesitate outside the door. Weird. I think I hear someone else's voice. If Ade has decided to help Sahara pack instead of visiting his parents, then I'm wasting my time. He'll protect her.

I knock, then step slightly to the side so she can't see me through the spyhole.

'I'm busy,' Sahara's voice is thin, unwelcoming.

She thinks I'm one of her flatmates. I don't speak; I want her to be surprised, perhaps shocked into telling the truth. I knock again. Nothing. Then I bang with my fist against the wood. It hurts.

'All right, all right.'

The door opens so fast it makes me jump. Her face is cross, the lines between her brows deep with irritation. But her eyes look . . . terrified.

She looks to her right, and then sees me. Her expression softens.

'Alice?'

I say nothing.

'What are you doing here?' She's smiling now. 'Have you come to help?'

'Can we go inside?'

'It's a god-awful mess. Why don't we go for coffee or—' She stops abruptly. It's taken her this long to look properly at me, to realise this isn't a social visit. 'Right. OK. Well, you'd better . . .' and she waves me inside.

I wait to feel the darkness as I step into the room. But there's nothing. No wave of evil, no inhuman coldness. It's not even that messy, just piled high with boxes.

What hits me is the similarity to my sister's room. Another thing I should have been prepared for. Same tiny pod bathroom on the left, same fake-wood bookshelves and desk, same double-glazed windows that won't open enough to let out the muggy July air. Even the curtains are identical: blackout-lined, navy blue.

It was in a room like this I had my first taste of being a grown-up, sleeping off my first hangover after a night clubbing with my sister. In the morning, we ate toast with

47

Marmite till midday. We only stopped because we finished the jar.

And it was in a room like this that she was murdered.

Sahara closes the door behind me and I turn round to look at her. That long, bony face of hers is oddly blank and, as I prepare to ask my first question, I feel like I'm about to kick someone when they're already down. Why do I even care?

'You've been following me, haven't you, Sahara?'

She giggles. 'Me?'

'It's not funny. I don't know why you've been doing it, but it freaks me out.'

She doesn't move. 'God. You're serious, aren't you?'

I nod. It's one of the things I've learned from my 'investigations'. Give away as little as possible. The less you say, the more *they* reveal.

'Why on earth would someone follow you, Alice? Especially me?'

'There's only one person who knows the answer to that. And that's what I came here to ask you.'

She looks more puzzled than angry. 'Sorry, sorry, but this is totally surreal. You've come all the way here to . . . accuse me of following you? Why would I? I see you often enough as it is. We're friends, aren't we?'

'Like you were friends with Meggie?' It's the wrong thing to say. Too hostile. But it's too late.

'What is this, Alice? An *ambush*?'

I stare at the grey carpet. I can hardly see it for stacks of files, assignments, textbooks. 'I know someone's watching me. And who else would it be?'

'Sit down, Alice.' Her voice is soothing. She thinks I've lost it – which could give me the advantage. So I *do* sit down on the end of the bed. She squeezes next to me, her thigh touching mine. I feel sweat breaking out on my forehead.

'Now, first of all, what makes you think someone is

following you?' Sahara is so close I can see a tiny nerve pulsing under her eye.

'It's instinct,' I say. 'I'm feeling it. I'm not making it up.'

'No, no, of course you're not. But you haven't actually *seen* anyone?'

I shake my head. 'Except for you, outside school.'

She tuts. 'If you must know, I was in the area to refresh the flowers on your sister's grave.'

Flowers? I won't mention those. 'Right.'

'Look, I'm not saying you're making it up, but why would someone follow you?'

I shrug.

'OK. Why do you think it's me?'

I'd planned for this bit. 'Because . . . because I know your behaviour used to worry Meggie, sometimes.'

Sahara reels back. '*Worry* her?'

'She told me you could be overbearing.'

And freaky and needy and a whole host of other things.

'Rubbish. We were best friends. *Soul* mates.'

Except my sister never had *best* friends. Meggie was always at the centre of the circle, with endless girl chums and hopeful boys and hangers-on. But she never let anyone get close. There was no Cara for her to confide in, no Lewis to take the piss out of her. Was my sister never lonely?

If she was, she hid it well. And she'd make you feel like you were the centre of her universe while she was with you. I think that's why Meggie was such a hit on the reality show: every viewer believed she was singing to them alone.

'I know you argued before she died,' I tell Sahara.

'Not that again, Alice. I told you before. It was nothing.'

I look straight at her. 'I don't believe you.'

She can't hold my gaze. She looks at her hands, which are clenched in tight fists.

'I want you to tell me what you argued about, Sahara. To

49

convince me that it's not you that's following – no, *stalking* – me.'

'Don't say that!' she spits the words at me. 'You knew, didn't you?'

'Knew what?'

'Come on,' she says, her voice icy. 'You wouldn't even suspect me if she hadn't told you, but here you are, playing dumb . . .'

'Told me what?'

'That she accused me of exactly the same bloody thing right before she died.'

'Accused you of what?'

'Of stalking her, of course. Even though it's the last thing I'd ever do.'

9

The word echoes in my head.

'My sister thought you were *stalking* her?'

Sahara nods. 'Don't pretend you didn't know that. How else would you have got this crazy idea in your head?'

My carefully planned questions seem irrelevant now. *Meggie had a stalker.*

'Believe me, Sahara. I *didn't* know. I knew you'd had a row.' *Because Meggie told me so on the Beach.* 'But not *why*; that's the reason I was desperate to ask you.'

'Yeah, right. You must think I'm stupid.'

Anything but stupid. I want to leave; there's something chilling about the way she's looking at me. But I have to keep pushing. 'OK, I can see why you think I might have known, but there's another explanation, isn't there? Maybe I *am* being stalked – by the same person who stalked my sister.'

It's better to pretend we're in this together, that I need her help.

'I suppose that's me, is it?' Her eyes are locked on mine now.

'No, I—'

'And that means you think I killed her, too?' she whispers.

'I'm not saying that,' I choose my words carefully, 'but I need to know more about what Meggie told you she'd seen or heard or—'

'Your sister had a vivid imagination, Alice, that's all. She felt she was being watched, or followed. I told her it was probably just fans recognising her. It only started after the show was aired. She got drinks bought for her, was stopped on the street for autographs. Fans used to send her presents: make-up, accessories. She loved the attention.'

'Except it doesn't sound like she loved this kind of attention.'

She shrugs. 'There was no proof it was even happening. The week before she died, I told her she should go to the police if she was that worried, and that's when she came out and accused *me*. I said the same as I just said to you, that there was no reason for me to stalk my best friend, and then she—' Sahara stops mid-sentence.

'She what?'

Her face twists at the memory, as though it's causing her physical pain. 'She *laughed* at me. We . . . we were sitting on her bed, as close to each other as you and I are now. I felt her breath on my face as she laughed. She told me I was kidding myself. That we had nothing in common, that we'd never see each other again once the first year was done, that I got on her nerves, that . . .' Sahara gulps.

Even though I don't want to believe my sister could be so cruel, it sounds too familiar. Just because no one talks about Meggie's tantrums any more, that doesn't mean they didn't happen. I can imagine her turning on Sahara like this, knowing how much it would hurt her 'friend' but not really caring at the time.

Afterwards she'd have regretted it. She always apologised later if she'd hurt someone.

But there was no later for Meggie that last time. Within days, she was dead.

'I couldn't listen to her any more, Alice,' Sahara continued. 'It was awful. I . . . I think now that she didn't mean it. She was feeling stressed and she only took it out on me precisely *because* we were so close that she knew I'd forgive her.'

'You made it up with her?'

'No. It's my biggest regret. She tried but, at the time, I felt so sore. *Humiliated.* We still went out – me and Adrian, her and Tim – but I avoided being alone with her. I would have got over it in time, but time's what she didn't have.'

It sounds so plausible that I want to believe her. Part of me even feels sorry for Sahara. Yet she's had over a year to come up with a decent explanation. She's probably convinced herself it's all true. That's what psychopaths do.

'Is it possible that she *was* being stalked, Sahara?'

'Well, obviously she was.'

'What?'

'By someone she loved. By Tim.'

I think it through. 'Why, though? He was dating her.'

'Because he was possessive and hated the idea of sharing her with millions of viewers. Because he wanted her to himself.'

I discounted Tim long ago, but the way the killer left the body always suggested something done calmly, not in anger. Almost with love. And Tim could easily have been the one who took those horrible close-up photos – not just of her, but of me too. He sent them to Zoe. Was it all a double bluff?

'Did you tell the police? About the stalking stuff?'

Sahara nods. 'Yeah. And my suspicions about Tim. He was an intense guy, wasn't he? Quiet. There was so much he didn't say, but it didn't mean he didn't *feel* it.'

Maybe Sahara saw her chance to pin the murder on him. The motives she's describing could equally apply to her.

'It's why I stayed in touch with you after Meggie died, Alice. I wanted to protect you, in case Tim came after you too. Then, by the time he killed himself, I was so fond of you, well, I didn't want to lose touch once the danger had passed.'

'And you really think the danger *has* passed? Despite what happened to Zoe?'

She frowns. 'Alice, have you thought about talking to someone?'

'Someone?'

'A . . . specialist.'

She's trying to convince me I'm going crazy. I'm about to defend myself, to turn the accusation back on her, but then I realise that playing along might be the best thing to do. If I pretend I've accepted I need psychological help, she might disregard my visit and relax again.

And the more she relaxes, the more likely she is to make a mistake.

'Maybe I *should* see someone,' I agree.

Sahara pats my hand. Her nails are bitten and the skin around them cracked. But her fingers are long, thin, *powerful*. Are those the hands inside the gloves that I've seen bearing down on my sister in her last moments?

'Alice, counselling is nothing to be ashamed of. I only wish Zoe had gone down that route instead of leaving the country and . . .'

I stand up. If we start talking about poor Zoe, I might lose my cool again.

'I should go. Before the traffic. I drove over here and I'm nervous about getting back.'

'You *drove* all this way to see me?'

I need to underplay this. 'For driving practice. And I wanted to catch you alone. Ade's always around when you come to see me.'

'He's very protective. I'm lucky.' She stands up too. 'But why were you so desperate to see me on my own?'

'I thought there might be things you could say that you wouldn't say in front of him.'

She looks away. 'We're completely honest with each other. That's what relationships are about, Alice. I hope you find that out for yourself one day.'

She's wrong, though. Lying is the only thing that keeps me safe. I lie to everyone, here in the 'real' world and on the Beach. Sahara, my parents, Cara, Danny, my sister . . . Lewis is the only one who gets anything near the truth and, even then, I keep my craziest secrets hidden.

I walk towards the door, then look back at her room. This will be the last time I see it, I suppose. 'How do you feel about moving out, Sahara?'

She shrugs. 'Relieved, mainly. The end of this chapter of the story for Meggie and me. But I won't forget her any more than you will, Alice. And at least I have you to remind me of how special she was.'

I manage not to shake until I reach the hallway. Instantly, the tremors overwhelm me and I have to lean on the wall, next to a noticeboard packed with flyers promoting long-past parties and round-the-world flights.

I've failed. What she said was so believable, and yet I *know* I'm missing something. The same person who was stalking Meggie could be stalking me – could my assumption that it's Sahara be too lazy?

Her story was perfect. Too perfect? Rehearsed, almost. The words made sense but the way she said them: it was emotionless. I'm groping for answers that won't come. But I've wasted enough time. There's one more thing I must do here, while I still have the chance.

The two flights of stairs make me feel dizzy and, in my hand, the metal of the key grows impossibly hot against my skin.

Once, almost a year ago, I stood by the Thames, about to throw Sahara's stolen key into the murky river. But then I imagined I heard my sister's voice, telling me to hold on to it, that the time to use it would come.

Is that time now?

I don't know what I'm hoping for: a flashback, a moment to connect the stripped room with the glimpses I've had on the Beach of Meggie's last moments? The rational part of me is arguing against going back to her room but I have nothing to lose.

Except when I push the fire door at the top of the stairs, I realise it was a terrible mistake. Why didn't I listen to my instinct, turn away before it was too late?

My sister's floor is a building site. Half a dozen guys in fluorescent jackets are working behind the glass door, drum and bass on the radio not quite drowning out the sound of drills.

I lurch forwards. I can just about see a slice of her room through the pane. Last time I saw it, it was a bare cell, stripped to wall and cement. But now carpet is going down on the floor, into the hallway. There's a large shrink-wrapped box leaning against the wall, labelled SANITARYWARE POD.

Will the person who takes this room next term feel my sister's presence? I don't. Not now. There are no clues or lessons for me here.

Unless the lesson is that the world is moving on, and so must I.

I drive home in silence, trying to focus on the road.

But it's impossible. I'm thinking, analysing everything I know about the days before my sister was killed. Tim must have known that Meggie thought she was being stalked – did he suspect Sahara too? But if he had, wouldn't he have warned Zoe – and me?

My hands grip the steering wheel. I need to get back online, find a way to get Meggie to tell me about this stalker stuff without getting banned from the Beach.

The traffic crawls along and I switch on the radio. It's tuned to a rock channel. Not my thing, but I turn it up full volume, trying to block out my thoughts with the drum beat.

When I can finally turn off into my close, I realise my jaw has been clenched for the whole journey and my shoulders are locked, hunched up near my ears.

Home. I'm looking forward to my bed, a chance to recover so I'm completely alert for the next stage of my investigations.

But as I turn the corner towards our house, ready to park *my* car in *my* space, I see there's another car there already. A flash black convertible. One of Dad's partners at the solicitor's, maybe? None of my parents' friends drive a car like that.

And then the front door opens and I wish I hadn't come home at all.

10

There are three people in the reception committee. Mum is trying to be brave, with a smile that doesn't reach her crumpled brow. Dad has his arms folded across his chest.

But the sight of the third person is the nail in my coffin.

Olav.

For a moment, I consider driving off again. But where? Cara's away. To Lewis's, then.

Yeah, like that wouldn't be the first place they'd try.

Did Sahara call them about my visit, tell them I need *help*? Because that's what creepy Olav offers: group therapy, one-to-one counselling, online forums. Mum's been through the lot and is a total convert, though so far she's let me make up my own mind about whether I want to get involved.

My own smile is as fake as my mother's as I lock the car and walk up the drive. 'Wow. A surprise party!' I say.

Olav nods to himself, as though my joke is a Bad Sign. He reminds me of a mannequin, with a face so smooth it looks airbrushed, and sandy hair that could be made of moulded plastic.

'Come in, Alice, darling,' Mum says, 'we need to chat to you about something.'

You don't say.

They're ready for me in the dining room, but this is no tea party. A sheet of paper lies face down on the table.

'Alice, we want to help,' Olav says once we're all sitting down. 'There's nothing to be worried about.'

Aren't those the most worrying words I've ever heard?

'What's this about, Dad?' I figure he's the only one who'll give me a straight answer.

'It's . . . the flowers, Alice.'

I look behind me, towards the living room. The bouquet is in a vase, overwhelming it. Some of the buds have opened and others are drooping already. The smell is intense, more like rotting than blooming.

'We *know*, sweetheart,' Mum says.

'Know what?'

'I was checking my online balance and—'

'Did *you* send them after all, Mum?'

A flicker of irritation crosses her face. Olav's still smiling.

'Alice, please don't pretend any more,' Dad says. 'We know you sent them to yourself. What's most important now is to find out why you'd do such a thing.'

'Sent them to *myself*?'

Olav picks up the paper, turns it over and hands it to me. It's a list of credit card transactions, printed from the web. Mum's name's at the top, and it's all the usual – supermarkets, mobile phone bill, a restaurant meal.

Until the bottom entry. £47. *The Flower Faeries Florist, Richmond-upon-Thames*.

Dated yesterday.

'I rang them, Alice,' Mum says. 'They confirmed that order was for your flowers – rung in just after you passed your test. There was a mobile number given but it doesn't work.'

'Well, that obviously wasn't me. This is crazy. Why would I send flowers to myself?'

Olav tries to take the paper from my hands. 'Recovery begins when denial ends, Alice.'

I hold on to the page. 'Denial. Of *course* I'm denying what I didn't do!'

Dad won't look at me, but Olav's smoothed-out gaze doesn't falter. 'Your parents are worried about you. I think that, deep

59

down, *you're* worried about you, too. Otherwise why use your mother's credit card when you must have known she'd see the payment sooner or later? It's a cry for help, Alice. We're here to answer it.'

I drop the sheet, close my eyes. Could I have done this and forgotten? Maybe the Beach stuff, my one-woman murder hunt, are more signs that I've lost touch with reality.

Except that, even if I was deranged, I didn't have the *time* to order the flowers. I went straight from passing my test to being driven home by my instructor.

I tell them that.

Dad just sighs. 'Darling, there's nothing to be ashamed of. What happened with Meggie isn't the kind of thing that stops affecting us simply because it's been more than a year. It can hit us at any moment.'

'Especially if you haven't *really* talked about it,' Mum adds, and Olav beams.

I realise with absolute clarity that there's no way to persuade them they're wrong. The evidence seems overwhelming. 'So what do you want me to do?'

'The therapeutic options are very wide,' Olav says. 'They can be tailored to what works for you. We'll begin with a session to discuss those, see where it takes us. It may seem strange at first, but so many of the people I work with end up looking forward to their time to be open about whatever they're thinking or feeling.'

That's never going to be me.

'It's not just about treatment, Alice,' Dad says. 'We want you to have fun. Get out and about.'

'And off the bloody internet,' Mum mumbles.

'What do you mean?'

'It's off limits, Alice, and completely this time. Like I wanted it to be after the last time,' Mum says. 'We're disconnecting the broadband.'

Thank God for Lewis.

'And before you go running off to your friends' places,' Mum continues, 'we've told them to do the same. Including Lewis. You can still see him, of course, but only offline. Hey, maybe you could even go outside. In the fresh air. It is summer, after all.'

'Bea,' Dad says.

'Sorry, sorry. I don't mean to be sarcastic. I'm just so very worried about you, Alice. We all are.'

'Oh, Mum.' I get up, put my arms around her. It's unbearable to think that I'm causing them so much pain, on top of all they've suffered already. If only I could explain why Olav is not going to solve the problem.

Why I have to solve it myself.

Dad sits on his hands and it's Olav who gets up and places a hand on my mother's shoulder, so he's close to both of us. I can smell his aftershave, as cloying as the flowers.

'Beatrice, please don't worry. Accepting help is a brilliant sign, and at least now you know your daughter is in good hands.'

And he rubs his good hands together, relishing the challenge.

Poor Alice. There are few things worse than being disbelieved.

I wouldn't have done it if it hadn't been absolutely necessary. I am primarily concerned with protecting her. It is in her interests that the rest of the world does not take her seriously.

Of course, I would love to have seen her face light up when she received the flowers. The first bouquet from a secret admirer is something all girls remember.

But I admit, my motives are more complex. I cannot know for sure what's going on in her head, but I have my suspicions. The strange things she does point in one direction: mine.

The less seriously she is taken, the safer she will be.

There is something delicious about being the only one who knows the truth about Alice. That she is sharper, smarter, brighter than the tedious people who surround her.

We have so much in common.

11

'So how is my favourite crazy chick today?'

For once, I don't laugh when Lewis makes a joke. 'Really, *really* crazy. Plus I've had a bit of a sense of humour bypass,' I tell him.

'I've got the straitjacket in the boot, just in case.'

He puts his foot down and we leave the close of houses behind. After two awful days, I can be myself again; I don't feel like everything I say or do is being analysed by my parents for evidence of mental instability.

'Where are we going?'

'Surprise.'

'Lewis, I've had enough surprises to last me a lifetime.'

'It's hot out, right? So I thought we'd go to the seaside.'

Almost like he knows how much I'm missing the Beach . . . except he knows nothing about the place that matters most to me. No one does. Sure, he knows I was sent 'hoax' emails after Meggie's funeral, but as far as the world is concerned, they stopped almost a year ago.

Two days without going online has made me desperate. I miss my sister, Danny, the ocean and the soft sand. But my parents are taking no chances. Lewis has had to promise to keep me away from any internet connections.

'Good idea? Not a good idea?' he asks.

'What? Oh. The seaside will be OK,' I say, then realise how ungrateful I sound. 'Sorry. I'll perk up by the time we get there.'

He nods. 'Music?'

'No thanks.'

So there's silence, except for the purr of the engine. Only now that I've passed my test myself do I notice how well Lewis drives. When I went out with Cara after she got her licence, it felt like she was trying to tame a bucking bronco.

But Lewis treats his beloved sports car like a dance partner. He's confident and calm, with a huge smile as he accelerates. The ride's so smooth I don't notice how fast we're going – until he brakes rapidly when he sees a police car on the motorway hard shoulder.

He glances at me. 'Whoops. Sometimes I forget what she's capable of.'

Instantly, I think of Sahara. What *she's* capable of. When I saw her on Wednesday, she'd already have known that her little trick with the flowers was about to blow up in my face. She must have taken Mum's credit card details when Ade and I left her alone on Sunday.

Her plan to make me look crazy worked a treat.

But does the fact she *needed* a plan mean I'm getting closer to the truth?

'Lunchtime, I think, Ali?'

Lewis has brought me to Brighton. When Mum used to drive me and Meggie down here, it took two hours. Despite the holiday traffic, Lewis has shaved forty minutes off the journey time, but I didn't once feel unsafe.

Or *watched*.

'I'm not that hungry.'

'You sure? I've booked a table at somewhere *very* nice.'

And he steers me away from a crowd of Italian language students and a tangle of pushchairs, into a restaurant built into an arch under the promenade. It's busy inside, full of people chatting and laughing and enjoying the view. The waiter checks the booking and takes us upstairs to the best table, right by a floor-to-ceiling window. When we sit down, it's like we're suspended in mid-air. I don't notice the people outside any more, just the waves and the wispy clouds against the blue sky, and the skeleton of the old pier in the distance. The sun's so strong I have to put my shades on. Through them, Lewis looks cooler than ever, a real *dude* in his designer glasses.

Two girls inside the restaurant are giggling. When I look up, I realise they're pointing at Lewis, and I feel proud to be with him. We're just friends, but those girls don't know that, do they?

'How come you always know the best places, Professor?'

'Interweb, obviously. There are nerds everywhere and even though they don't actually go out in daylight themselves, they know the places they'd go if, say, they lucked out massively and found a girlfriend.'

When the waiter hands me a menu, I almost faint at the prices. It's *exactly* the sort of place where you would bring a date to impress them, but the thought makes me embarrassed. 'So this must be their recommendation for where you bring a girl who needs psychiatric help, as a favour to a mate's little brother?'

That's how we met: my ex-boyfriend asked Lewis to keep an eye on me, because he was worried the hoax emails were messing with my head.

But Lewis tuts. 'I'll treat that comment with the contempt it deserves.'

'Even so, there must be times when you wonder why the hell you let yourself in for all this, Lewis.'

He looks at me evenly. 'There are definitely times when I think it'd be an awful lot easier if you'd tell me what's really going on.'

'You know I would if I could.'

'The thing is, Ali, I used to buy that. But now I'm wondering what else exactly I've got to do to get you to trust me. I've broken the law for you more times than I can count. Ferried you on endless wild-goose chases. Lied to your parents, your friends. All because I trusted you. Yet you don't feel the same . . .'

The waiter approaches the table.

'The clams and the sea bass,' Lewis says, even though I didn't see him look at the menu.

'Um . . .' I focus on the food.

'The gazpacho soup is a very refreshing starter on a day like today. And the chicken's our bestseller,' the waiter says.

'I'll have those, then, thanks.'

'Drinks?'

'White wine OK, Alice?' But Lewis doesn't look at me when he asks. He sounds angry.

'And water please,' I say. 'It's so hot.'

When the waiter's gone, I speak before Lewis can say something to make me feel even guiltier about not telling him the truth. 'I know, all right? I know I should trust you. I know you've done amazing things for me. But if I told you, you'd . . .'

The thought is so scary that it makes me stop. He'd hate me. Disbelieve me. Dismiss me as someone way too unhinged to be worth bothering with.

'What? What would I do, Ali?'

The wine turns up, in a bucket. Beads of condensation decorate the bottle.

It reminds me of the Beach. I *long* to be on the Beach.

I look out of the window at *this* beach. There's a touch of haze blurring the horizon, so it's hard to tell the difference between sky and sea. Not quite the perfect day I thought it was, but maybe they only happen online.

In my imagination?

Lewis says nothing. The two girls are glancing over again. We must look like a couple who've had a row. God knows why

66

he hangs out with me. I'm moody and demanding and now I'm officially delusional and attention-seeking too.

'I didn't send myself those flowers. Just so you know.'

When I look back across the table, his face is half amused. 'Not even as a cry for help?'

'I don't need help. Not that kind, anyway.'

The starters arrive. My soup is cold, blood-red, with salsa piled up in the middle. One minute I think I'm going to struggle because I'm not hungry, the next the bowl is empty.

'Just imagine, for a minute, that I *did* understand, Ali. What would that be like?'

I look back out to sea. What *would* that be like? After nearly a year of being alone with this secret, it would be incredible to share it, to have someone believe in me.

For the first time, I consider what might happen if I *don't* tell Lewis. I'm pushing him further and further away. Most people would have given up on me by now.

When I think it through, I wonder if I have a choice at all.

And as he carries on eating, I begin to plan. How do you explain the inexplicable? I suppose it begins with that first email.

After the waiter takes our plates, I take a sip of the wine – tart, like gooseberries – and take my sunglasses off. I want Lewis to see my eyes, understand that this isn't a fairy story.

'OK. You win.'

'I win?'

'Let's try it your way. I'm taking a risk, Professor. But before you judge me, imagine living with this, doubting yourself every day – as I have since Meggie's funeral. If I wanted to invent a story, I wouldn't dare come up with anything this crazy.'

He nods. I'm glad of the chatter in here. Everyone else is too busy with their own conversations to eavesdrop on ours.

'It started with those emails. The ones that Robbie asked you to look into. The hoaxes.' *Robbie.* My first proper boyfriend. I haven't thought about him for months and months.

Lewis says nothing but his brown eyes are focused on me, as though there is no one else in the restaurant.

'What if they weren't hoaxes? What if for the last ten months, I've been spending time on a website which has helped me to do the thing I wanted more than anything else?'

Lewis leans forward. 'You responded to the emails?'

'How could I *not*, Lewis? If there was even the tiniest chance that she might have been . . . reachable, well, of course I had to.'

He nods.

'And . . . she was there. I found Meggie. On the site.'

'Found her? What do you mean?' His voice is cautious.

'I know it's hard to believe. Impossible. But the site I found . . . It's like a virtual beach, with *people*. People who died. Including my sister.'

'A memorial site?'

'Not exactly. It's . . . another world, I suppose. At first I saw nothing except the place itself. It's called Soul Beach. It's beautiful. A tropical beach, pale sand, deep turquoise sea. It was so realistic, Lewis. I really felt like I was there, walking by the shore. Feeling the sunshine on my skin.

'And then I started hearing voices.' I pull a face. 'I know how that sounds. Really, it was one voice, actually. My sister's, calling my name.'

Lewis says nothing. I'd have no idea what to say if I were in his shoes.

'I wouldn't have believed me either, if I hadn't experienced it. I *didn't* believe it, at first – thought my grief was making me see things that weren't there. Or even that someone was playing the cruellest trick I could imagine.

'But then I saw her, Lewis. *Meggie.* And the others. Other

teenagers who'd died before their time, with something left to be done or said or fixed. Like . . . remember the girl whose brother we visited?'

'Triti?'

I nod. 'She was on the Beach. It's how I knew about her. I was obsessed with her story. Not for the reasons I gave you, but because she was suffering.'

Lewis gulps. 'I never did believe that you just read about her online. But *this*? You're saying you met her somehow? That she told you about the bullies who hounded her to her death?'

'I knew her, yes. And she told me enough to know something had to be done to make things right.'

'And your sister? What has *she* said?' Lewis can't stop the hardness creeping into his voice. 'Has she told you who killed her?'

'She doesn't know. She never saw the person or, if she did, she doesn't remember. Lots of them forget, perhaps as a way of protecting themselves.'

'You're sure she's not just protecting you?'

'Hmm. She genuinely doesn't know. But now Tim's there too, and he wouldn't be if he'd been guilty because then the murder would have been resolved and—'

'Hang on? You're saying Tim's *beach-combing* too?'

I stare at the table, wanting to scream with frustration. 'Lewis, don't mock me. Why do you think I haven't told you before? Because I wouldn't believe me, either. But there is evidence there, if you listen.'

'Like Triti?'

'Triti, yes. And I made a difference in Barcelona, too. You can look it up. There was a boy called Javier. He fell off a roof to his death. I can give you dates, details, his address. I couldn't have known any of that without the Beach.'

'Made a difference, how?'

'I helped him get away. The Beach is kind of an online limbo, I suppose. When something changes here, in real life, then the Guests are finally set free. It happened with Gretchen, too. The German girl with the hacker dad? She disappeared from the Beach.'

'Where to?'

I shake my head. 'No one knows, any more than the living know where they go after death. But—'

'Summer chicken, and sea bass fillet.'

I'm almost relieved when the waiter brings our main courses, because it forces me to stop for a moment, to let my words sink in with Lewis. My dish is beautiful to look at: the chicken in a white porcelain pot, with fresh green herbs floating in a garlicky broth. It smells amazing but I won't be able to eat any of it. I can hardly even swallow as I wait for Lewis to speak.

He barely glances at his own plate. 'I honestly don't know what to say.'

Which is his way of saying he thinks I've lost it.

'I could have made up something, you know. Something credible. But I couldn't bear to lie to you. Was that a mistake?'

Lewis picks up his knife and fork, but then puts them down again. I've silenced him.

'I can't take much more of this,' I say, and I push my plate away. More people are watching us now. *Look at that girl, doesn't know how to behave in a good restaurant. Is he dumping her or is she dumping him?*

'Ali . . .'

'Don't "Ali" me. You asked me for the truth, you've got it. Now I need the truth from you: do you believe anything I've just told you? Because if you don't, I think I should leave. Now. And I'll never bother you again.'

12

I regret the ultimatum the moment it's out of my mouth.

Why alienate the last person on this earth who still takes me seriously?

I try to think of something to say to make it better.

Lewis holds his hand up. 'Wait, Ali. I'm thinking.' He smiles. Is that a sad smile – because he's finding the words to tell me our friendship is over – or a smile that says, 'I get it now'?

'I don't know what I was expecting, but it wasn't *that*,' he says eventually. 'It's the perfect storm for me. I'm a scientist. A rational person. I believe in matter and gravity and what's observable. Evidence.'

'I know, Professor.'

He smiles again. 'I'm not convinced there's an afterlife. I've always thought we invented it to make us feel better about the big unknown. Wouldn't bet my life on it, but, you know, odds on we die and, well, that's it. Except for the memories of us that the living hold on to. *That's* how we stay alive.'

I nod. I'm not noticing the restaurant any more. Just him.

'If I'd heard what you just told me from anyone else, Ali, I'd be raising my eyes to the heavens I don't even think exist, and asking for the bill. But you're not a flake. Eccentric, yeah, but not a flake.'

Is there a chance he could believe me?

'Plus, I don't see why you'd lie to me. Like you said, you've had the best part of a year to come up with something more plausible. So, there are two possibilities. One, this beach of yours does exist. Two, *you* sincerely *believe* it exists, even though it doesn't.'

A wave of disappointment smashes into me. 'So you *do* think I'm crazy—'

'Ali, you had *your* time to talk, now let me, will you? It's not a case of *crazy*. More that the brain can be . . . ingenious in finding ways to adapt to horrible events and, God knows, you've had enough of those in the last year.'

'I am afraid I might have lost it,' I say.

'Oh, Ali.' He rests his hand gently over mine. 'What makes me so sure you haven't is the fact that you've still got insight. You know it defies belief, yet you still trusted me. I'm honoured you told me, despite the risks.'

I feel as though someone's watching us.

I spin round and realise it's just the waiter. We should have finished our food by now, but our plates have barely been touched. He floats away again.

'So, what now?'

Lewis peers out of the window. I don't know if he's seeing the sea, or is lost in Lewis Land. Maybe we all have private places we escape to when we need to.

'What's the best way to test a hypothesis?' he says thoughtfully. 'Experimentation. There must be a way to analyse what you're seeing when you are convinced you're on this virtual beach.'

'Really? How?'

Lewis puts his napkin on the table, runs his hands through his hair. 'I need to work on that part. But there has to be an explanation for what you're experiencing.'

'And that'll help me?'

He sighs. 'I can't promise anything. There's pure science, and then there's the application. Two very different things. But knowledge is better than ignorance, right?'

'I thought a little knowledge was meant to be a dangerous thing.'

And then he smiles. His eyes crinkle at the edges and he looks like he might be about to laugh. 'Life's dangerous, Ali, especially when I'm with you. But I kinda like it that way.'

After lunch, we head for the amusements on the pier.

Salt and vinegar, smoking oil, burnt sugar, seaweed. It's exhilarating. Perhaps I also feel so good because I've shared it now: my darkest secret.

I never smell anything this real on Soul Beach.

I try to stop myself thinking about it, but it's too late. What is Meggie thinking, and Danny? They were expecting me to be hanging out more, not less, now it's the holidays. And after what they said to me about leaving, might they believe I've left without saying goodbye?

The thought is *horrible*.

I should sneak away from Lewis, find an internet café, so I can go online, explain to my sister and Danny why I'm never there.

'Cheer up, love, it might never happen,' Lewis says, and he makes me giggle. He's watching me so closely that there's no hope of getting away without him noticing, so I might as well try to enjoy the time before I return to top-security prison, i.e. home.

We play air hockey – I win. We lose countless tuppences in the coin waterfall, and our hands smell of dirty money.

We watch through the window of a downmarket beauty salon as women have their toes nibbled by carnivorous fish, and we watch kids staggering off the rollercoaster, unsteady on their feet.

Occasionally I catch Lewis glancing at me oddly, but I say nothing. He's entitled to wonder about me. The main thing is, he's going to help.

'Dodgems, Ali?'

I laugh. 'With your driving? I'll be behind the wheel, thanks very much.'

As we clamber into our bumper car, there's barely room for the two of us, and Lewis almost has to fold himself in two to fit inside. Maybe we should have taken one each.

Except there's something comfortingly solid about Lewis next to me. His height makes me feel protected. No, not just his height. It's his integrity, too, and his brain most of all.

Despite everything I told him, he's still here, at my side. If I could choose anyone in the real world to help me wade through this mess, it'd be him. No doubt.

13

My car tyre's flat.

Of course, it could happen to anyone. Punctures are annoying but *normal*. You get them driving over a nail, hitting a kerb too hard.

Except I haven't driven my car anywhere since the bouquet showdown. Could Sahara have done it, to keep me 'safely' confined to home?

'Bad luck, Alice,' Dad says. 'Time for a vehicle maintenance lesson, don't you think?'

I follow him to the side of the car. He's already rolling up his sleeves. It's Monday morning, and I'm meant to be driving myself to my first session with Olav, like a condemned prisoner making his own gallows. Though Dad is still going to chaperone me before he goes to work, in case I change my mind en route.

If this *is* Sahara's doing, I could almost thank her for it. Every minute spent fiddling with hub caps and wheel nuts means one less minute being patronised and psychoanalysed by the creepiest therapist in England.

Mum comes out, hands on hips. 'This is silly. Take her in your car, Glen. You can show her how to change a wheel later. What Olav is doing is much more important.'

Dad looks a bit hurt: I think he was getting into the whole 'father-daughter bonding over car maintenance' idea. Plus, I suspect he's not quite as behind the Fixing of Alice Forster as he's pretending to be in front of my mother.

In the car, he offers me a wine gum. The pocket of the

75

driver's door is stuffed with crinkled family-size bags of sweets and peanuts. Empty ones. At least he's eating *something*.

He doesn't speak till we've turned out of the close. 'You know, if it's not for you . . . this Olav. Well, I can talk to your mum.'

He must notice the hope in my face, because he adds, 'Talk to her about alternatives, that is. Clearly you're still not one hundred per cent, and though I'm no fan of therapy, we need to get you shipshape before university.'

'Alternatives like what, Dad? Knock-out drugs? A mental hospital?' I regret it as soon as I've said it.

He sighs. 'We realise this is hard for you, Alice. I'm just saying there are other therapists. You're a smart kid. No, a smart young woman. I know once we've got the right approach, it won't take any time at all to get you fixed.'

Olav beams when he comes into reception, his swollen lips pouting like a puffer fish's. Finally he's got his two fiercest opponents into his soft pastel territory.

OK, maybe I *am* being paranoid now. If everyone watches you for signs of insanity, after a while you start showing them.

'Alice. Glen.' He shakes our hands in turn. 'So pleased you could make it.'

'I'm off,' Dad blurts out, as though he's worried he'll be frog-marched to a padded cell and forced to reveal his feelings. 'I'm going to run some errands.'

Like buying himself more three-for-two wine gums?

'Shall we?' Olav says to me, dismissing Dad with a nod and showing me upstairs.

The therapy room is painted lemon yellow, but when Olav pulls the blind to stop the sun shining in my eyes, the colour seems muddier. There are two chairs facing each other, and a table with a box of tissues in the middle.

Whatever happens, I won't cry for him.

'So, Alice, shall we start by looking at how it feels to be here, right now?'

The fifty minutes go faster than I expected. It's a game. Every question he asks, I try to think of the most evasive and confusing answer.

By the end of our treatment, I want him to be doubting his *own* sanity.

'Right, Alice, time to leave it there, OK? But I do want to say something about getting the most out of our sessions together.'

'Hmm.' This is my default answer for when I can't think of anything cleverer: I learned it from Olav himself. It's the ultimate in noncommittal mumbles. Says nothing, gives no clues.

'Alice, I can tell you're resisting. That's normal.'

'I'm glad something about me is normal.'

His eyebrows dart up. Funny, I was sure he'd had too much Botox to manage that. 'But the sooner you commit to working with me, the sooner we can make things better. We could easily spend the next four weeks playing games—'

'Four weeks?'

'That's the minimum that your mother and I agreed would give me a chance to help you. Individual sessions twice-weekly, plus we're hoping your father will agree to a family discussion or two.'

So much for offering me 'alternatives'.

'Alice, I'm not your enemy, OK? It's pretty common to resist change.'

Now I'm *common* as well as crazy.

As he walks me back down to reception, I wonder what would have happened if I *had* told him the truth. The Beach, Triti, Javier, my theories about Meggie and Tim and Zoe. My certainty that Sahara is stalking me. My fear that Lewis, my only ally, might now run away as fast as his long legs can carry him.

I can't help smiling. If I'd 'fessed to all that, I'd have made Olav's day.

Dad doesn't ask what happened. He just hands me a warm doughnut in a bag, the oil oozing through the brown paper.

'What are your plans for the rest of the day, then, Alice?'

'More of the same, I suppose.'

My father gives me a sympathetic look. 'I guess these aren't turning out to be the most exciting summer holidays you've ever had.'

'You can say that again.'

All weekend I sat in the living room, trying to find a book I wanted to read, a movie I wanted to watch on Sky. I couldn't focus on anything. What I really wanted, of course, was to be on the Beach. But Mum locked the broadband router in the garage and announced that if we went out at all, it would be 'as a family' – she made it sound like a threat.

I kept remembering what Sam had said about how hard Meggie was finding things. And of course I miss Danny's kisses, even though . . .

It seems disloyal to admit it to myself, but his words keep coming back to me: *I won't ask you to sacrifice yourself for this limbo.*

He meant the Beach, of course. But I'm in limbo here too, aren't I? Trapped between his world and mine. The kisses always close that awful gap, but is it possible they're a distraction from the reality? That we're going nowhere.

I don't have anything to offer you except this, and this is not enough.

But not going onto the Beach was just about bearable because I knew Lewis was working behind the scenes on a scientific solution. I waited and waited for a call to reassure me that he had found some technology that would be able to work out what Olav can't: what's really going on in my head.

But he didn't call. Four days now since the Brighton trip. With every day, the dread grows. No texts. No calls. No unexpected visit.

Has he had second thoughts about me? I don't know what I'll do if he has.

'I might have good news, Alice.'

For a moment, I think Dad's guessed how I'm feeling, and is going to tell me Lewis is waiting for me at home.

'Your mother's talking about booking a short holiday. I'm in enough trouble with the other partners already about how much time off I've had in the last year, so it'd be just the two of you. She was wondering about New York?'

He glances at me, to assess my reaction. I try to summon up the right level of enthusiasm. 'New York! *Wow!*'

And I really hate myself, because they're trying so hard, and only an ungrateful cow like me would not be thrilled at the prospect of a trip to NYC.

'Let's see how it goes with Olav, eh?' he says, and I realise the holiday is conditional on my progress. A bribe, like a promise of biscuits to stop a toddler having a tantrum in the supermarket.

Back home, Dad changes my tyre before he heads out to work. Mum makes me tea and I can tell she's itching to ask how it went, but is trying to respect my therapeutic boundaries or whatever.

'Olav was great,' I say.

She stares at me. 'Really?'

'So understanding.' I know she's bound to tell him what I said, so I might as well say something that will make Mum happy *and* confuse Olav even more.

'Oh. Fantastic. I'm so pleased, Alice.'

'I might go out,' I say. 'Olav thinks it's important I don't mope around the house all day.'

'Fine,' she says. 'I'll come with you.'

'Three might be a crowd at Lewis's.' I say it as though he's invited me round for tea. But I have to see him. I have to know.

Mum frowns. 'Will you call me when you get there? I'd love to say hi.'

Check up on me, she means. And make certain he doesn't let me online.

I get in the car. He won't like me turning up unannounced, especially if he's already written me off.

Better to find out, though, right? Better to be put out of my misery if the last person on my side has decided I'm a lost cause.

14

I have to ring the bell three times before I get an answer.

Lewis comes to the door with headphones round his neck, his chin covered in dark brown stubble and his eyes half open.

When he sees it's me, he frowns. For an agonising moment I think he's going to shut the door in my face.

'Oh. Hi.'

'Sorry. I know you weren't expecting me. You're probably in the middle of something. I can go, if you want.'

Please don't make me go.

'No.' He grinds his knuckles into his eye sockets, trying to wake himself up. 'No, you're all right. I threw an all-nighter on a project. I could probably do with some human contact.'

I pretend not to hear the doubt in his voice. Inside, it's so dark that I can't see anything for a few seconds. Then the tropical plants that form a living curtain beyond the patio doors come into focus. The room smells musty, of pizza and cold coffee.

'Maybe I should have pulled up the blinds and let the light in, but I was . . .'

There's a pile of papers on the floor next to the chocolate-brown sofa, along with the remains of last night's takeaway. And the night before's.

'Busy?' I finish his sentence.

'Yup,' he says, and walks past me to open the doors that lead onto the tiny patio. 'Fresh air. Now why didn't I think of that before? Can I sort you a coffee? Or a Coke? You know there's nothing un-caffeinated in the entire flat. Even my shower gel's stuffed with it.'

'Coffee, please.'

It really is a mess in here. If I had to guess, I'd say he hasn't left his place since he got back from Brighton on Thursday. This is a Lewis I'm not used to. Yes, he's a workaholic, but he's image-conscious, too. Everything is just so, from his designer glasses and man-bag, to the plant varieties he's chosen and nurtured, and the caffeine in his shower gel.

'Before you ask, I'm still not quite there with the Fixing Alice research. Irons in the fire, but none of them glowing.' Lewis is talking incredibly fast, but he hasn't looked at me once since he's let me in.

He *has* had second thoughts. Even though I'd considered the possibility, I couldn't imagine it happening. He's always been so loyal and kind.

This time you pushed him too far, didn't you, Alice?

It's over. Without Lewis to tease me and reassure me, I don't know if I can carry on. I feel dizzy.

'Maybe . . . if you don't want me here, I can go. I drove, anyway, so—'

He turns back towards me. 'Eh? What are you going on about? Did I *say* I didn't want you here? Forgive me if my manners aren't as gentlemanly as they usually are; I had a rough night. But, Ali—'

I look away. I can't let him see I'm on the edge of tears.

Too late.

'Hey. What is it? Has something happened?' He comes closer, touches my arm. His fingers are warm against my skin but I'm cold with fear.

'No.'

'It's not because I'm grouchy, is it? After everything you've had to deal with, don't say it's grumpy old Lewis who's tipped you over the edge?'

'You think I'm crazy, don't you? You're trying to find a way to tell me to go.' The harder I try not to weep, the more choked I get. And I'm not a crier, not usually.

'What?' Then he slaps his own forehead – too hard, judging from his pained expression. 'Bloody hell, Ali. No. That's not what it's about. I had everything go wrong on me with some stupid project overnight and I'm sulking. Nothing to do with you.'

That's all it takes for me to believe him. Instincts aren't only about negative stuff, like Sahara being dangerous. They're also about who you can trust.

I want to change the subject away from my own paranoia. 'Tell me about what went wrong. Lewis. We're always talking about me.'

I don't know nearly enough about what Lewis does, though I know his heart's not really in his day job. He only does the boring projects to fund some kind of Robin Hood style campaign against hackers. Perhaps he needs someone to confide in too.

'Ali, you don't want to know. Too tedious. Let's lighten up, shall we? You're banned from the web, but I've got every video game you can think of. Not just the shoot-'em-ups, either. Some girly ones, too. We could Zumba. Build a virtual zoo.'

Banned from the web. I'd hoped I might be able to talk him round, but I get the impression it's not a good time to push him.

'I'm not that into games. I haven't had time lately . . . what with the Beach and everything.' I try to smile and he smiles back. 'Oh, before we do anything else, you need to call my mum, please – to tell her I'm here and I'm not up to no good.'

He whistles. 'Like *that*, is it? Surprised she hasn't fitted you with an electronic tag.'

'Whatever you do, don't suggest it. I bet they sell them on Amazon.'

I hand him my phone, already calling Mum's number.

'Mrs Forster. Lewis here. Just checking in, to tell you your daughter's safe and well . . . Yes, absolutely . . . We thought a country walk might be in order. Maybe to a nice country pub. No . . . Ha ha, don't worry, I won't let her drink during the day. Same to you, too. Bye for now.'

He hands the phone back. 'How was that? Reassuring enough?'

'Perfect.'

'In which case, Ali, shall we work out what we're *really* going to do?'

We *do* go for a walk, by the river.

'Ugh! The great outdoors. I can't take any more,' Lewis says. He threw himself under the shower before we came out and now he looks like his old self again, sleek and geeky at the same time. I waited on the sofa, staring at his three high-def. monitors. I had to sit on my hands so I wouldn't rush over to log on to the Beach.

'Daylight must be quite a shock for a hermit like you, Professor.'

We stop on the bridge, looking over at the weir. Water crashes down angrily but by the time it gets to where the little boats are moored, it's calm again, so the *Mallard* and the *Port Out Starboard Home* bob as gently as toys in the bath. The sky is a very English blue; we could be in a kids' cartoon world.

'How are you feeling, Ali?' Unlike everyone else who asks that question, he really wants to know.

'Up and down. Right now, I'm good. But the rest of it . . . being offline. Not hearing from you.'

'I didn't want to call till I had something definite to tell you.'

I gulp. 'So you don't know how you're going to fix me?'

Lewis turns to me. 'I just don't want to get your hopes up.'

'Trouble is, Lewis, I've nothing else to feel hopeful about. My summer holidays involve nothing but therapy sessions with a guy who wants to enslave me in his bereavement cult.'

He laughs. 'I'll keep an eye out for that blank look in your eyes. Or if you start wearing cheesecloth and getting your hair crimped. Sure signs of cult membership.'

'Seriously. I could do with something to believe in. Anything.'

Lewis nods. 'I get that. OK, well, I'm looking into brain scanning.'

'To check I've got one?'

'It's a little more sophisticated than *that*.'

'Sorry. Go on.'

'The thing about scanning is it can show which parts of the brain are being used when we're doing different things: the pleasure zones, the Stone Age instinctive parts, the visual or imaginative areas. My theory is we can use the same tools to find out if what you're seeing is really there or if it's . . . well, if it's a delusion.'

Delusion. The word is frightening, though it's not the first time I've been scared I might be going crazy. But I *must* know one way or the other. 'That's possible?'

'The truth is, I don't know. I've been making contacts, finding out where the UK facilities are. Obviously, most of the sophisticated scanners are in hospitals but it's harder to sneak you into those. So I'm looking at commercial companies, games research labs, that kind of thing. These are seriously expensive bits of kit, you see. And I also need to find the right kind of person to analyse the results.'

I nod. 'But if you do find someone . . . it could change everything.'

'Yup. Or nothing. But, you know, Ali, there is another, simpler way.'

'What?'

'I could try visiting Soul Beach myself.'

15

I shiver, no longer feeling any warmth from the sun.

'No. No, you can't.'

Lewis frowns. 'Why not?'

'Because . . .' Reasons flood my brain, faster and more urgent than the water on the weir. 'Because it's wrong. I'm sure the rules won't allow it. Because I bet you wouldn't see it anyway.'

'In which case, there'd be no harm done,' he says gently.

'No! You don't understand, Lewis. It's too big a risk. I could be banned like that,' I snap my fingers, 'for good. And then where would I be?'

His face is unreadable. Does he not believe me? 'It has to end somehow, Ali, unless you're going to carry on living this double life forever.'

'Maybe. But not yet. I'm not ready. Letting someone else see, it would be . . . unnatural. You can't do it. I won't let you try.'

'OK. OK.' He places his hand on mine. 'I'm sorry I even suggested it, then. I only thought it might be the fastest way to get an answer. The last thing I wanted was to upset you. We're in this together, right?'

I nod. Yet already I'm plotting. Will he let me go online on my own, or is that going to make him cross?

He squeezes my hand. 'Can I say something else? Something important.'

'I guess.'

'If I can organise a lab, then we'll scan you while you're

online on the Beach, to see which parts of your brain are most stimulated by it.'

'Right.' I'm picturing electrodes, electric chairs, mad boffins. 'It won't hurt, will it?'

'No, no. It's noisy but not invasive. But there is one thing you can do, to prepare and get the clearest results. From what I've read, it's recommended that subjects avoid similar stimulus in the days leading up to the research.'

Subjects? Stimulus? It takes a moment for me to work out what he's talking about. 'Oh. You mean, I shouldn't go online before it happens.'

'Right. I mean, you're not supposed to be online anyway, while you're being "treated" by this Olav character, but I know you, Ali. You're determined.'

'Do you really think it'll make a difference to the results?'

'It's uncharted territory. There've been no experiments like yours because, obviously, this situation is unique. But it's like any addiction – the craving for it, and the response once it's available again is bound to be intensified by a wait.'

We step down from the bridge and head for the bank opposite the lock gates, where there's a queue of families waiting to buy ice creams from a kiosk.

Addiction. Am I addicted to the Beach? The same way my mum's addicted to therapy and Cara can't stop herself chasing bad boys?

And Meggie was addicted to being centre-stage?

It's not quite so clear-cut in my case. At least the others involve human contact, whereas the Beach . . .

'Do you think . . . it'll be a long wait?' I ask.

He looks at me. 'I hope not.'

I nod. 'OK, then. It seems like the best chance of understanding. So I'll do it. I'll stay away. Except . . .'

'What?'

'Let me go there today. *Please.*'

'Online?'

'To the Beach. For the last time before the experiment. Please? It's been six days offline now. *Six*. Meggie and—' I'm about to say Danny's name, but I stop myself. I don't want Lewis to know about him, 'and the other Guests will be worried. Scared something awful's happened. All I have to do is go for a minute or two, let them know I'm OK.'

Lewis keeps walking, slowly, staring into the river water.

'You *are* addicted to it, aren't you? Your mother would kill me.'

'She doesn't need to know. It's just once. Then I promise I'll go cold turkey.'

He smiles at the joke, then sighs. 'How come you *always* manage to persuade me to let you do what you want, Ali? I'm such a pushover where you're concerned.'

For some reason, that makes me blush. 'Thanks.'

'One condition.'

I wait for some other awful demand, except I can't think of anything that will make my life duller or tougher than it is right now.

'You buy me an ice cream.' He nods towards the van. 'I think this is a two-scoops kinda favour.'

And I laugh, because Lewis always knows the right thing to say. 'Two scoops *and* a chocolate flake,' I tell him. 'Because you're worth it, Professor Tomlinson.'

I sit down in front of the middle one of the bank of screens. The largest one.

Lewis has taken his spare laptop – actually, he's got *three* spare laptops – into his bedroom and closed the door to give me some privacy. But he has set an alarm to remind me that this *must* be the briefest of visits.

I log into my email, find the original invitation that's my only gateway to the Beach, click on the link.

Because it's been so long, I'm scared. I hold my breath while I wait for the place – the only place I can truly be myself – to appear. I just never know if . . .

It's there. I breathe again and feel the warmth of the sun on my face.

Danny and Meggie and Tim are stretched out on the sand, as though they haven't moved since I was last here, six days ago.

My sister jumps up when she sees me, and gives me a hug. The vision of the black gloves and the white pillow is so fleeting it only registers because I was expecting it. What I *do* feel is the softness of her breath against my cheek, the thump of her heart against my chest.

Addictive? You bet.

'You've been *naughty*, baby sister! Too busy with your real life to come and hang out with us nobodies.' She smiles, but I can tell she's been worried.

'You don't want to know why, Meggie, but I'm here now.'

Tim gives me a half-wave, then gets up and walks away. He started this whole 'Alice shouldn't be on the Beach' discussion. Does he have a hidden agenda? With me out of the way, there'd be no competition for my sister's attention.

Or might he even be afraid I'm going to find out he was the killer after all? No, I ruled him out months ago.

Meggie follows him with her eyes, but stays next to me. 'Don't judge him too harshly, Florrie. He cares about what happens to you. And he didn't exactly have the easiest time of it when he was living, being hounded by the press and police. Whereas at least I died when I was at my happiest.'

Even though you were being stalked? I need to find some way of prompting her to tell me more, without getting banned, but Danny's already putting his arm around my waist and nuzzling my neck.

It would be so easy to melt into the embrace, to let the kiss be all that matters.

And yet, Danny's own words come back to me again: *I don't have anything to offer you except this, and this is not enough.*

'Missed you, Alice,' he says.

'Missed you too.'

Meggie tuts fondly. 'I won't interrupt this touching reunion.'

Before I can stop her, she's heading off after Tim. I should follow her. It can't be long till the alarm goes off and I have to leave the Beach indefinitely.

Danny will understand, surely, that I have to prioritise. That affection has to take second place to justice and finding out the truth at last.

'Hey,' says Danny, 'what's with the frowning? Anyone would think you weren't pleased to see me.'

'Oh, I am.' And as he holds me tight, I know I'm not ready to break away from him yet.

Does that mean I will be one day?

'Danny,' I whisper. 'There are things happening. Things that might keep me away from the Beach for a time.'

He loosens the embrace, looks down at me. 'What things?'

'I want to tell you, but I daren't take the risk.'

'It's happening finally, isn't it?' His voice is sad, but almost resigned. 'You're moving away from this . . . from *us*?'

'No. No, that's not true. It's about Meggie, not the two of us. Putting things right. I'll be back as soon as I can.'

But I can tell from his eyes he doesn't believe me. 'Whatever happens, you should know I've never felt like this about anyone, Alice.'

As he holds me tight again, I whisper back, 'I love you too, Danny. So much.'

We stay like that, for as long as I dare. Time loses meaning on the Beach, but I know I can't stay much longer. Just one more second . . .

'Alice, something's wrong.'

I force myself to pull back, then look up. 'What the hell?'

The sky's gone dark. One second it was bright blue, now it's the purple-black of a new bruise.

Danny looks up too. Light slashes across the whole sky, as though it's tearing it in half. Lightning. Not just one fork, but five . . . no, ten, or more. I'm losing count. Dark. Light. Dark. Light. It's like someone's playing with a floodlight.

The noise starts. Thunder so brutal and loud it makes my eardrums pulsate.

There's alarm on Danny's face. Some of the Guests are screaming. Many are running towards the bar to shelter. A few head for the jetty, instead, for a better view.

And one girl has crouched down on the sand, her hands covering her ears. Her eyes are wide with horror.

I feel something cold on my skin.

Rain.

It's *never* rained on the Beach before.

Danny is staring at me, his eyes blood red. I don't see love. I see terror.

His arm grips mine. Except . . . it can't be Danny touching me, because he's backing away.

I look down. There is a hand on my arm but it's not Danny's . . .

'Lewis?'

He's here. Next to me. Not on the Beach, but in his flat, his hand on my arm as he looks over my shoulder . . .

'NO!' I scream. I wrench my arm away, shut down the Beach as fast as I can.

But I already know it's too late.

16

He stares at me as though I'm speaking a foreign language.

'Lewis. Tell me. Did you see the Beach?'

His eyes are half closed, as though he's trying to hide something. 'No. I saw nothing. I've only come in because the alarm was ringing and I needed to turn it off. I was calling across the room for ages but you didn't hear that either. So I came over. But I didn't look.'

I don't believe him.

The phone alarm is sounding, shrill and insistent. I didn't hear it at all while I was in Danny's arms.

I try to make sense of what just happened, to guess how many seconds the thunder and lightning lasted before I realised Lewis was there. Ten. Maybe fifteen? 'How long have you been next to me?'

'Not *that* long.'

'It only takes a split second to see something you shouldn't, Lewis. And I warned you how dangerous it might be.'

He sits down on the sofa. 'Look, maybe I did see . . . I need some time. To . . . process it. To make sense of what it was.'

'You promised you wouldn't look.'

'I didn't mean to. It wasn't *planned*. But you seemed to be in a trance. I had to try to wake you somehow, so I touched your arm and then—'

'Then you couldn't resist a peek, right? And because of that, I might have lost *everything* that matters to me.'

Hurt crosses his face, but I'm too furious to care.

'I almost lost the Beach before when I asked questions

I shouldn't have. I can't imagine what the penalty is for showing someone *else.*'

Lewis is running his hand through his hair, and it sticks up like he's a cartoon character who's seen a ghost. 'Alice, we don't even know this place exists, so how can we have broken the rules?'

'Doesn't exist? So all that stuff about researching the Beach, helping me discover the truth? You were only fobbing me off. You think I'm mad too!'

'No, I didn't meant that, but surely it can't have changed in a split second—'

'Shall I tell you what changed? Why I turned round? It was because . . .' I remember screams, sudden darkness. My refuge transformed into a place of terror.

Lewis stands up again. 'Ali. Ali, you're right. I'm sorry.' He reaches out for my hand but I back away. 'I promise I didn't do it on purpose. I was afraid for you.'

His voice is so contrite that it takes the heat out of my anger.

'What if it's too late?' I say.

'I did see something,' he murmurs, as though he can't believe what he's saying.

Those words change everything. 'Say that again.'

'I *did* see something, Ali. A beach. At least, I think I did. Unless all this talk has put ideas in my head . . .'

'Don't backtrack, Lewis. You might doubt yourself but I believe it. I have to.' Despite the horror of my last moments on the Beach, my heart hums with excitement. If he saw it, then *it exists.* 'Were there people?'

He shakes his head. 'Just landscape. Colours. Blue and gold. But it did feel . . . very real.'

Part of me is desperate to try going online again right now – but I'm scared of what I might find. 'So does that change things? Do you believe me now?'

'Ali, I always have. But I'm rattled. That's an understatement, by the way. I don't know what to think. But it's made me even more determined to set up this experiment as soon as I can.'

I nod. 'It wouldn't do any harm for me to go online again now, though, would it? Because if I've been banned, it's not even worth getting access to a lab.'

Banned? Saying it out loud makes it real. My future without the Beach will be one of unfinished business, not knowing what's become of my sister or Tim or Danny.

He frowns. 'Please. Stick to what we agreed, Alice. I want to get to the bottom of this more than anyone, especially now. But you've had your chance to tell your friends that you need some time offline. Please do what we agreed. Enjoy normal life, time with your folks, while I work on it. You keep your side of the bargain and I will keep mine.'

I leave a few minutes later; Lewis is distracted and so am I. Plus, Mum's already texted me, suggesting we go out for a 'girly' lunch.

The engine turns over, I pull on my seatbelt, take a breath, check my mirrors.

They've moved.

Not the rear-view one in here, but the ones at each side. Not by *that* much. And wing mirrors are always being smashed or clipped, even on a quiet road like Lewis's.

But *both* mirrors?

The air inside the car could melt plastic, but my skin prickles with cold fear.

I adjust the mirrors, so almost every angle of the street is covered. Of course, there's always a blind spot, so I check that, twisting in my seat.

Once.

Twice.

Three times.

No Sahara. No Lewis. No one at all behind me.

But someone must have been here. It's a reminder – like I need one – that life offline isn't without its dangers.

17

I try to enjoy my 'normal' life, really I do.

But every minute I'm checking my mobile for a call or a message from Lewis. It never comes.

Doubts begin to creep in about whether he *ever* believed me, and then fears about the consequences of what damage he may have done by glimpsing Soul Beach. I even drive round to his place, but he doesn't answer the door. Either he's out, or he's hiding.

Meanwhile, Mum keeps coming up with *activities* to keep me busy. It feels like the stuff they give psychiatric patients to do to take their mind off their insanity. One day we go to a bloody pottery, the next to a pasta-making class.

I try to smile as I stuff floppy envelopes of dough with hot spinach. I hate spinach. None of it distracts me from the black despair I'm feeling as I contemplate being without the Beach forever.

'Fun, isn't it?' Mum says.

More fun than family therapy, I'll give her that. That was Tuesday: the day after Lewis took hold of my life without telling me when he planned to let go.

It was hard to know which of us least wanted to be at therapy: me or Dad. All Tuesday I'd felt I was being followed again, so when Olav took us to a different room – the pastel-painted *Family Space* – and I realised one chair had a view onto the street, I asked to sit there.

Which led to a full twenty-minute discussion about where my feelings of paranoia and control-freakery might stem from. It was the perfect chance to play my silly game with Olav, to twist and turn his words and make him doubt his own sanity. I tried – suggested a game of musical chairs, and then said I could only talk if everyone else sat on a beanbag – but my heart wasn't in it.

All the way through, I could imagine Lewis sitting behind me, whispering sarcastic comments in my ear: *just because you're paranoid doesn't mean they're NOT out to get you, Ali.* Or, *do you think Olav would be drummed out of the shrink's club if he shaved off his goatee beard or dared to wear socks with his sandals?*

But Lewis doesn't even seem to be speaking to me any more.

At least Mum was happier by the end of the session. 'It's the start of a journey, Alice.'

A journey that involves eating home-made pasta off hand-painted plates and wanting to smash both onto the floor.

The only thing that's keeping me going is knowing that Cara's back from holiday tomorrow. I've never needed my best friend more than I do right now.

Even jet-lagged, Cara has the look of a reality TV-show star.

Like my sister.

Her hair is braided, her skin is golden and her gel nails are so sharp I'm surprised security allowed her to board the plane home.

'Honey.' She hugs me tightly on my doorstep, and I don't want to let go.

I'd texted her to say I wanted to talk to her urgently, so she's come to my place straight from the airport, leaving her mum to go home in a cab with the luggage.

We walk to the pub by the lock and she orders a cranberry juice.

'Cara! Have you gone teetotal on holiday?'

'I've become a fruitarian. No toxins will ever enter my body again.'

I stare at her.

She giggles. 'Had you going! Actually we got upgraded on the plane home and I had so much champagne that I don't fancy any more booze right now.'

'Ah. That makes more sense. Life would never be the same if you decided you'd had enough of partying!'

Cara frowns. 'Plus I need a clear head. Your text made no bloody sense. What's all this about *flowers*?'

I look away. I don't want to see her judging me when I tell her. 'Well, I passed my driving test—'

'Yeah! I got your text! Big hug!' She squeezes me tight, then lets go. 'And?'

'And I got this huge bouquet delivered.'

'Ooh, Lewis. Bound to be.'

A short, sharp pain hits me somewhere in my chest. 'Not Lewis, no. Or my parents. It . . . turns out they were ordered on my mum's credit card. Cara, they think *I* sent them.'

She laughs. 'But why would you send flowers to yourself?'

'I didn't. Obviously.' I sip my water. 'But someone did and it's persuaded everyone that Meggie's death has driven me mad. Literally, mad. Mad enough to send flowers to myself to make it look like I have some . . . I don't know, secret admirer.'

Cara closes her eyes. 'Maybe it's the jet lag but I'm struggling. You've got a secret admirer?'

'No! Of course not. Though sometimes it *does* feel like I'm being followed.' I want to see how she reacts before I tell her the other stuff: the mirrors, the flat tyre and the rest.

'But who'd do that, hon?' she asks. 'I love you to pieces but you're a seventeen-year-old sixth-former, not a spy or a master criminal. What would be the point of tailing you?'

I shrug. 'I suppose you're right. I'm too boring to be followed.'

Cara blushes. 'Sorry. Jet lag is making me sound like a right cow, but I'm back now. We're going to have so much fun that no one following you will have a hope of keeping up, right?'

I nod.

'I want to hear a *yes* from you.'

'OK,' I say.

'It's time, Alice. Time to move on with your life.'

18

I'm dead to the world when my phone's ring wakes me, urgent and insistent.

I scrabble round for it in the dark.

Dark? It must be very late – or very early. The weather's stifling this week, it's impossible to tell what time it is from the temperature alone.

Lewis? Please let it be Lewis.

But the name on the display reads *Ade*.

I almost don't answer, but it must be serious for him to call at . . . I squint at the time . . . three-forty a.m.

'Ade? Is that you? What's going on?'

In the moment before anyone speaks, violent scenarios fill my head: Ade under attack from Sahara. A stranger discovering their bodies and picking up Ade's phone, scrolling through the frequently dialled numbers.

Sahara calling to confess.

There's been no direct contact from her since the day I visited her in Greenwich – the day Mum and Dad confronted me about the flowers.

'Sorry to call so late.' Ade's voice is urgent, but he doesn't sound sorry at all. He sounds angry. 'Sahara is very upset. Well, hysterical is probably a more accurate description.'

'Why?'

He tuts. 'I think you *know* why, Alice.'

'If she's got a problem with me, surely she's big enough to sort it out herself.' I don't care if I sound fed up. 'Preferably not in the middle of the night.'

'I've had to force it out of her – what happened, how you accused her.'

'*Force?* Come on, Ade, Sahara never needs to be forced to make up stories.'

I hear a whimper in the background and realise I must be on speakerphone. Anger makes me feel hotter. Will she never leave me alone? 'What is it, Sahara? Is it not enough to stalk me – now you want to deprive me of sleep too? Or something worse?'

'Stop lying, Alice!' she shrieks. 'I've never stalked anyone. I'd never do anything to harm you. Or Meggie.'

Her voice is so loud that I pull the duvet back over my head so my parents won't wake up. I've gone too far. She isn't supposed to know I suspect her directly. But the fear and the stress, it's pushed me to the edge. I have to ring off before I say something else I regret. 'I can't see the point in this phone call. Goodnight, Sahara.'

'No. Don't!' she calls out. 'I need to see you! Talk to you—'

Then I hear rustling.

'Alice, I've switched off the speakerphone because Sahara is finding it so painful to hear your voice. But I have to ask – why did you accuse her of being involved in your sister's death, after all we've—'

'I never said that.' *Even though it is what I think.*

'You must understand how devastated she is,' Ade sounds calmer now, but there's still an edge to his words.

'I haven't spoken to her in days, Ade. Perhaps she's got confused.' Though I bet she's *seen* me, before moving the mirrors on my car or letting the tyres down.

'I think you're the one who is confused, Alice. Look, we know you're getting psychological help now. That's why we're not going to say anything to your parents, but as Sahara's boyfriend, I need to ask you to be more considerate in future. She's on the edge.'

Something's wrong about this conversation. Something doesn't add up.

My parents only staged their intervention *after* I'd visited Sahara in Greenwich.

So how could Ade and Sahara possibly know I'm getting help?

'What do you mean, "help"?'

He sighs. 'Alice, it's nothing to be ashamed of. Sahara mentioned it but of course it won't go any further. You can trust us completely.'

His words echo in my head, because trusting them is the last thing I can afford to do. The only way Sahara could know about Olav is if she's been following me, surely? Mum and Dad would never tell, and the only other people who know are Cara and Lewis and they both loathe Ade and Sahara.

'You woke me up for *that*?'

There's a long pause, then Ade says, 'Maybe I made a mistake. Since she's been living with me, I've realised how much Meggie's death, and all that's happened since, is still affecting Sahara. Things were getting a bit fraught just now and I guess I wanted to warn you—' He stops abruptly.

'*Warn* me? About what, Ade?'

'Forget it. It's nothing.'

'Tell me. Please.'

'Seriously, it's *nothing*. I over-reacted. Things always look bleaker in the dark, don't they, Alice?'

I say nothing, hoping he might change his mind and tell me what he meant. But I can hear Sahara breathing by the mouthpiece and I sense the moment's passed. I wonder how often things get 'fraught' with Sahara, and if he has any idea what he's dealing with. Surely if he did, they wouldn't be together.

'I'm going to ring off, now, Alice, I'm sorry. I guess everything will look better in the morning. Goodnight.'

After the call ends, night lingers, darker and deeper than

before. What was that phone call really about? A warning – or a threat? I try to remember the exact words he used. *Fraught. Painful. Devastated.*

Is Ade afraid of Sahara himself?

The only comfort I can take from the call is barely a comfort at all – my suspicions about being followed *are* right. Sahara must be hanging out in the shadows most of the time, tailing me from home to Olav's to Lewis's.

And then she goes home to Ade and he has to listen to her lies and hysteria. It must be suffocating.

I shiver as I realise something else: the conversation felt incomplete, as though he were trying hard to tell me something else, or warn me, even. My thoughts circle endlessly around his words and his unfinished sentences. Perhaps I should have been sympathetic, listened more.

What the hell was it that Ade *didn't* say?

Hot.

Suffocatingly hot.

When I wake up again, I'm sweating, the duvet twisted round me like a straitjacket.

I wrestle it off. Light is streaming through my windows, the room fuggy with stale, hot air.

Eleven o'clock.

My alarm didn't go off and my parents have left me to sleep. They know as well as I do that I have nothing to get up for.

I change my sweaty t-shirt, pull on some tracksuit bottoms and go downstairs. Dad's reading the paper in the living room, Mum's trimming something in the garden. They wave, but don't try to talk to me. Maybe that's Olav's latest strategy: wait for me to spill the beans of my own accord. Well, I'm not playing.

I pour out a bowl of cereal and catch my reflection in the

glass in the oven door. No one would mistake me for Meggie right now. For a short while, I started to resemble her, but maybe my brief moment of prettiness has been and gone.

Or maybe I should stop feeling sorry for myself and have a bloody shower!

I take my bowl upstairs and am about to hit the bathroom to wash away the pointless self-pity and wake myself up, when I notice the light on my phone is flashing.

Missed call: Lewis.

That's woken me up.

He's left no voicemail but there is a text, sent a minute later: **I've got access to a lab. If you're still sure it's what you want.**

I don't hesitate. There's no *if* about it. Maybe the truth is going to hurt, but it's all I have left.

I dial his number.

'Lewis! How are you?'

My mother greets him at the front door.

'Very well, thanks, Mrs Forster. Are you going out? You're looking very glamorous.'

Mum laughs. 'I've told you before, call me Bea. Glamorous! Hardly, we're just having some old friends round for supper. So where are you taking my daughter tonight? She seems very excited.'

'Ah, well, it's a surprise, you see.'

I catch sight of Lewis as she lets him in. There's something different about him. What? He's dressed in his normal working-from-home uniform of designer jeans and crumpled shirt. His hair's slightly more dishevelled than usual, but he might just have overdone it with the gel.

It's his face that's different. His eyes.

They're blazing.

When he looks at me, it feels like he can see right through

me: my doubts, fears, wishes. Though he knows all of those already, or at least more than anyone else does. Even Danny doesn't know me so well.

'Ready, Ali?'

My throat is so dry that my 'Yes' comes out more like a croak.

'Drive safely,' Mum says, ruffling my hair on the way out as though I'm five and heading off to school.

'I'll have her back before the clock strikes twelve and she turns into a pumpkin,' Lewis says.

Outside, he's left the engine running. There's not a moment to waste.

Just before Mum shuts the door, I turn back. She looks so small standing there, waving me off. How hard must it be for her to let me go, after what happened to Meggie?

I run back up the path and give her a hug. Her bones feel fragile.

'What was that for?' she says, when I let go.

'Just . . . well, if I can't hug my mum, who *can* I hug?' I say, trying to make a joke of something that, a few seconds ago, didn't feel like a joke at all.

'Hug me any time you like, Alice. Any time,' she says, blowing me a kiss as I climb into Lewis's car and he puts his foot down.

19

The evening air smells of barbecues and summer idleness.

But Lewis is anything but chilled. He's driving way too fast. OK, he *always* drives too fast, but usually I still feel safe. Tonight, not so much.

'Are we in a hurry?'

'Whatever gave you that impression, Ali?'

The car almost flies off the roundabout and straight into the fast lane of the motorway. Luckily the entire population of London must be at a barbecue; the road is so empty you'd think there'd been an apocalypse.

He accelerates so hard that I'm pushed back in my seat. The Lewis I'm seeing tonight isn't the person I know. Has that glimpse of the Beach affected him, too?

'Where *are* we going, Lewis?'

'It's better if you don't know too many details.'

'Why?'

'You're safer if you know as little as possible about the lab.'

His speech is much faster than usual, and his words more alarming. *Lab. Safer?* 'You're sure this isn't dangerous?'

'Yes. I told you before: it's completely non-invasive. But it isn't exactly mainstream either. The lab's private and the technology is cutting-edge.'

Cutting-edge? Nerves knot my stomach and make my head throb. 'But it should tell us whether the Beach is real or not?' I ask.

'There are no guarantees, but it's the best chance we have.'

'Lewis, if we get there and I . . . change my mind, that'll be OK, won't it?'

He turns to look at me. 'Of course. Right up till the last moment, or even while it's underway. You just say the word.' His voice is softer now, more like the old Lewis. 'The only thing is, I've had to call in some pretty big favours for this. There will be no second chances.'

After forty minutes, we turn off the motorway and take a twisty route via back roads to a little trading estate. I strain to hear cars or life, but there's no sound at all. The place is dead.

Lewis slows right down and the car crawls past a tile warehouse, a pine workshop, a tool-hire depot. As he drives, Lewis checks his mirror, his blind spot, his watch. In the yellow street lamps, the whites of his eyes look jaundiced.

I want to make the usual silly jokes, but I don't know how he'll react tonight.

Right at the far end of the estate there's a long, squat building backing onto an embankment. There are four shuttered windows along the front plus a glazed door, but no light shows at all. Lewis parks next to a white van with no number plates. When he turns off the engine, I hear rumbling and feel a slight tremor. What are they *doing* in there?

Then I spot the railway line running along the top of the embankment.

'Ready, Ali?' Lewis asks.

'I guess.'

Outside, the air is still, but now it smells of diesel instead of barbecues. Once the train's gone past, the only other sound is a regular hum coming from the building.

I notice a white unit attached to the far wall. Air-conditioning. Otherwise there's nothing. No birdsong at dusk, no laughter from distant parties.

Lewis doesn't go to the front door, but walks towards the

other end of the building. There's a metal door but no bell and no signs, except one that reads ANTI-CLIMB PAINT: KEEP OFF.

He sends a text.

Moments later, the metal door opens. Inside looks even darker than outside and the man who opened the door says nothing, but lets us in, locks up behind us, then leads us through a maze of corridors. There is very low-level emergency lighting that gives the space a green glow, but he helps guide us using the torch beam from his mobile. He's slim, not that tall, and I can just make out the silhouette of his square glasses. But I can't see anything else, not even enough to guess his age.

You're safer if you know as little as possible.

As we shuffle along, I lose any sense of where the back and front of the building might be. In the gloom, my hearing becomes more acute. What *is* this place? I listen out for the squeaks of lab rats or the cries of human guinea pigs.

I tut to myself. Ridiculous. I'm safer in here than I am in the outside world, surely. At least Sahara can't get inside.

Finally, there's a brighter strip of light ahead of us, shining from the gap at the bottom of a door, plus a smaller dot of red light at waist level.

'Ladies first,' the man says after he waves a swipe card and the dot of light turns green. His voice is young, nervy. *Nerdy*, too, maybe, or am I just playing to the stereotype of mad scientist?

My head pounds. If I could remember the way, I have a feeling my body might take over and race back out. But I need to do this, however much it scares me.

And I've missed the Beach so much – despite the fear, part of me is desperate to see Meggie and Danny again, no matter what it takes.

Inside the secure area, it's a little brighter, thanks to the glow from endless high-tech equipment. I guess this is what you'd call a control room and, to the left, there's a door marked SERVERS. Through the reinforced glass of the door I can see banks of computers lined up like library shelving.

An electronic hum fills the space and makes my head throb.

To our right, there's a long desk, with keyboards and controls built in, and flat-screens mounted above, ten or more. And beyond that, a pane of glass that reflects our own faces back at us.

Lewis's eyes look wild in the reflection. But the lab guy has a beard below his glasses, covering the bottom half of his face. It looks like a joke-shop disguise.

Finally my own face is reflected back at me. In the dark mirror, I resemble my sister again. A reminder of why I'm here – and why I have to stay put, however scary it gets.

'OK, Alice. This is what's going to happen. This set-up allows us to monitor your brain responses while you complete an activity.' The man sounds almost bored, as though it's a script he's read over and over again. 'What we usually do is monitor what you're seeing on one screen, your responses via camera on a second screen, and then your brain scans on a third.' He points at the bank of screens.

'But there are more than three,' I point out.

'Yep, we're set up to monitor up to four subjects at any time during working hours in the main booths, through there.' He points. 'But they don't always get the full MRI treatment. Tonight, you're centre-stage.' There's a sarcastic edge to his voice, as though he doesn't believe my brain is interesting enough to be scanned.

'I've told the operator there's no need to monitor what you're seeing, Ali,' Lewis explains.

'Whatever,' says the operator with a shrug. 'You're paying. You get what you ask for.'

Paying? Lewis said he'd called in a favour. I wonder how much this has cost.

'It's absolutely critical that no one gets to see what I see,' I say. *If there is anything to see at all. If it's not too late already.*

'Like I said, no skin off my nose. I'll disconnect the lead, so whether it's porn or the best of bloody LOLcats, whatever you're seeing will be strictly between you and our super-fast broadband connection. Though there's no need to be embarrassed. We've monitored the effect of pretty much everything on the human brain, from snuff movies to Australian soap operas and Viking role-play games.'

He thinks I'm *ashamed* of what I'm hoping to see? He couldn't be more wrong.

'Ready, Ali? We ought to get going,' Lewis says.

I nod.

'All right, I'll set you up in the scanner,' the technician tells me, his voice slightly impatient. 'Thing to remember, it's safe as houses. Noisy as the depths of hell, but that's the magnets. Forewarned is forearmed.'

He pushes open a door to the left of the monitors and it makes a swooshing noise. The pounding in my head's much louder now, a deafening drum beat.

Lewis goes ahead of me. The door closes softly behind us. Dark, again, though those eerie green emergency lights do provide enough glow to stop us falling over each other. There's an awful synthetic smell like cheap carpet. My lungs are struggling to get enough air and I'm not even in the lab yet.

It's only when the operator guy opens another door that I realise we were in an ante-room. We step into another space, and he flicks a switch.

'Ouch.' The strip lights blind me for a few seconds. When my eyes adjust, I'm surprised at how *medical* the room is, all white tiles and metal fixtures.

And a huge doughnut-shaped machine that's familiar from TV medical dramas.

'Our two-million-dollar baby,' says the operator. The cynicism is missing. He sounds awestruck.

The operator shows me where to lie down, and how. He positions a headset with built-in microphone around my ears, puts a moulded foam cushion under my knees and then explains that the mouse and keyboard sit on a tray on my chest, while the screen with a webcam on top is suspended over my face. 'Please try not to move or the scanner won't work properly.'

When I'm in the right position, he fastens some straps around the upper part of my chest and arms, pulls a strange plastic cage over my head and positions dense cushions either side of my neck so I can't change position.

I feel trapped.

He must see the alarm in my eyes because he smiles. 'Nothing to worry about. More of a reminder not to move than anything else.'

'And you'll tell me when the machine starts up?'

I hear him laugh. 'Oh, don't worry, you'll know.'

His footsteps bounce off the tiled walls and floor, making them impossibly loud. I test the straps by trying to move my arms. He's right, they don't feel that strong, but they're still unsettling.

'Lewis? Are you still in here?'

'Sure.' He steps forward so I can see him close by, smiling down at me. It's reassuring. 'Everything OK?'

I try to smile back. 'It's a bit freaky. What do they *really* do here? I feel like a lab rat.'

'Games and media research. But some of it is quite *extreme*. Not just which virtual car we most want to drive, or which gangster we most want to shoot. The scanning they do here focuses on the areas of the brain that relate to primal emotions and experiences. Delusions. Fear. Love. Addiction.'

Those words again.

'Do you really think that's what it's about?'

He shakes his head. 'I don't know, Ali.' He pauses. 'All I know is that knowledge is power, and this could unlock what's going on.'

'Oh. OK.' I try to nod, but my head's fixed in position. 'And the guy . . . the caretaker or whatever he is. He does know what he's doing, right?'

Lewis chuckles. 'Ian's not the caretaker. He's one of the UK's rising stars in neuroscience.'

'Really?'

'Only the best for my freaked-out friend.' He hesitates. For a weird moment, I think he's about to lean down and kiss me, but he moves a strand of hair off my face, away from my eyes. 'It'll be OK, Ali. Whatever you see, or you don't see, it's fine. We're getting closer to the truth. Shall we rock and roll?'

'Yes.'

'Good luck, Alice. I'll be right next to you.'

And then he leaves the room too.

I'm alone.

'Alice, give me a thumbs-up if you can hear me.' Ian's voice comes through the headphones. I do what he asks.

'In a moment I'll turn on the machine to give you a few seconds to get used to the sounds it makes. Then the platform moves you into the scanner. It'll be noisy at first. Maybe claustrophobic. Most people can deal with it once they're used to it, but any time you think it's too much, there's a panic button by your right hand. Shaped like a diamond.'

I can't see it, but I grope around to feel for it. 'Got it.'

'Good stuff. Once you've been in for a minute or so, you'll notice the blank screen above your head will be replaced by your normal PC desktop. Though only you can see it, remember? We'll let you surf away for as long as you need to; simply press the diamond button when you're done. We'll be monitoring your reactions all the way so don't worry, we won't abandon you in there. You ready?'

I nod.

The rumble comes from nowhere.

What the hell? I couldn't ever have been ready for *that*: a noise so intense that it seems to take over my body and my brain. *Whirr*, rumble, *whirr*.

Breathe, Alice, breathe.

I begin to count backwards from a hundred, a trick Meggie told me she used when she had pre-show nerves.

It's not helping.

The sound of the machinery is nightmarish. Like I'm a product in a factory on a processing line, being tested for defects, ready to be thrown on the reject pile if I don't pass.

Focus, Alice. Maybe you're just seconds away from all the answers.

My finger hovers over the panic button. I could so easily press it right now. This is *terrifying*.

But above my face – only a few centimetres – the screen is changing already.

My desktop wallpaper.

It shows all the same icons and the background shows that familiar paradise: the Beach. *So close.*

I can't let myself sound the alarm. I must go through with this.

I take my hand away from the panic button and fumble with the unfamiliar controller, trying to select my email program. All I can hear and feel is the rumble.

As I type my password, my fingers feel disconnected. I wait.

My inbox loads.

Nothing in there but spam, these days.

I click to the bottom, and there it is: the original Beach

invitation. My gateway to the place where everybody knows who I am, where I really matter.

If I'm even allowed back after what Lewis saw.

I click on the link and hold my breath.

20

The sounds of the Beach usually begin before the image appears. I listen out for paradise above the rumble of the machinery. I hope for birdsong, or someone strumming a guitar.

But I can't hear any of that. Memories of the Beach race through my head: Javier, before he left, warning me about consequences; my sister, tears running down her face when she realised that he'd gone, that she'd lost yet another friend; Danny, his eyes blood red with terror as the storm began to rage.

My doing. I allowed Lewis to catch a glimpse of the world of the dead. Surely that can't go unpunished, even though it wasn't my fault. Soul Beach is not a forgiving place.

But now I think I hear . . . *something* natural. It's higher-pitched than the mechanical roar of the scanner. Whistling?

Something's happening on the screen, too. I wait for the white background of the email to dissolve away like morning mist, to reveal the blue sky behind, as it always does.

No!

The sky is not blue any more but a fiery red flecked with streaks of orange. And as I move the mouse, down towards the shore, I realise it's not *my* Beach at all. It's some other place, a wasteland. There's no jetty, only debris in the choppy sea. The water is a dark crimson and a slick of silver stretches the whole length of the bay, reflecting a mean slice of sun that penetrates the clouds. It looks oddly beautiful, yes, but sinister too . . .

Oil. I can smell it: it catches in the back of my throat, heavy and toxic.

I try to move my head but I can't. My hand on the mouse has to do the job for me. Like Soul Beach, *this* bay is bordered by rocks and palms, but the trees here are ravaged. Branches are strewn across the dark brown sand. The spear-like leaves are dried out and brittle.

I reach out to touch one. It turns to dust under the gentlest pressure.

The oil is making me choke.

'Who's there? Is *anyone* there?' I can hardly hear my own voice above the machinery.

It's almost impossible to think straight but a horrible realisation is dawning. This place follows the same contours and geography as *my* Beach, except with a pile of sticks where the beach bar and huts should be.

I can't see any sign of human life, either now or in the recent past.

That feeling of familiarity grows and, with it, fear.

But it can't be true. I can't possibly have the power to destroy paradise by accidentally allowing a stranger to see it.

I'm not that *important.*

Unless it was in my head all along.

I remember that Lewis and Ian are observing every click of the mouse and every eye movement. Perhaps they already have the evidence to prove that none of this is real.

'Please? Anyone?'

Was that something moving behind me? I fight to screen out the sound of the scanner, to focus on the shore.

Wishful thinking. Maybe that's true of everything else I've conjured up since we laid my poor sister to rest in her poppy-patterned dress. For these last eleven months I've felt pleased with myself for being the only person who refused to give up on Meggie.

What if I've been lying to myself?

Please, no.

Alice.

Someone said my name. *Who?*

Aaa-leese.

'Who is that?'

'Alice, it's Ian here. In the control room. We wouldn't normally interrupt but we noticed you're crying. Are you OK for us to continue?'

I try to touch my face but the strap round my upper arm stops me. I force a smile, knowing they're watching me. 'Something in my eye. Can't reach it. But it's been washed out now. I'm happy to carry on.'

I blink, hard. Move the mouse again. Look at my feet, sinking into the dark brown sand. Why is it that odd colour? Then I realise: it's soaking wet. The storm that began the last time I was on the Beach – surely it couldn't have caused all this damage?

I walk, not knowing what else to do, but continuing for the good of the experiment if nothing else. At the waterline, where the jetty should be, are two stumps. The wood that remains is split, as though a giant has wrenched the pillars out of the seabed in a fit of rage, yet the splinters left behind smell rotten, not fresh. You'd think that years had passed since anyone came here.

Perhaps I should leave. This place torments me with memories, with could-have-beens and should-have-saids.

I call out, 'Meggie, can you hear me?'

My own words bounce back at me, off the rocks. I keep walking, keep calling out.

'Danny? I came back. I love you. If you're here, tell me. Show me. Do *something.*'

My voice is breaking and I'm aware that the tears are really falling now, though what Ian and Lewis don't know

118

is that they're tears of frustration as well as grief.

This really *is* the Beach. I can't deny it any longer. I see the gap in the rocks ahead of me, the place where Danny and I snatched what little privacy we could. I know the contours of those stones as well as I know the shape of his lips and the flecks of gold in his deep green eyes. I want to touch him. What if those stones are the closest I'll ever get to being near him again?

I clamber through that gap, scraping my shin along the sharp edge. I cry out, but part of me is ashamed. *Insane* to think I can feel pain or anything else here, when none of this can really exist.

The stone is hot and smooth under my fingers. An illusion, but a comforting one. I sit down and close my eyes. What now? The scanner will be switched off soon, I guess. And then Lewis will confirm I've imagined everything.

It'll be the end of the Beach. Does my fight for justice end here too?

No. Even if I've imagined all of this, Sahara can't go free. I won't allow that to happen . . .

'You came back.' Danny's voice. So close that the sensation of his breath warms my skin.

I jump but I daren't open my eyes. 'I'm imagining you. You're not really here.'

The lightest touch on my shoulder feels like searing pain because it's so real. Then that sensation of falling from the sky, the fear as the desert earth gets closer and closer . . .

'Turn around and tell me that's what you believe, Alice. I waited for you, even when they told me I shouldn't.'

'They?' I still don't face him because I'm afraid of nothingness.

'The other Guests. They said you must have done something terrible, to bring this destruction. I defended you. Please, tell me what you've done.'

The brain is dangerous territory.

Unpredictable things happen there. So I can think of nothing more unnatural than trying to pry into its secrets or analyse how someone else interprets the world.

It is true that sometimes even I long for understanding, for one good person to see me for the person I really am and, better still, to accept me completely.

But I realised after what happened to Meggie that few people can forgive, and almost no one can forget. Offering someone the truth about your innermost thoughts and desires is too big a gamble. You risk judgement, condemnation.

Let me rescue you, Alice, before it's too late . . .

21

Still I'm afraid to turn round and look at Danny. Everything feels misshapen and wrong.

Half of me is here on the wrecked Beach with my back to Danny, longing to touch him and be touched by him.

But the other half knows I'm being monitored in a scanner, that what I'm experiencing can't possibly be real.

Is this what schizophrenia feels like? Perhaps Olav has hit the jackpot; I really am in need of psychiatric help.

'Alice? You can't wait forever.'

Slowly, I turn towards the voice.

Danny. A different Danny from the one I know so well. His sandy hair is matted, his arms and legs are covered in scratches and he has a blackened eye that makes the green of his iris look even more intense.

'*Danny*. Oh God. What happened to you?'

When I reach out for him, he backs away. On any other day, we'd already be in each other's arms, kissing, but no wonder he's keeping his distance. I might have caused the destruction of paradise.

If it even exists.

My head throbs in time with the thunderous machine.

'I'll live,' he says, then lets out a single laugh. 'Or survive. Or whatever. But I need to know what happened. One moment we were talking, the next all hell broke loose.'

I nod. 'Someone saw the Beach. Someone who shouldn't have.'

Disbelief clouds Danny's face. 'You *showed* it to a stranger?

What the hell were you thinking? Didn't you realise that would make the Management angry?'

The scene of devastation behind him shows just *how* angry. 'It wasn't deliberate. The person . . . he walked in on me when he shouldn't have.'

'He?'

That one-word question has so much behind it: suspicion, jealousy, *fear.*

'My parents have banned me from going online and the only place I could go to try was a friend's flat.'

A friend who must be able to hear every word I say.

'You were in his place, then, were you? Just the two of you?'

'Danny. *Please.* He doesn't matter.'

I look away, hoping Lewis hasn't heard that part, or doesn't realise I'm talking about him. It doesn't seem fair. Or true.

Danny stares back.

'What I need to know is what's happened here. And where Meggie is. Please?'

Danny's face changes suddenly, from hostility to fear. He's cowering as though someone is about to hit him.

And I realise it's not only the scanner machinery that's rumbling.

'It's starting again, Alice,' he shouts. 'We need to move. I don't know what will happen this time—'

Before he can finish, the first bolts of lightning break up the sky and a wild wind comes from nowhere. He grabs my hand and pulls me backwards, towards the sharp rocks that enclose the Beach, where Sam's bar used to be.

The force of the storm is intensifying so rapidly that we're struggling not to be pushed over into the sand as we run. I can feel my skin being warped by the wind like Plasticine.

'Here!'

There's a tiny overhanging section of rock which forms a shelter. Danny lets me crouch down, then squeezes in beside me. Finally, we kiss. But it's different. Not the all-the-time-in-the-world embrace we've lingered over before, but the briefest touch to prove we are still in this together.

It makes me shake a little less.

I watch the storm in awe. So much rain is pouring, like a whole ocean is being tipped down from the heavens. Thunder makes my teeth vibrate, and flashes of lightning turn the Beach from night to day and back again a hundred times a minute.

The rawness is almost exciting. I wonder how the Guests felt when confronted with this after months or years of nothing but endless sunshine and bland blue skies.

'What about the others?' I ask Danny, though of course there's only one other I care about: *Meggie*.

He kisses the top of my head and I feel comforted, till I realise that he's doing it so I don't have to see his face as he tells me what happened. 'I don't know for sure. When the storm really got going, it was hellish.'

'But Guests can't be hurt, can they?' A memory of poor Triti comes into my head. She wanted to escape from the Beach more than anything, but couldn't injure herself or end it, however hard she tried.

'All bets are off now, Alice. You haven't noticed how bad I look?'

I touch the bruised skin under his eye. 'Still gorgeous. But maybe a little rougher around the edges.'

Danny smiles briefly, then goes back to the story. 'Perhaps no one would have been hurt, who knows? But it's instinct to flee from a storm. You see what it did to the bar, to the huts?'

'But where did they flee to? I thought there was no way out of the Beach. People have tried hard enough.' A horrible dread is rising inside me. *Meggie?*

'Not as hard as they did when the storm struck.' He closes his eyes as he remembers. 'The Guests started to clamber up the rocks. At first, it was every guy or girl for him- or herself, but pretty soon they realised it could only work if everyone helped each other, so they kinda got a human chain going. People fell, were pulled up again.'

'Including my sister?'

'She was one of the last, Alice. She hung on for hours in case you came back, even though Tim was the one who organised the whole escape chain.'

'Tim?'

'Weird, right? I never thought he'd lead anyone, but the Guests just seemed to trust him. We're talking total panic when the storm first hit. But there was this quiet English guy thing about him, like nothing could be bad while he was giving orders, you know, like in a war movie.'

'But Meggie didn't stay with you.' My voice is small and scared.

'Alice, Tim left her no choice. They both tried to make me go but I refused. I couldn't leave without saying goodbye to you. They said they'd come back for me.'

Goodbye? Who mentioned goodbye? I ignore that part, focus on the practical. If I created this mess, then surely I can find a way to put it right, bring Meggie back.

The alternative is too awful to contemplate.

The rain is even heavier now. 'Have they come back?'

Danny shakes his head. 'No. A few times I tried to climb up on my own, far enough to see over the cliffs, but it takes two to get any grip.'

I look above us. The rocks are unforgivingly smooth and sharp.

'Where could they have gone?' I think back to the last time I saw my sister. She was walking away with Tim, to give me some time alone with Danny.

He doesn't answer. There *is* no answer, I suppose.

'I might never see my sister again, Danny.' It's been my

worst fear from my very first moments on the Beach, but I can't believe it's actually happened.

He squeezes me tighter. 'We don't know that. We don't know anything.'

'Sam might know,' I say.

He points towards where the foundations of the bar form a low square in the sand. 'We'll go ask her, shall we? Maybe see if she can rustle up a couple of daiquiris while we're there.'

Danny doesn't usually *do* sarcasm but I understand why he's talking this way.

'And you? How do you feel?' I ask him.

He shrugs. 'Not that excited about the prospect of eternity here without even a softball to keep me company.'

'You've got me.'

'No.'

'Of course you have. Forever and always! We could try to clamber up now, together.'

'And then what? Alice, there might be no going back once you've seen what's at the top.'

That silences me.

'We have to be realistic, Alice. And you must promise not to be sad. Not about me, not about your sister. I've had plenty of time to think while I've been alone, and I have to tell you I wish you'd never come to the Beach at all.'

'*I* don't.'

'Only because you can't imagine what your life woulda been like without it, but I *can* imagine it. You'd have been sad for a long while, but slowly you'd have accepted that the police had solved Meggie's murder. It would have been easier to move on.'

'But then I wouldn't have met you, Danny. I wouldn't have known how it feels to be in love.'

'Another bonus, huh?' His voice is bitter. 'Loving you has been wonderful, Alice. But it won't be like that now. What lies ahead of us is nothing but pain. And I don't want you to think that's what love is about, this *twisted* version. Loving someone you can never really have is a poor imitation of the real thing, don't you see?'

'This is the real-est thing I've ever known.'

He shakes his head. 'No. Nothing here is real. Not even me.'

'Not that again, Danny, please. I *know* the real you. The old one you told me about before, the rich brat, I've never met him. What he did, how spoiled he was, doesn't matter to me.'

'Even if the brat caused his own death?' He turns away from me. 'Even if he caused someone else's death too?'

I shake my head. 'Don't torture yourself. You died in a plane crash. There were inquiries. OK, so you took the controls for a moment, but the pilot shouldn't have let you do that if he wasn't confident you'd be safe. It was his responsibility.'

Too late, I remember he never told me *any* of that. I found it in news reports online. Have I gone too far in talking about the past? Will I be banned?

But nothing changes: Danny's still there and the rain is still falling and the thunder is still growling. Maybe the Management aren't listening any more.

He laughs. 'So that's the story the world bought? How *cute*. But if it were really an accident, I wouldn't be here, right? There'd be nothing to resolve.'

It *is* the one part of his story that's never made sense to me.

'Well, try this on for size, Alice. Dumb rich kid decides to prove that there's more to him than his daddy's money. Dumb rich kid wants to play the big man in border country, down Mexico way. But it's not enough for super-dumb rich kid to fly down in the family jet and buy a few pills from your local *farmacia*. No. Danny decides to play with the big boys. He—'

'You don't have to tell me this.'

'*Someone* has to know what I did.'

I want to block my ears because I don't want to hear bad things about the boy I love; yet I sense he needs to do this and I owe it to him to let him confess to me. I nod for him to carry on.

'Drugs are sexy, right? That's what I thought back then. So I got myself a gang contact and began making deals *so* much riskier than the legal stuff Daddy did – though it was all funded by Daddy's allowance, obviously. I made the pilot take a detour on the way to a family party. We went right over the border, even though he didn't think too much of heading somewhere with more cactuses than people. But what Danny wants, Danny gets.'

'And that's when you took the controls?'

He shakes his head. 'No. I never did that. The dealers must have brought us down, then played around with the wreckage to conceal what happened, before taking the cash I had for the deal. I don't remember much except losing height . . .' Danny sighs. 'Five thousand dollars. That was all. The pilot had two daughters – orphans now, for the sake of five thousand dollars. All *my fault*.'

I remember the news footage I watched online. His funeral. The pilot's widow and children. The image of the smashed plane on the floor of the plains.

I don't know what to say to him.

'I disgust you, right? I disgust myself, too.'

He's hunched up against the rock, centimetres from me. His shirt is soaked through and his eyes are full of pain.

'No! You don't disgust me, I . . .' I should reach out for him, but I need a few more seconds to process this. As soon as I touch him, I know I'll glimpse his last moments again. It'll feel different now I understand what really happened and why.

I *am* shocked. What he did was stupid and irresponsible, the consequences pointless and tragic. No wonder he's been telling me the same things since we fell in love: that he doesn't deserve me, that he is a terrible person. Living with that knowledge would be enough to drive anyone crazy.

And yet does it change the way I feel about him? No. He had no way of knowing it would end like that. It was childish rebellion, not premeditated killing. Danny has suffered every day since he arrived on the Beach. More than I ever knew until now.

'Alice, say what you think. It can't possibly make me feel any worse than I already do.'

Instead of looking at him, I focus on the bleak landscape in front of us. What seemed like paradise has always been a kind of hell for Danny. He's tried to make up for it here, by supporting Triti and Javier and my sister, spending his time trying to solve the mystery of the Beach itself. I won't turn my back on him because he made a single mistake.

'You're not a monster, Danny. You're just a guy who got it wrong.'

He stares at me, as though he can't believe what I just said. I shuffle along the rock towards him and reach out, putting my arms around his shoulders and pulling him into me.

Burnt earth fills my vision. And guilt – Danny's guilt – fills my brain. What did the pilot think as they went down?

Danny's crying but trying not to let me see. Even now, he wants to protect me.

'It must have been torture keeping this a secret,' I whisper.

I feel him nodding against my chest. 'I couldn't tell you because I was so afraid you'd leave me and you've been the only thing . . . the *only* thing . . . that stopped me going crazy. See? I'm selfish too.'

I realise something important. 'That's why you stayed behind to wait for me?'

He lifts his head to look at me. 'A devastated beach with you here is still better than paradise without you. But it can't go on.'

The storm rages on. Were we always heading for this moment? Maybe my fate is as entwined with Danny's as my sister's is with Tim's. 'What do you mean?'

'I can deal with my punishment, Alice. Hanging out here alone. I guess it's what I deserve.'

'No. It's too cruel. Forever is too long to be alone with so much guilt. There must be some way I can make this right – as I have for the others. You deserve peace.'

Even though if he finds peace, it must mean I will lose him too.

'I don't deserve peace and, anyhow, what can you do, Alice? There's no way to make up for the death of the pilot, or change things for his widow and daughters.'

'I don't believe that. There *must* be a way to resolve it, otherwise, why would you be on the Beach, Danny? I promise I'll work it out, right? Whatever it takes.'

'Not everything has a solution.' He sighs. 'There is something more important I want from you.'

'Anything.'

He pulls away from me properly now. 'Actually, it's two things. First, you *must* leave here, and for good this time. It's not a place for the living, not now.'

'But I don't want to leave you. Or cut myself off from the chance to see my sister again—'

'Alice, stop kidding yourself. Nothing here happens by chance. You must accept she might be gone for good.'

I'll never leave the Beach until I've seen her. The idea makes me feel hot and faint. The sky is lightening and, as the wind drops, heat breaks through: intense heat, like the sun is burning a hole through the cloud. 'Is the second thing any easier?'

'I need you to try to forgive me.'

'That *is* easy. I already have.'

'What the hell did I do to deserve you?' Danny smiles at me but I can still see tears magnifying the little flecks of gold in his eyes. 'I can't let this carry on. I must do the one good thing in my control, Alice, and say goodbye to you now, for the last time.'

'I won't let you do that.'

'It's my decision, Alice. You said it yourself, I need peace. How am I gonna get that if I spend every hour of every day knowing that not only did I deprive the pilot of life, I'm depriving you too. Because this, here, is not enough for you.'

The heat is building, but it's not the brilliant sunshine that used to light up languid afternoons on Soul Beach. It's harsh and relentless, like midday in the desert.

Could he be right? Should I be putting my energies into solving Meggie's murder and trying to help the pilot's family, instead of hanging out here, reminding Danny of all the things he can never have again?

Here, now, I'm facing the question I've been avoiding since the night I first realised I was in love with Danny.

What does the future hold for us?

And as the sun beats down on my head, I finally let myself answer it honestly.

Nothing.

'You know it's the right thing, don't you, Alice?' Danny whispers. 'You know that if you keep coming, it'll only get harder when the inevitable happens. For both of us. That the only good choice now is for you to walk away. And stay away.'

I don't speak. I won't admit it to him. He lifts my chin with his hand and begins to kiss me and, with my lips, I try to tell him all the things that words can't say: how happy he's made me, how I will never forget him, how I couldn't have asked for a better person to be my first love.

I don't want the kiss to end.

'Not yet,' I whisper.

It's him that breaks away. 'Alice?'

I hold on tight, trying to focus on his beautiful face, but my eyes are hurting, and my throat stings too.

'Something's wrong,' I tell him.

He's staring at me. Behind him I notice something changing in the sea. A backwards tide, like the water draining out of a bath. It reveals the sand below, dark and greasy-looking from oil deposits.

I try to warn Danny but I can't speak. It feels as though I'm hurtling away from the Beach now, being pulled out by a force much greater than either of us. Something eternal.

God-like?

Now I hear the noise of the scanner machinery again and remember where I *really* am. The din is as intense as it was, but beyond that there's something else.

Screeching?

The screen goes black.

'Danny?'

'Alice, stay where you are, we're investigating, but everything's fine, don't move.'

I don't recognise the voice at first, but then I remember – it's Ian.

'What's that noise?' My throat stings. 'What's going on?'

It's not just the screen that's black. The room is completely dark. Not even the green glow of the emergency lighting is penetrating this oppressive gloom. I try to pull myself free from the straps but the more I move, the tighter they seem to become.

Is that what this is? Some kind of *trap*?

Someone is pulling me, grabbing hold of my arms and fumbling with the buckles. The headphones slip off my ears and now the noise of the scanner is painfully intrusive.

Beyond it, there's another sound. A wail or a screech.

Sirens.

Finally, my body comes free of the straps and someone is helping me up, but I can't tell who it is or where we're going and I can't breathe properly.

Sahara?

The darkness I feel when I'm with her is exactly like this.

Suffocating.

Paralysing.

The noise is fading as I'm lifted up into someone's arms. I try to fight whoever's carrying me but I have no strength left. Only fear.

'Stay still, Alice, for God's sake!'

'Lewis?'

'Save your breath!'

The voice is sharp. I can't reply. I don't have enough air in my lungs.

Faster, faster. There is light now, low light. I think we're in the corridors. The maze.

Then he's ramming into the wall – no, the door – with his shoulder. Each thump I feel in my own body.

Twice. A third time.

It's not going to give.

And then it does, and we're falling – hard against the tarmac. Too hard against my head.

Like Zoe when she fell.

Before the world goes dark, I see his face.

Lewis – my friend, my confidant.

Except he no longer looks like either, his expression twisted almost beyond recognition.

Is that blind fury – or pure hatred?

22

Charcoal
  Choking
  Pine trees
  Zoe
  Raw
  Plastic
  No air
  Acid
  Tim
  No air
  Meggie
  NO AIR

Alice? Alice, love, can you hear me? Everything's all right, sweetheart. You're in the ambulance, on the way to hospital. Don't fight the mask. We're just giving you a little help with your breathing. Absolutely everything's going to be fine . . .

My hearing returns first.

A sucking, whooshing noise.

Now I can feel. Feel how much everything *hurts*. As though my skin and throat have been grated. When I try to breathe, air comes painfully and not nearly fast enough.

I'm struggling. To wake up, to stay awake.

Am I dead?

No, death shouldn't hurt. That much I *do* know.

So what . . .

'Sweetheart, you're all right. There's no hurry. Wake up when you need to. We'll be here.'

Mum?

When I try to open my eyes they resist. Unless they're already open and I can't see any more?

NO!

Blood red.

Soot black.

Nothingness.

Suddenly, I know *exactly* where I am.

'Hospital,' I croak. Each syllable takes as much effort as a marathon.

A soft touch on my hand. The peachy smell of Mum's perfume, the one she wore when I was little. It's all wrong here in this antiseptic world. Too cloying.

'Yes, sweetheart. That's right. But not for long, not now you're back with us.'

'Feel . . . foggy.'

'Foggy? They gave you something to settle you down. You were thrashing about a bit, especially when they put the tubes in to help you breathe.'

Now I wonder how I didn't notice them before: tubes in my nostrils that feel wider than car exhaust pipes. When I close my mouth, the struggle lessens. My heartbeat slows and my chest rises and falls less furiously.

Until I try to open my eyes. I half remember fighting to do this before. 'Mum?' Nothing's happening. 'MUM! I can't see!'

I lift my hands to my face and feel gauze, rough under my fingers, but then my mother's warm hands grip mine, stop them tearing at whatever's covering my eyes.

'Don't struggle, Alice, it's just a bandage to help you recover. But the doctors say you'll be fine, soon. You've had a very lucky escape.' Her voice falters.

Escape.

I remember Lewis's eyes boring into me. The lab. The darkness. The smell.

'What . . . happened?'

I hear Mum sigh but she says nothing for a long time. 'We're hoping you can tell us that, but not now, eh? Nothing should stress you out right now.'

'But my eyes?'

'It's not your eyes, it's just the lids. They're swollen from the smoke.'

Smoke?

'The doctors say it's normal. Everything will settle back down and then we'll take you home.'

More fragments of memory are flooding my brain. Danny kissing me as a storm raged around us on the Beach. And then his words . . .

The only good choice now is for you to walk away.

Forgive me.

Goodbye.

Did he find some way to banish me, forever?

'No! He can't have—'

'Alice, please, settle down. I'm sure he didn't mean for this to happen.'

'He said it was over . . .' but I stop myself. *Mum doesn't even know Danny. How* could *she know him?* He's nothing but a dead stranger, like all the other Guests on Soul Beach. Except Meggie, of course.

'We feel responsible, darling; we should have realised that he wasn't a good influence.'

'What happened to him – it wasn't an accident.'

'Oh, sweetheart, don't say that. Lewis wouldn't have put you in danger on purpose, even though we have no idea what he thought he was playing at, taking you there. But don't worry, you won't ever have to see him again.'

She's talking about Lewis, not Danny.

'Lewis? What did he do? Where did he take me?'

'Let's leave that till later—'

I grasp for memories, reasons, clarity. There was something we were trying to do. Me and Lewis. What was it?

'Not later, Mum. Now!'

She grips my hand so hard it's almost painful. 'There was a fire, Alice. In some rubbish bins at the back of a lab-laboratory.' I hear her voice tremble over the word. 'It was an accident. But what we don't understand – what your so-called friend refuses to tell us – is what you were doing there in the first place.'

A laboratory? The harder Mum holds my hand, the faster my brain seems to lose its grip. I'm closing down, even as I try to cling on to now, to make sense of this.

Lewis? What did he do?

But it's Danny whose face I see as the dark overwhelms me again.

When I come round properly, it all floods back. An experiment. A confession from Danny. Being dragged from a building.

Mum's told me more about what the police say happened. A 'rubbish fire' in bins at the back of the lab. Probably caused by teenagers who'd been smoking and didn't stub out the butts. An 'accident'.

It should be the final piece in the jigsaw of what happened last night. Except I don't recognise the picture. What I *do* know is that there've been too many 'accidents' in my life lately. Kids smoking on an industrial estate miles from anywhere? A discarded cigarette that just happened to ignite when I was strapped into a machine in an isolated lab?

This was no more an accident than what happened to Zoe in Barcelona was an accident. I was *that* close to ending up the same way as her.

I shiver.

'And you're sure you don't need any more painkillers to take home with you?' the doctor is asking.

I shake my head. 'Everything feels numb.'

The doctor nods but I can't make out his expression because my eyes are still not opening properly, and what I *can* see through the narrow gap is blurred. That'll get better soon, they say. Now I'm conscious again, they can't wait to kick me out of hospital.

'That's normal, isn't it?' my mum is asking.

In only a few hours I've gone from being terrified of blindness, to feeling relief that I can't focus on the pain in my parents' faces. It's bad enough to hear it in their voices.

And all because of Soul Beach.

'Delayed shock, probably. But Mrs Forster, do call us immediately if any of the symptoms on the printout recur. Particularly any change in skin tone. Sometimes the body's response to carbon monoxide can be delayed. Don't worry about bothering us; it's what we're here for.'

'Thank you. We really are very grateful.'

The porter pushes my wheelchair and I let my head fall against the fabric. I'm not ill, but the fight's gone out of me. I let myself be transferred into the back of Dad's car, and Mum does up my seatbelt, unzips my coat. A two-year-old does more for herself than I am capable of right now.

'There we are, sweetheart. We'll soon get you home,' she says, patting my hand. I see her doing it, but I don't feel it. My body's numb but my brain is swollen with awful thoughts. Grief dominated my life after Meggie died. I thought there could be nothing worse.

Now I know different. Grief is pure, an emotion so close to love that it's almost welcome.

This is worse. Fear of everything and everyone. With my body weakened, all I can do is go over and over what happened, trying to fill in the gaps. The same three questions circulate, more damaging than smoke.

Why did Sahara try to kill me?

Did the brain scans show the Beach was real?

And why hasn't Lewis – the person I trusted with my secret – come to tell me what that life-threatening experiment in the lab has revealed about my own sanity?

23

Mum's sleeping on the floor in my room tonight.

I told her not to but she insisted, and there *is* something comforting about the sound of her voice whispering through the dark. I try to focus on her words, not on the fears that threaten to overwhelm me completely.

She's telling me the stories she told me when I was small: how she met my dad at a gig, their wild hippie wedding and the Indian fortune-teller they met on their honeymoon who predicted that Mum would have two beautiful daughters who would make her happier than she thought possible . . .

My sister has a leading role in the stories.

'And she was *so* jealous after we brought you home from hospital. Kept asking when we could take you back or swap you for a puppy. She even had names ready for a dog – Trixie or Tinseltoes.'

I start to cough. It's terrifying, not being able to get enough air. Panic makes it worse. Something is clawing at my throat with ragged nails.

Mum's sitting me up, patting my back quite forcefully. I can see nothing but shapes through my puffed-up eyes. 'You're all right, lovely girl. You're just bringing the bad stuff up, out of your lungs.'

The bad stuff.

I nearly died. Death itself doesn't scare me as much as it should, because of the Beach. What scares me is what I'd have left behind. My parents would have been destroyed. And justice could never be done without me to fight for it.

'There, there, Alice.'

Even when the coughing finally lessens, my lips burn because they're so dry and cracked. I think of that last kiss with Danny, and the sudden heat, and how fast the fire took hold.

Mum and Dad are desperate to know what I was doing there, but I've said nothing.

I need to make sense of it myself, first. I imagine how Sahara must have tailed us to the lab. Watched us go in. Lit her fire.

Did she wait, to make sure it took hold? I picture her hiding nearby. Was she smiling as the smoke snaked into the building? Does she know I got out alive – and if so, what the hell will she do next?

The coughing gets more brutal, as though I'm trying to force the fear out of me.

'That's it, sweetheart, let it go.' Mum shifts away from me to go back to the sleeping bag on the floor.

I hold on to her hand. 'Stay here with me.'

So she squeezes in next to me in the bed, on the edge so that if we move it'll be her that falls out. Her arm is around me. Right now, I'm safe, aren't I?

'Where had I got to with my story?' she whispers.

'Meggie was jealous of the baby me.' I try to lose myself in the story, to forget everything bad.

Mum chuckles. 'Yes. So she refused point blank to have anything to do with you, till one night when we couldn't get you off to sleep. You were wailing as though your little heart was about to break, so your dad suggested Meggie sing to you . . .'

I know the rest of the story word for word, even though I haven't heard it for years. How my big sister never could resist an invitation to sing, even though her audience that night was a cuckoo in her lovely cosy nest.

How the first thing she thought of was one of her nursery rhymes.

How I stopped crying within seconds, and my big sister then always ran through her entire repertoire whenever I was inconsolable.

'Three blind mice . . .'

My mum is singing softly. This one was my favourite, according to family legend.

'They all ran after the farmer's wife, who cut off their tails with a carving knife.'

Despite the sinister words, the melody is comforting.

'Did you ever see such a thing in your life

'As three blind mice?'

Maybe I dream; I don't remember. Six or seven times I wake up gasping and coughing, convinced I can see a tall woman looming over me, with a pillow about to come down on my face.

But there's no one but Mum and me.

When it's morning, I sense her right next to me. I try to open my eyes as far as they'll go but the world is still out of focus.

'You look a little better, sweetheart. Do you feel it?'

I nod. Sitting up makes me dizzy, but perhaps my throat feels a bit less raw, my lungs less full of crap. Then I notice a dark stain on the pillow and bedclothes.

'Just what you've coughed up overnight, Alice. I'll get that changed. If you can make it downstairs for some breakfast, I thought I'd make eggy bread with honey.'

Another childhood treat.

Getting downstairs is hard enough, but I can't imagine ever getting back up. Is this how it feels to be a hundred years old?

As I hobble down, I squint towards the front door,

imagining Lewis is on the other side of that glass, coming to tell me what he's discovered, what it means.

But there's no one. *Where is he?* I know Mum and Dad might give him a hard time at first, but he's determined, isn't he? Unless the scan showed the Beach is all in my imagination and he's written me off . . .

While Mum makes breakfast, I collapse onto the sofa to give me time to get my breath back. *So* humiliating. At this rate she'll have to cut my bread up and feed it to me because the idea of lifting a fork to my own mouth is too daunting.

Sahara did this to me. She wanted to do worse.

It must mean I am closer than I've ever been to the truth.

At least I don't need physical strength to go over the night in my head, to seek reasons why Lewis might be staying away. I try to reconstruct the night in order. The dark corridor. The straps, and sounds of the machinery. The shock when I realised that wasteland was the Beach.

More shocks: Danny's smashed-up face, his confession about the drug deal, the awful goodbye.

And, even worse, learning that Meggie had gone.

A tightness spreads across my chest. Gone forever?

Am I alone again?

My puffy eyes are closing and the world goes dark. But I won't feel sorry for myself, or let myself believe I've lost her for good. I need to focus on getting well – so I can finally make sure Sahara gets what she deserves.

Before, it was about revenge and justice. Now she's tried to kill me, it's about survival.

'All right, sweetheart?'

Mum brings a tray in for me. The bread will hurt my throat, but I'm determined to build up my strength. When I lift up the fork, it falls out of my hand, clattering on the plate.

My mother sits down next to me and begins to slice.

'Haven't done this in a while, have we?' she says, and that makes it a little less humiliating.

'So long as you don't start doing the thing about the little aeroplane flying into my mouth.'

We laugh. She seems happier, somehow, taking care of me.

But she wouldn't be so happy if she knew that while I'm being fed like a baby, I'm plotting how to trap my sister's killer once and for all.

Eggy bread is a miracle worker.

I can feel myself getting stronger, hour by hour. Going upstairs to the loo leaves me totally breathless, but there's no way I'm letting Mum or Dad take me there. I manage it, step by step, and coming back down is OK.

Every time I weaken, I imagine Sahara thinking she's got away with it and it makes me more determined to get well, fast.

My second night at home is better than my first. Mum stays in the room with me at first, though when I wake at eight, she's gone back to her own bed. My eyes are still swollen but at least there's no dirty soot mark on my pillow.

'Good to see some colour back in your cheeks,' Dad says as I make my way downstairs. He's holding his briefcase.

'What day is it?' I ask.

'Tuesday, darling. I thought I ought to show my face in the office, but I'm only ten minutes' drive away if you or Mum need me.' He gives me a hug which goes on longer than I expect, and I feel so guilty because I can tell how worried he's been.

I stand in the doorway and wave him off, even though the sunlight hurts my eyes. When he's gone, I pour myself some cereal, and Mum lets me, even though I realise most of it ends up on the worktop because I still can't see all that well.

Now what? The day, the week, the holidays stretch out in front of me like a prison sentence. I turn on the TV and . . .

'Alice!'

I jump. I'm on the sofa, the TV on mute. The clock reads eleven-twenty. I must have been dozing for hours.

'Alice. You have a visitor. Do you feel well enough?'

A visitor? *Please let it be Lewis.*

Except even as I strain to hear his voice in the hallway, I know it can't be him. He'd have to fight his way past my parents.

I freeze. Please don't let it be *her*.

'Alice Forster! I know I said you should live more dangerously but I didn't mean *that* dangerously.'

'Cara!'

It's the only person apart from Lewis that I actually want to see. She bursts into the room and holds me so tight that it makes me cough.

She jumps away in shock.

'When did you start smoking fifty a day?'

'Reckon I inhaled a year's worth of Silk Cut on Saturday night,' I say and she scowls.

'You've got a hell of a lot of explaining to do, Alice,' she snaps, but I can hear the fear underneath her anger.

I sigh. 'It's tricky, while Mum's here.'

'Can we go to the caff, then? I've got some sunglasses to cover up your bloodshot eyes.'

I'm stupidly dizzy just from standing up to greet her. 'Still under house arrest.'

Mum comes in, jacket half on. 'Can I trust you two girls not to get up to anything too terrible while I nip to the shops?'

'Absolutely, Mrs Forster. I'm a fully qualified babysitter. I won't let her go near any matches.'

'That's not funny, Cara. I'm on my mobile. Ring me if her

skin turns blue or her lips go red or she's short of breath. Or anything, really.'

'Mum. I'm getting better. Honestly.'

When she leaves, Cara squishes next to me on the sofa. 'What the hell happened, Alice?'

'It's . . . a fuss about nothing.'

'My best mate almost dies in a fire and she tells me it's *nothing*?'

'I didn't almost die.' If I say it often enough, I might start believing it. 'What do you know already?'

'That you were rescued from some weird lab in the middle of nowhere. That the police are investigating. That you ended up in the bloody *hospital*. I mean, what were you doing?'

'It was . . .' I try to think of an explanation she – and the police – might buy. So far, my parents have been too scared of stressing me out to ask many questions, but that won't last. And apparently the police want to take a statement. The only comfort is I guess they won't push too hard. It's not like *they* think it was arson.

'If you're thinking of lying to me, Alice, don't you dare. You're rubbish at it. I can always tell.'

I sigh. She's right and, anyway, I'm fed up with lying to her. 'It was to do with my brain. With what's been happening since Meggie died. Bad thoughts. Memories.' So far, so true. 'I asked Lewis for help. He found the place. It was all going fine and then . . . Mum said that some rubbish caught fire outside, near the air-con unit. Could have happened any time.'

'Hmm.' Cara doesn't sound convinced. 'Bit of a coincidence it happened when you were there. Plus, top-secret brain labs? It's insane, Alice.'

'No. *I'm* insane. That's what Mum and Dad think, what Olav thinks, what you probably think, too. I begged Lewis to help me find out for sure, one way or the other. If I really am nuts, then I'll take the horrible counselling, the group therapy.'

She sighs. 'Oh, honey. I hate that you were feeling so desperate that you resorted to *this*.'

'I'm *still* desperate,' I say, because she's the only one I can confide in. 'Especially because Lewis hasn't tried to get in touch. I don't even know if I was in the scanner long enough to get any kind of result. It might have been a waste of time.'

Cara stares at me for so long that I begin to feel seriously self-conscious.

'Either I have eggy bread between my teeth or I'm turning into a werewolf,' I say at last.

'It wasn't a waste of time,' she says, so quietly I only just hear her.

'What?'

'The experiment. Lewis came to see me. He's got some information but . . .' she puts her head in her hands. 'I came here to make up my own mind.'

'About what, Cara?'

'About whether you should know the truth.'

24

'What has he told you, Cara? What did the experiment show?'

It must have shown that I'm crazy. Otherwise she'd have told me when she first arrived.

'Nothing, Alice. He wouldn't tell *me*. That'd be like, I dunno, breaking an oath of confidentiality. But he came over to my place and begged me to talk to you.'

'When?'

'First thing Sunday morning. He'd tried to get to see you at the hospital, but your parents wouldn't let him near you. They threatened to call the police. He was in a bloody awful state, Alice. To start off with, I couldn't even make sense of what he was saying. I thought there'd been some kind of car accident.'

'Was he hurt?'

Cara frowns. 'No. Well, he was coughing and he smelled like a bonfire, but he certainly looked in better shape than you do now.'

I realise something. 'You already knew about the lab. Even though you just pretended you didn't.'

She looks away. 'For your sake. You've not exactly been telling me the whole truth and nothing but the truth about your life just lately, have you?'

She's right: I've been lying to her since I found the Beach. I say nothing.

'I needed to be sure I was doing the right thing, Alice. That putting you back in touch with Lewis wasn't going to do even more damage.'

For the first time since I came round in hospital, I feel the tiniest glow of hope. Though if he's desperate to see me, it could just be to tell me I need the kind of help Olav offers. 'Did he hint at whether it was good news?'

'No. Only that he thought you should know. And soon.'

'If Mum and Dad are that determined to keep him away, we'll need your help,' I tell her.

Cara nods. 'If it's what you really want. Personally, I just want you to be safe, but it's not like I ever take anyone else's advice.'

'It's what I really want.'

'OK. How soon do you think your parents will let you out of the house?'

The idea of leaving these four walls makes me shaky, but I need to know. 'Tomorrow, maybe? But there's no way they'll let me go anywhere that Lewis might be.'

She shrugs. 'They don't need to know. I can sneak him in while Mum's doing one of her bloody meditations. As far as our parents are concerned, you're just coming over for a sleepover. And what could be safer than that?'

Mum is tougher to crack than I thought; she doesn't let me leave the house for two more days. I complain, but secretly I'm relieved. My lungs still hurt and the swelling in my eyes hasn't gone down as fast as I'd hoped.

With my sight still hazy, I focus on what I hear. Like Mum and Dad whispering about how soon Olav can get back to work on me, and whether they should talk to the doctor about some kind of *medication* when I visit for my check-up.

I try not to get my hopes up about Lewis, but what else is there to focus on? Saying goodbye to Danny? Sahara's attempt on my life?

Finally, Mum relents and lets me go over to Cara's for the afternoon – she's not ready to let me sleep over and I guess, given my best mate's reputation, that's not surprising. Even my afternoon 'get out of jail free' pass has only been granted after a phone call to Cara's mum to guarantee she'll be on hand in case I need emergency treatment. If she hadn't been a GP, I doubt it'd have happened for ages.

Mum almost changes her mind on the doorstep, but Cara jollies her along and then drives me over to her place, a huge glass-walled apartment overlooking the river. Her father's loaded and her mum had a mid-life crisis after her divorce, so the two of them are more like flatmates than mother and daughter. The living space is strewn with drying tights and Magnum wrappers. Somewhere in the middle of the mess is a tabby cat who lives mainly on takeaways.

'Alice, you poor lamb!' Cara's mother says when she sees me, eyeing me suspiciously to make sure I'm not about to collapse. 'My darling, are you all right?'

'A lot better, thanks.'

'What an awful thing to go through. Your poor parents, it's the last thing that should have happened. Compared to Cara, you and Meggie were so well-behaved.'

'*Mother!*' Cara says. 'I can't believe they haven't struck you off yet for tactlessness.'

But it *is* strange. Cara should be the one causing her parents sleepless nights.

'Sorry,' her mum says. 'I'm always saying the wrong thing. I mean, I didn't mean to— Anyway, I'll be in my office if you feel unwell. Enjoy your afternoon!'

I smile back as Cara leads the way to 'her' wing of the flat. You notice the difference as soon as you step into the corridor. It smells of candles and the pictures on the walls aren't wonky and the wood floor is clear of shoes and abandoned magazines. Cara likes everything just so.

'Lewis is here?' I whisper to Cara.

'Yup. Mum was so deep in her yogic trance that I could

have snuck in the entire Manchester United football team and she wouldn't have noticed.' She smiles. 'Don't worry, though. It's just you, me and the dangerous Professor Lewis.'

Dangerous? I hesitate before pushing open the door, suddenly nervous. This could be the time when I finally have to face the truth: that I am ill.

Cara gives me a little push. 'Don't keep him waiting, Alice.'

He's sitting at her dressing table, in an ornately carved chair. He has his back to me and the sunlight is shining through the floor-to-ceiling window, so his hair is golden.

But when he turns, I catch my breath.

Despite my blurred vision, I can see he looks wrecked. Eyes as red as mine, washed-out skin and a dark shadow of stubble that makes him look much, much older.

'Lewis?'

He jumps up from the chair and holds out his arms. I fall into them.

For a very long time, I can't speak. My hands grip his back, tracing the solidness of him: shoulders wider and more muscled than you'd ever guess from the loose t-shirts he wears, strong arms keeping me close.

This is the first time I've felt safe since the fire. Which I know makes no sense, but still . . . I close my eyes.

Lewis smells so familiar, but not of his posh aftershave. He's a cocktail of coffee and green leaves and a hint of fire. I know I must smell worse; even now, almost six days after the fire, I can still detect the scent of charred plastic on my skin.

'You're OK, you're OK, you're OK,' he whispers.

In my head, I repeat, *so are you.* Then I remember Cara's here and I wriggle free, though Lewis doesn't seem to want to let go.

When we're at arm's length, he studies me, scrutinising me from head to toe.

'It's all right. Nothing's missing,' I say, trying to lighten the mood.

Lewis sighs so deeply it's as though he's been holding his breath since Sunday. 'I am so, *so* sorry, Ali.'

'What for? You were trying to help me. I begged you to.'

'You could have died. It would have been my fault.'

'No, not yours.'

'I'll leave you two to it,' says Cara. 'Gooseberry green isn't my colour. I'll take the fire escape to the residents' gym downstairs. I'll be back in half an hour, ready to deliver you home, Alice.'

'Make it an hour,' Lewis says, his eyes not leaving my face.

'Ooh, don't you just love it when he gets all masterful, Alice?'

I say nothing. Cara grabs her gym bag, then goes onto the balcony and scrambles across to the steel ladder. It's not the first time she's used this as her escape route when she's meant to be grounded.

But I'm more worried about what Lewis has planned. Why does he need an hour with me? I try to prepare myself for what he's about to tell me. I wasn't in the scanner for anything like an hour, so why does he need so much time to explain what he's found out?

'So Professor—'

'Sit down, Ali—'

We speak at the same moment.

I sit on the bed, opposite him.

'You first,' I say. 'I need to know, Lewis. Am I mad or is Soul Beach for real?'

25

'It's *real*,' he whispers. 'Or at the very least, you're definitely not mad.'

I blink. My vision seems to clear and everything shines with certainty. Lewis's face – half smiling, half frowning – is full of kindness.

'I still don't understand what's going on,' Lewis continues. 'But I am as certain as I can be that you're not imagining the Beach. That it exists somewhere, somehow.'

I feel . . . reborn.

'I can't believe it,' I murmur. Except that's not quite true: the Beach has always *felt* real. It's just I haven't dared to believe it till now.

Part of me wants to hug Lewis for making this happen, but before I can, he sits back down at Cara's dressing table. 'It's the news you were hoping for, isn't it?'

I nod. 'God, yes. I didn't know what to expect, but – wow, Lewis, Soul Beach exists.' The words I never thought I'd be able to say out loud. 'Tell me how you know! I want all the details.'

'OK. Well, I'm no neuroscientist, but luckily, Ian is. He does games research now, but his PhD involved working on a team looking at delusions suffered by people with mental illness, comparing them to people who didn't. The people with delusions all showed what they called neuronal hyperactivity when they were seeing things. But the way your brain responds when you're on the Beach is completely normal. No signs whatsoever that you're seeing things that aren't there or imagining it. Ian was adamant.'

I know I won't remember the scientific term, but I don't care: it's proof that *I'm not crazy*.

'When you were on the Beach, Ian said that every part of your brain was active exactly as though you were moving through a *real* place: as though you were *there*, Alice. In two places at once. Ian went through it all with me: the way the occipital lobe was processing what you were seeing, the way your temporal lobe was responding to what you were hearing, plus your orbitofrontal circuit was lighting up like crazy – that's the part that deals with empathy, with understanding other human beings.'

Was that while I was trying to make sense of what poor Danny was going through? I wonder. The moment when I realised I still loved him and knew I had to forgive him?

'That's all definite proof that I'm not delusional?' I ask.

'Ian couldn't see any signs at all that you were delusional. Though he did also say he'd love to study you some more.'

I frown. 'I'm never going anywhere near one of those scanners again. Why would he want to make me do that?'

'Apparently you have a very developed . . . let me get this right, paracingulate sulcus. It's a fold in the brain that helps people tell the difference between truth and reality. Anyway, it confirms what I've always thought – you, Alice Forster, are a very special person. No wonder I love spending time with you.'

The compliment makes me blush slightly. 'I . . . don't know what to say, except, well, thank you. For doing this, for taking such a huge risk, for everything.'

He looks away. 'Even though it could have got you killed?'

'What actually happened, Lewis? In the fire? I don't remember very much.'

Lewis sighs. 'It was so sudden. We were watching your

face and your brain scans. That was pretty uncomfortable, like voyeurism. Some of the things you were saying, this *conversation* you were having with a figure we couldn't see or hear. I turned down the volume to protect you.' He laughs, but it sounds sad. 'Which is ironic when you think what comes next.'

I remember the emotional things I was saying to Danny towards the end and I hope Lewis didn't hear any of that. 'Tell me.'

'When the siren first went off, Ian said it was a false alarm – that the systems were incredibly sensitive because the owners are so paranoid about break-ins and the sensors were being triggered all the time, so he reset everything.

'But then the camera on your face went out of focus. Ali, it was weird. And horrible. I couldn't tell why, but I knew you were in danger. I raced into the lab, even though Ian was telling me that it was fine, the lab was fireproof.

'But it wasn't *smoke*-proof. The room was dark with this *fug* of chemicals and plastic and—' His eyes are wide.

I think about how convinced everyone else is that the fire was an accident. Surely Lewis is suspicious too? 'So it wasn't an ordinary rubbish fire?'

Lewis blinks hard, as though he's trying to get rid of the memory. 'Of course it was. Rubbish is the worst. There were plastic containers, aerosols, carpet from one of the other units on the trading estate. And you know how hot the night was. A cigarette can smoulder for hours and then . . . It was just seriously unlucky for you that the fire started right by the air-con system that serves the labs.'

Seriously unlucky?

Meggie, Tim, Zoe. Statistically that's way too much bad luck for one small group of people. Lewis must see that too. So why is he sticking to this 'whoopsadaisy' theory?

Unless . . .

No. Of course he's not involved. He didn't even *know* Meggie. Plus he's done so much for me.

And anyway, if I lose faith in the one person I can trust, then the world really will feel like the darkest place.

'The police talked to you?'

He nods and begins to fiddle with the perfume bottles on Cara's dressing table, placing them in height order. 'Yup. Second police interview since I started hanging out with you, Ali. You're a dangerous person to know. Worse for Ian, though. He's been suspended. He'll be lucky not to get the sack.'

'Oh, no! I feel awful.'

'He'll find something else. He's too smart to be doing this commercial stuff. He wants to get back to medical research. Find a way to help people. The way you do, too, I guess.' When he smiles at me, there's a strange sadness there too.

'Lewis. Is everything OK? I mean, I feel better for knowing this, but you don't seem so thrilled.'

He sighs. 'It's hard for me to accept. I'm Professor Rational, right? I don't believe that raindrops are falling on my head unless my iPhone weather app confirms it. Yet suddenly this place is real. Not only that, but – *I* saw it, remember. How?'

He looks so confused that I want to hold him, reassure him as he's reassured me so many times. Yet I feel awkward. Something's changed today, not just for me, but between the two of us.

'I know how it feels. To be . . . different.' And I force myself to overcome the uneasiness, to reach out to take his hand.

His skin is hot and when his fingers close around mine, a wave of something like heat passes through me too. I blush and let go.

And then I realise something significant. That time Lewis saw the Beach, he was touching me, as he leaned towards the screen. Is *that* why it was visible to him and no one else?

155

Perhaps I should tell him? But this has all freaked him out, too. Maybe adding yet another layer of strangeness will make it even worse for poor, rational Lewis.

He looks away. 'I don't see where the hell we go from here.'

To the Beach again, I think, but then I remember the wasteland that remains. Not to mention that agonising goodbye – should I really disrespect Danny's plea for me to stay away?

Except this isn't just about Danny. It's about Meggie, too.

The relief I felt about the scan result is trickling away. 'I have to try again, Lewis, to go back. There'll be something I've missed, some clue that will help me resolve what happened to Meggie.' *And to Danny,* I think, but I don't say it. 'My parents aren't letting me look at the internet again till I'm at least forty, so we'll have to do it at your flat.'

'Ali, your mum's probably got a private detective tailing you to make sure you don't go anywhere near my place. I've never seen anyone so angry as when she threw me out of the hospital. Not that I blame her.' He runs his hand through his hair, and it sticks up, as though he's had an electric shock. 'Face facts. We can't even be friends, now.'

Even? What else does he think we are? 'Cara will cover for us. She always does. We can meet back here: once Mum's realised I survived today, I'm sure she'll let me come back. And you could bring one of your vast collection of laptops, surely. Tomorrow night?'

'Tomorrow? What's the urgency?'

'I guess I want to be put out of my misery.'

'Why? Did something else change when you were on the Beach in the lab?'

I don't want to tell Lewis about Danny. I can't explain exactly why I'd hate Lewis to know all that, but it makes me feel deeply unsettled.

'I just don't think there's any time to wait. But you've done more than anyone else would have, Lewis. I understand if you don't want to help me any more.'

Finally he laughs properly, as though what I've said was meant to be a joke. 'You're right. I should stop here, shouldn't I? But in all the time you've known me, Ali, tell me when I've ever been able to say no to you.'

Despite all that's wrong, and my many doubts, that makes me smile. I count my blessings. Whatever it is, the Beach is real in some way and not just a figment of my deluded imagination. I'm sane.

And I'm not fighting alone any more.

26

I sit in my bedroom, listening to my parents rowing downstairs.

Dad's putting his foot down about Olav. 'We can't leave her in the care of some amateur any more, Bea. It's not worth the risk.'

'Amateur? You think I've spent the last year being helped through my grief by some . . . charlatan? I've dealt with it a bloody sight better than you have—'

And they're off again. *My* fault. Before the fire, they'd been getting on better, but now it's almost as bad as the months after Meggie's funeral, when they dealt with the loss by tearing each other apart.

I put my headphones into my ears, turn up the music and try to focus on tonight, when Mum's given me permission to go to Cara's again for a whole two hours. This time, Lewis is bringing his kit, so I can try to go back to the Beach.

And then what?

The fear that the Beach is a dead end and Meggie's gone forever is all I can think about. If only I'd made the most of it while she was still there – found a way to get more information. Yes, now I know it was real, but how does that help me get justice for her?

Sleep is the only escape. I've learned to look forward to being dead to the world.

Both of my worlds.

*

Sahara.

In my bedroom.

She's hazy, yes, but it's definitely her. A nightmare.

She's speaking to me, but though her mouth is moving, fast, I can't hear a word. I blink, try my hardest to wake up. She's reaching out with those long, gnarled fingers. Is she going to suffocate me too? She came close enough when she sent choking smoke into the lab, knowing how little it would take to kill me.

The hands are coming closer. Slowly. Surely.

Perhaps this dream is trying to tell me something Meggie no longer can.

'No! Get away!'

I feel tugging. Then the touch of her nails against my face, my ears.

'. . . was it a bad dream, Alice? I've discovered these amazing herbal teabags, they take everything awful away. Only the deepest, loveliest sleep remains.'

'I . . .'

The headphones drop out of my ears onto the bed and I realise, *I'm not dreaming.* Sahara really is here.

'Who let you in?' I ask sharply.

'Your mum. Oh, Alice, it's wonderful to see you. You had such a lucky escape.'

She's acting as if everything's totally normal. Has she forgotten about the visit that Ade said left her 'hysterical'? Blanked out the night-time phone call?

Does she have amnesia about trying to *kill* me?

I rub my eyes but her face is still blurry, which makes me feel vulnerable. 'Sahara, what are you doing here?'

'Alice! That's not much of a welcome!'

I'm too rattled to pretend. 'Seriously, I don't understand. Last I heard from Ade you were so devastated by what I'd said that you never wanted to see me again.'

She laughs nervously. 'Ade's just over-protective. But he's got both our interests at heart. And I *was* hurt, but when I heard what had happened, I had to come and check you're all right.'

Or check how close you came to finishing the job?

'I'm not great company at the moment, Sahara.'

Of course she doesn't take the hint. Instead she sits down on the bed, so close I can smell boiled sweets on her breath. She sighs. 'What are we going to do with you, Alice? Your sister would have hated to see you this way.'

No, my sister would have hated to see Sahara here, sinking her fangs into me like a grief vampire.

'I need to rest . . .'

The door is opening. Thank goodness, Mum must have realised she shouldn't have let Sahara in. I can tell her to send her away again.

Framed against the light is a figure so pale that it could be a ghost.

'You look better than I'd feared, Alice.'

Ade. No show without Punch, as my dad says. But at least with two of them here, I feel slightly safer. Sahara will have to behave herself.

'I survived.'

I'm not embarrassed by the awkward silence that follows.

'Thank goodness,' he says. Out of focus, his pale face reminds me of the man in the moon. 'We were so worried.'

So he's in on this pretence that we're all the best of friends, too.

'We almost didn't come,' Sahara says, 'but we had to see you in person.'

'I look bad and I feel about eighty years old,' I tell them. 'The smoke can affect your lungs for weeks, apparently.'

Is she feeling guilty yet?

'Fresh air is what you need,' she says. 'And a change of scenery. That's what we've come for – as well as to check up on you.'

'To check you're all right, she means,' Ade puts in.

'There's no chance of a change of scenery now,' I say. Dad hasn't mentioned that New York trip lately. Cara's flat is the furthest I'll be allowed to go now for . . . well, as long as they can keep me here.

'Which is why we want to invite you to stay with us, Alice!' Sahara's voice is high-pitched, as though she's offering me the best treat she can possibly imagine. 'Now we've moved in together we've been jazzing the place up. And there's a spare room in our flat.'

It's not a *spare* room. It's where Tim used to sleep.

'We're on holiday from college so we can take you anywhere you like in the car.' She picks up one of the uni prospectuses Mum has stacked up on my desk. 'We could head off to one of the campuses you're considering.'

The pitch of her voice keeps rising. Going to stay with them is the last thing I'd consider – but why is she so desperate to stay close to me?

'I'm not sure . . .'

'Your mother thinks it'd be an excellent idea to take your mind off things,' Ade says. His voice is more measured. I can't imagine he wants me as a house guest, but perhaps he's scared to disagree with his girlfriend.

I can't believe Mum would let me go, unless it's part of Olav's therapy – to send me off to 'have fun'.

Even though it'll be fun with someone who seems to want me dead! Panic rises again.

'Mum? MUM?' Maybe it's childish to call for my mother, but I don't want to be alone with these people for a second longer. As I cry out, it feels as though my throat is being hacked with razor blades and the sound I make is pathetic.

Ade backs away. 'I'm not sure she can hear you. Mrs Forster? Can you come up here, please?'

'Alice, you know it's the right thing. You'd get better so fast with us taking care of you. I'm an excellent nurse,' Sahara whispers urgently. 'I promise you wouldn't be out of my sight for a single second.'

Mum's here, finally. 'Well, can I get you folks a drink or– Oh! Alice, are you all right? You look frightful.'

'I'm feeling very tired.'

'We're going, now, aren't we?' Ade says, and there's a steeliness in his tone that even Sahara can't miss.

Mum's leaning forward. 'Oh, sweetheart, we'll leave you alone to rest. You've done so well, I keep forgetting it's less than a week since the fire. Is there anything else I can get you?'

I shake my head, wishing she didn't look so worried, but my visitors have genuinely made me feel ill. Together they have a kind of toxic energy that drains the life and the hope from the air.

Like breathing smoke.

Mum kisses me on the cheek. She hustles the others out. I hear her whispering in the hallway.

'. . . sorry about the long journey but, really, the doctors have warned us that the effects can be very unpredictable . . . probably better to leave the Greenwich idea for now, till we know she's definitely on the mend . . . sure you understand.'

But my relief at that is diluted by the knowledge that Sahara is too self-obsessed – or ruthless – to ever take no for an answer.

27

I have to work really hard to persuade Mum I'm well enough to go to Cara's after my relapse.

Cara's mum reassures her on the phone. 'It'll be absolutely fine, Bea. I won't let her out of my sight.'

Except when Cara picks me up, she turns right instead of left onto the main road. Away from her flat.

Towards Lewis's place.

'There's been a change of plan,' Cara says, seeing my face. 'Mum's just come back from Pilates where she managed to do her back in. Which is good news for us, as she's self-prescribed some knock-out painkillers. She won't even notice if a herd of elephants *and* George Clooney do the samba through our place, so we're safe to take you to Ground Control. Assuming you're OK with going there?'

I nod, even though the thought of being alone with Lewis makes me nervous. The last time I trusted him, I almost died.

But that was nothing to do with him. I try to slow my breathing, but when Cara pulls up outside his flat, I feel my heart beating so hard I'm surprised she hasn't commented.

'Back in two hours,' she says, kissing me on the cheek. 'Or sooner if the mother troll stirs.'

She waits until I knock on the door and Lewis answers.

He's still drawn, his pupils large and his forehead creased with worry.

'How are you, Ali?' he asks. No jokes tonight, I guess.

'Better every day. Nervous about this, though.'

He nods. 'Sure. But I feel we're getting towards the end, don't you?'

Maybe, I think. If there is an end. In a strange way, the worst possible result is no ending, nothing conclusive at all. Just spending the rest of *my* life with no more idea about how my sister ended *hers.*

His flat smells of smoke, too. We must both still be oozing it through our skin. But the freshness of all those plants masks the worst of it. Outside, the sun is setting and the living room is half in darkness.

Is this where everything ends? The Beach, hope, my fight?

'Do you want me here, or . . .'

I'm aware of Lewis close to me, can hear his steady breathing and sense how tall he is compared to me.

I turn my head. His face is startling in the half-light, all angles and drama. Like a stranger's.

A good-looking stranger's.

Bloody hell, Alice, where did that come from? I turn away again. 'It's probably better if you let me try on my own.'

He nods. 'Call me. I won't come out until I hear you. Not like last time.' And he backs out, towards his bedroom, leaving me alone with the bank of screens.

OK. I can do this. I try to convince myself that even though Danny told me he didn't want me to go back, he didn't really *mean* it. The Beach might be a different place, but it's still somewhere we can *be* together – somewhere that holds the answers I've been seeking since Meggie was murdered fifteen months ago.

And she might be back, waiting. She wouldn't just leave me. Would she?

I log in to my email and my inbox appears. I have to blink constantly so I can read, because my eyes are still not focusing properly. There are dozens of new, dull emails; it's been a week since I last logged in. A week since I nearly died.

At the top there's a newsletter Mum subscribed me to, with uni reviews by students. Going to college is the last thing I care about now. I scroll down to find the original Soul Beach invitation. It's there, at the bottom of the page.

In red?

I try to open it, but it won't work. The heading – *Meggie Forster Wants to See You on the Beach* – is in italics, and I try everything: right-clicking, highlighting, closing my email program and starting it up again. But it still won't work.

My breathing is rapid, blood is rushing in my ears.

'Lewis? Lewis!'

He comes running, perhaps hearing the panic in my voice.

'It's frozen!' I shout, when he's next to me.

'The Beach?'

'No. This.' I point at the screen. 'There's only one route onto the Beach – the invitation I was sent by my sister. And I can't open it!'

Lewis frowns, takes hold of the mouse and tries the same things I did to open it, to move it, to right click. 'I think it's . . . expired.'

'Expired?'

'Mmm. That's why you can see it was there, but can't do anything with it. Like, I dunno, the shadow of what was there.'

Or the ghost, I think. 'Why would that happen?'

He sighs. 'It would have been set to do that when it was sent. By the original sender. Perhaps the invitation was only meant to last a certain amount of time.'

The original sender. In other words, *The Management*. But how would they have decided when to make it expire? They couldn't have *known* this would happen, could they? Perhaps this was always going to be their final trick: taking the Beach away from me as though it never existed.

'But you could get the message back, surely? Hack into it somehow?' I plead.

Lewis shakes his head. 'Because you're on webmail, not a standalone program, any files won't be cached. Plus, if they've taken the trouble to set an expiry date, whoever *they* are, then I doubt they'd be lax enough to then let you access the site via a deleted email.' He spreads his hands out. 'I don't know what to say, Ali.'

I grab the mouse back from him and try all the same things again, in an increasingly manic cycle, until my hand looks like a claw on the mouse. He doesn't try to stop me. He knows me too well by now, knows that I won't give up, can't give up, till I accept there's no chance.

'Unless it's something Danny did when he said goodbye,' I say.

'Danny?'

I shake my head. I hadn't meant to say his name out loud. 'It's nothing. No one.' I feel guilty at dismissing someone who meant – *means* – so much to me, yet it also seems disloyal to mention him when I'm with Lewis, who has done more than I could ask of anyone. 'Lewis. Help me. I don't know what to do.'

For the first time since I took my initial walk along Soul Beach, I am completely lost. I have no more evidence against Sahara. No way to talk to my sister. No clue about how to resolve her death, or Danny's, or the tragedies of a hundred lost souls who must surely still be . . . *somewhere*, in their own personal limbos.

Lewis takes my hand and leads me to the huge sofa by the fireplace. '*I've* been thinking – since last time. I mean, it might be nothing, but . . .'

'Go on. I'm in a grasping-at-straws frame of mind.'

'OK. So we established in the scan that the Beach exists, somehow, in some other dimension.' He laughs. 'Listen to me. "Other dimension". I've always taken the piss out of Trekkies, and now I sound like one.'

166

I smile. 'Welcome to my world.'

'What if the Beach is a real place?'

'I thought that's what we'd already worked out.'

'No. There's a difference. A subtle one, but what I'm thinking is, what if the place itself – the landscape, the sea, the geology – what if they're based on a genuine beach?'

I understand what he means now. 'Somewhere on earth.'

Lewis nods. 'You know I only caught the tiniest glimpse of the place but it seemed so real to me.'

I know how hard it's been for him to accept that he saw it for real and it makes me even more excited. 'You think they're really there? *The Guests*? That there's a place we could even visit . . .' I don't dare say any more; it seems too good to be true.

He shrugs. 'Maybe. Or it might be that I'm losing my grip. Listen, Ali, this whole business is unknown territory for me. I'm totally out of my depth. But I can't see anything else left for us to try.'

I close my eyes, trying to imagine seeing my sister, holding her, hugging her again at last but this time for real.

Ninety-nine per cent of me knows it is too good to be true. But after all that's happened, how can I stop the tiniest part of me believing in this wonderful, life-changing idea? Especially as it's Lewis who's said it, the most logical person I know. 'How would we find it?'

Lewis walks across to his desk, fetches two pens and two brand new, leather-bound notebooks. 'We start offline. We write down everything we can remember about the *physical* aspects of the Beach. Separately, so we won't be distracted or muddled. OK, your observations will be more useful, but I might as well join in.'

'And also about the Guests – the people?'

'I didn't see any people, remember?'

Like me, the first time I saw the Beach.

Lewis crosses the room and begins to write with his shoulders hunched, as though this is an exam in which I might be planning to cheat.

I take my pen. It's almost painful to revisit my memories. My first thought is of the idyllic Soul Beach, but then it's replaced by the wasteland I saw the last time, with uprooted palms and polluted sea.

I try to remember both versions, before and after I made it all go wrong. As I write, I have to rub at my eyes so that I can see the ink and the page.

> _Before:_
> Paradise – skies so blue they're almost turquoise.
> Rocks the colour of granite, with green shrubs growing up the sides. Leaves shaped like spiky stars.
> Bay completely enclosed.
> Beach bar, huts on stilts, hammocks hanging from the trees.
> Wildlife: brightly coloured birds, shoals of ghostly metallic fish under the water, unfamiliar birdsong, tiny white crabs.
> Beautiful people. Bright clothes. Music. Games. Laughter.
> Wooden jetty but no boat, no way out.
>
> _After:_
> Hell.
> Red sky.
> Buildings blown to pieces, only the sharp-edged rocks left.

Did my sister hurt herself as she clambered up? Or is she as insubstantial as any other ghost? I try to focus and keep writing . . .

> Sea slicked with oil and debris.
> Screams. Then nothing.

Well, nothing except Danny, a single guilty soul, haunting the shore. But I don't want to tell Lewis about him. I have a powerful sense that something else happened before the fire started, before Lewis dragged me out of the lab. Something huge. But I can't remember what it was, though I can remember fear. Awe. What the hell was it I saw?

'You done?' Lewis is holding out his hand for my slip of paper.

'Yep. Now what?'

'Now we compare notes.'

I sit down next to him at the desk where he lays the two pieces of paper next to each other. I've never seen his handwriting before. It's rounded and regular, more flowing than I expected. Easy to read, even with my swollen eyes:

> *Birds flying: bee-catchers, kingfishers, kites.*
>
> *Strange song - rattling, shrieking, knocking sounds.*
>
> *A hammock swinging in the background.*
>
> *Bizarrely blue sky, like camera has a filter to turn it turquoise.*
>
> *Oversized palms, black-grey rocks, fine white-gold sand. Asia?*
>
> *One small pier for launching boats, but no boats moored.*
>
> *A building - bar - plus shacks on stilts. Six. Or eight? Rush roofs.*
>
> *No one on the sand - but footprints, hundreds of them.*
>
> *Thought I could hear laughter, like best party ever.*
>
> *Then it changed to screaming.*

I feel the paper slipping through my fingers but I do nothing to stop it. 'Oh, God, Lewis. You really *did* see it.'

He's still staring at my list. 'We saw the same place. Reading this, there's no doubt. I'm a rationalist, Ali. Everything has an explanation. But I'm lost.'

I know how that feels. 'Sorry. It's my fault.'

He says nothing for a moment, but then he puts the list down and reaches out for my hand. 'Yeah. Because you really asked for your sister to be murdered and then to be drawn into some bonkers world of conspiracies and dead–alive people.'

His hand is warm as he squeezes mine. But I'm still missing something. I close my eyes and try to fast-forward through my last emotional goodbye with Danny. The storm, the thunder, the lightning, the sea . . .

The sea.

That's what I'd forgotten. What I saw that made me terrified, but awe-struck, too.

The way it drew back from the shore as Danny held me tight. The sight of the sand beneath, oily and dark. That powerful sense that I was seeing something monumental.

And the strange familiarity. I couldn't work out why it would remind me of something, until now.

I open my eyes again. 'You think it looked like Asia?'

Lewis nods. 'Maybe. I mean, I've only been to that part of the world once – on a stopover from Kuala Lumpur.'

'Malaysia?'

'I stayed a couple of days. Coast, city, then on to Australia. But there was something about the landscape that reminded me of your Beach. Still, we have to narrow it down. Asia is a pretty big continent.'

'I might know how,' I whisper. 'When I was in the scanner, something strange happened, right at the end. I thought it was the same storm returning. The sea was pulling back from the shore. It's only now that I've realised just what it was.'

'What?'

'A tsunami. We watched a programme in geography about the Boxing Day one. The survivors all said that the first thing

170

that happened was that the water disappeared. Then, of course, minutes later it came back, and destroyed everything. Perhaps this is the final act in the drama. The complete destruction of Soul Beach.'

Lewis takes his hand from mine and tears at his hair. Thinking.

'Or perhaps it really happened, right, Ali? Somewhere in Asia?'

I look into his eyes. 'Could be. In which case . . . it might be easier to find. Will you help me look for it?'

I'm close enough now to read his face, despite my blurred vision. I see worry in his eyes, but something else too. Resignation? Or even a hint of excitement.

'Nothing would stop me now, Alice Forster.'

And I realise I couldn't ask for a better companion.

You look so weak, Alice.

What's the phrase? Weak as a kitten.

But appearances are deceptive. Just as I am not what people see, you are not as weak as you seem. A kitten has claws and teeth and the hunting instinct of a tiger passed down in her genes. And you have hidden strengths.

If only I could convince myself that you are vulnerable, represent no threat. Then life could go on as normal.

If only.

28

I wake on Saturday, feeling a hundred per cent better.

And a thousand per cent more restless. So much energy, but nothing to channel it into. I'm missing Meggie, trying to think of ways I could help Danny, wishing I could be working alongside Lewis, but I am still being monitored twenty-four seven. It's like living in a very cosy police state.

All I can do is wait for Lewis to play his part.

'Sweetheart, can I have a word?' Mum says after breakfast. Then she sits me down and tells me that my next appointment with Olav is on Monday, with another session on Friday. Plus on Saturday morning we have family therapy to look forward to. Repeated every week till I'm cured.

Even the thought of tormenting my least favourite shrink with mind games doesn't soften the blow. 'I don't get any say in it?'

My mother's face is stern. 'Not this time. I'm sorry, Alice. You need specialist help, urgently. Without it, we can't send you back to school. And if you don't go back to school, then there'll be no university and—'

'What about Dad? Is he behind this?'

'He agrees that we need to tackle this head-on now.'

'So why isn't he here?'

Mum examines her nails. 'Look, Alice. If your father had his way, you'd already have been to the GP and be on God knows what kind of cocktail of drugs for depression or anxiety. I persuaded him to try this first. But if you aren't willing to commit, I don't think I'll be able to keep you away from the medical approach.'

I gulp. No way. I need to stay sharp. Dumbing me down with drugs would be exactly what Sahara wants.

If it is Sahara.

Of course it is. There is no one else it could be.

'So will you go, Alice?' Only now does the desperation creep into my mum's voice.

I nod. What choice do I have?

Sunday. Three a.m.

The text wakes me: **May have found the Beach. Or, at least, somewhere that looks identical. When can we meet?**

I read it a hundred times. Click out of my texts and back, because part of me can't believe it's real. That Meggie might be there, wherever 'there' is, waiting for me.

Seriously? Where is it?

The reply takes less than three seconds: **Better to wait till I see you.**

My thumb keeps slipping as I type: **Will text Cara as soon as it's morning. She'll help cover for us meeting. She promised.**

And then he sends another message: **Damn. Sorry. Hadn't realised what time it was.**

I smile.

Wouldn't have wanted to wait a second longer. This could change everything. Thank you.

He sends back a smiley face, even though Lewis doesn't strike me as a smiley-face kind of guy.

I've never been so desperate for dawn to break. Every minute seems to last an hour and I nearly call Cara straight away but, if she is up, she'll be drunk, and, if I wake her up, she won't remember a thing in the morning.

So I stare out of my bedroom window. This is where we grew up, Meggie and me. Where we learned to ride our bikes, where we turned cartwheels, where she had her first-ever standing ovation after singing at the Golden Jubilee street party.

How did it come to this? My big sister murdered, me labelled unstable or worse. It's so hard to imagine where I go from here.

And then I realise I know *exactly* where I must go from here.

If Lewis has found a place, a real place, that might be Soul Beach, then there is nothing else for it.

I have to go there.

Five a.m. It's almost light now.

It's rubbish-collection day tomorrow – well, later today, really – and as I blink, a skinny fox comes into focus through the window. He's making his way from one bin to the next, tearing open the bags with a lazy arrogance, like a customer at a self-service buffet. Chicken bones from number six. A drink of spilled milk from number eight. A pot of what looks like rice pudding from number ten.

I tap the glass and he looks up at me. He doesn't run.

In his eyes, defiance. I never believed in reincarnation before but after the Beach, anything seems possible. Perhaps the fox was a person, once.

It's almost light, now, but I can't call yet. My brain keeps replaying my last trip to the Beach and what Danny said – how it felt when he held me, kissed me.

Said *goodbye*.

I picture him on the oil-blackened sand, alone. Is he condemned to walk that same shoreline forever, never seeing another soul? Yes, I suppose I might find him once more if Lewis is right about uncovering the site of the real Beach, but will that be enough to set Danny free?

No. There has to be a resolution to his death.

And then I realise. I've been so focused on returning to the Beach that I've missed the obvious: I don't have to wait to go online to look for the pilot's family so I can send them some lame email begging for forgiveness.

No, I can do something much more old-fashioned, which could at least ensure the pilot's daughters don't go hungry. I can write to Danny's father, explain what Danny did, ask him to take care of the orphans.

Then put the letter in the *post*.

Doubts crowd my mind even as I reach for a pen and paper. Why would a billionaire take any notice of an unknown English schoolgirl? Does a letter ever stand a chance of reaching him? But I focus on the task. This is the best hope of releasing Danny from his torment. The least I can do is try.

I rub my eyes until the blurring lessens and I can see the paper. I lower my pen. I don't remember the last time I hand-wrote a letter to anyone. But this has to be good.

> *Dear Mr Cross,*

It's a start.

> *You don't know me, but I know your son. Danny is*

I cross out *is*.

> *was a credit to you. A fine, funny, smart guy who could have changed so many people's lives for the better. But he made a mistake, and I think I might be the only person who can explain, and give you the chance to put it right.*

Is that going too far?

> *I'm not a crank, even though I know I probably sound like one. Please keep reading, then make up your mind. I'm not writing for my sake but for Danny's. I genuinely believe things must be resolved if his soul is ever to rest in peace . . .*

29

When Cara picks me up at seven-thirty, she's still in her pyjamas. I'm not even sure she's a hundred per cent awake, though her eyes are open and she waves at my mother through the windscreen.

She doesn't ask me why I phoned her at six forty-five, or why Lewis turned up at her place at seven. Partly because she's a great mate, but I also have a feeling she had a late night. I should know who she was out with, if I were as good a mate to her as she is to me but, right now, all I can do is think about that tsunami. I tell myself everything will change soon.

'Thanks so much for this, Cara. You're a legend.'

She nods. 'I am, aren't I?'

'Do you think we could just stop here? By the postbox.'

I've stuck on all the stamps I could find in Mum's stationery drawer, and written AIR MAIL in big letters all over the envelope. As I hear it drop onto the other post below, I make a silent wish: that this will set Danny free.

Even though the thought makes my eyes burn with pent-up tears.

When we get to Cara's place, she goes straight back to bed, pushing me towards her den where the TV and sofas are, and closing the door behind her.

I step out of the patio doors, shielding my eyes from the morning sun. Lewis is on the balcony, leaning over the edge of the metal rail, staring at the river below. He turns slowly.

'Hello, Professor.'

'Ali.' His designer glasses have darkened in response to the sun, but when he faces me, he takes them off. His skin's sallow with tiredness but his eyes are bright. In this light, they glow like amber.

There's a wooden table with a parasol – underneath the shade, Lewis has set up one of his laptops. He pulls out a chair for me and I sit down. The screen comes to life as soon as my finger hovers above the touchpad.

'Here.' Lewis reaches across me and his hand brushes against my shoulder. It gives me goosebumps. Must be the anticipation.

All I can see is his desktop wallpaper. The bay, the sea, the sky. It's the same as the one on my laptop and it makes me impatient; I don't want to see some standard image.

'Please don't play games, Lewis, I—'

And then I remember. No one except me has *that* wallpaper. Because it only appeared after I was invited to Soul Beach: it infected my desktop like a virus.

'Where is it?' I whisper.

'That's Thailand,' he says. 'The Andaman coast.'

He leans in again, and brings up another photo, and another, and another. Huts with the same six supporting struts buried in the same dazzling sand.

A close-up of an orange and green bird with a long curved beak and an aquamarine tail.

A jetty built from wood that's been weathered and bleached to palest silver. I run my finger along the screen, imagining the soft warmth of the planks as I touch them.

'What do you think?' Lewis asks.

'It . . . feels right, Lewis.' Though even as I say it, I'm not certain. Something about the image doesn't fit.

He changes the view, zooms out to show the shape of the bay, like a crescent moon of sand with a sapphire sea beyond.

'And that?' his finger traces the curve along the screen. 'Do you recognise the shoreline?'

I peer at it. 'I can't be sure. The sand is darker, and I've never seen it from this angle, so . . .'

'Ah.'

'It doesn't mean you're wrong, Lewis.' But the geography doesn't feel right either. Disappointment hits like a hard punch to the belly. 'How did you find it?'

'Combination of factors. Mineral analysis of the rocks I thought I saw. Research into the flora and fauna. Plus I eliminated anywhere that *didn't* get hit by the Boxing Day tsunami. Though, sadly, that left whole swathes of this part of the world that were devastated. Sri Lanka. Indonesia. The Maldives.'

We stare at the satellite image of the bay. Is this my Beach, or are we chasing shadows? 'It's *very* close to the place I know, Professor,' I say, trying to make him feel better.

He's frowning. 'Crap. I was *so* sure. I know I only caught a glimpse but to me, it looked so similar.'

'I can't explain what's wrong about it. The shape seems right, except maybe the shoreline is too wide. Not quite uneven enough.'

'Unless—' Lewis grabs the laptop and begins to type so hard that it sounds like he's punching holes in the keyboard. Finally he turns the screen back to me.

The curve is basically the same, but this time there are little notches and spikes in the pattern where sea meets sand.

And, this time, it feels so right it makes me dizzy.

'Oh, my God. That's it. It's the Beach. *My* Beach. But . . . how? What did you do?'

'This one is the archive image,' Lewis tells me. 'From *before* the tsunami.'

He presses another button and the images dissolve into

each other. Before and after – the after image smoothing away all the character and the sharp edges I know so well. Just as the Beach smoothes away the physical flaws that the Guests had before their deaths and leaves them . . . too perfect.

'I'm as sure as I can be that this is *my* Beach, Lewis.'

He nods, his face serious. 'Finally.'

I want to reach over, hug him to say thank you. But I stop myself. Instead, I focus on the laptop again, and begin to type. When I find what I'm looking for, I turn the screen back round to him.

'What's this?'

'Flight times between here and Thailand.'

Lewis says nothing.

'I'll understand if you don't want to get involved with this part, Lewis. You've done enough already.'

'You'd go on your own?' he asks.

'What other choice do I have? I've spent long enough trying to get closer to my sister on a laptop. The only chance of finding out the truth is to see it for real.'

He sighs, then reaches into his pocket for his car keys. 'I'd better get going, Ali.'

I've pushed him too far this time. But it's OK. I'll do it alone. 'Right. Well, I'll let you know when I'm going.'

Lewis shakes his head. 'I should hope so. Because, obviously, I *am* coming with you. I just need to get home and make sure my passport isn't about to expire.'

30

Despite everything – all the times I've let her down, the secrets, the lies – Cara agrees to our plan without a second's hesitation.

'Whatever you need. I'll cover for you. You've done it for me often enough,' she says, and we hug so hard that it triggers the worst coughing fit I've had in days.

When I've got my breath back, she frowns. 'So long as you're well enough. It's only a week since you were pulled from a bloody burning building.'

'I promise, Cara, if this works, it'll do more for me than any drugs or therapy.'

'I suppose it would be quite therapeutic to go on a forbidden holiday with a gorgeous man.' She shakes her head. 'Not that I think Lewis is gorgeous. I mean, he's attractive in his own geeky way but, you know, not my type.'

I smile. In the face of all this weirdness, it's funny and, well, nice, to be chatting like normal friends about the men we fancy. Not that I fancy Lewis, of course, but . . . 'Good.'

She touches my hand. 'Though it's a long way when you've been so sick. Wouldn't, I dunno, Paris, do the job just as well?'

I shake my head. 'It's complicated. But it has to be there. And it has to be him. He's the only person I can imagine going there with.'

I regret it as soon as I see her face.

But she brushes off the hurt. 'See, Alice, told you it'd be a man who would take your mind off your problems in the end. Sun, sea and—'

'Yes, all right, Cara. I get the picture.' My cheeks redden but I don't argue because it's easier to pretend that this *is* a mad, romantic escape. Well, the mad part is true. What we're really doing only makes sense to Lewis and me. And, even then, the doubts make me wonder if I've lost the plot, finally. But what is there left to try?

'I know there's more to it,' she says, suddenly serious. 'But you won't tell me even if I ask. So, if it helps bring the old Alice back, that's all I need.'

I hold her hand. 'Thank you. Not just for this – but for sticking by me for all of this time. I've been such a rubbish friend. And this could get all three of us into big trouble, but I promise I'll make it up to you as soon as it's over.'

Cara nods. 'Yeah, yeah. Just . . . enjoy yourself. Don't carry anything in your suitcase you haven't packed yourself, and please try not to turn into some kind of henna tattooed drop-out who ends up staying on the beach forever.'

Olav is totally confused when I show up for my first therapy session since the fire. I suppose he must have been bracing himself for an hour of me being surly and evasive. Instead I am obedient as a sheepdog, smiling as he outlines my treatment plan.

We're going to be focusing on what my sister gave me, and what I gave her, apparently. The bond that continues even now she's gone.

Oh, and anger will be very important, too, Olav reckons.

'I sense a rage in you, Alice. But a need to keep secrets, as well. By the end of our time together, I know you're going to understand that anger and frustration are much better out than in.'

I keep smiling, even though there's something creepy about the way he's relishing the prospect of stripping down my defences before building me back up again.

Thank goodness I'll be thousands of miles away when my next appointment is due. If weeks and weeks of Olav was all my future had in store, I'd be begging Mum to send me to the doctors for knock-out drugs instead.

Passport, sunglasses, SPF 25.

But what else do I take on my 'holiday'? Trashy paperbacks, strappy sandals, a barely-there dress to show off my tropical tan?

No. There will be no moonlit walks or dinners for two.

I pack just before midnight on Monday, laying out the things I need next to my backpack. T-shirts, shorts, the blue silky scrunch-up dress I always wear at night in hot countries. That's all I'm taking. It might look a bit obvious if I leave the house tomorrow for a 'sleepover' at Cara's with a crammed suitcase and a straw hat.

By the time my parents realise I'm not watching old rom-coms in my pyjamas on Cara's cinema surround-sound system, Lewis and I should be safely in Thailand and headed for the Beach. Yes, there'll be war, and poor Cara will be in the firing line, but she just laughed when I told her I was worried about what will happen to her when they find out.

'It'll blow over – and it'll be worth it if you're happy again. Just promise me that if I end up grounded, you'll find a way to tunnel me out.'

With luck, we'll have thirty-six hours in Thailand before anyone realises. Long enough to try one last time to discover the secrets behind Soul Beach.

I can't bring myself to consider what happens if we don't.

The plan goes flawlessly. Mum waves me off when Cara picks me up, and I try to look laid back, even though I'm feeling like total crap for lying to her yet again. Then Lewis arrives at Cara's looking every bit the international business traveller.

New sunglasses, a white shirt and his usual jeans swapped for go-anywhere chinos.

He pushes the down button on the lift. 'Ready?'

Suddenly I'm nervous. My first holiday with a man. I never imagined it would go like this.

'Ali, what is it?'

I fiddle with the strap on my backpack. 'Bit edgy, I guess.'

'Look, everything is going to be OK. The flights are on time. We've got a decent place to stay, separate rooms, of course, so we've both got privacy but I'll be close by you when you need me.'

'Why, though?'

'Why what?'

'Why do all this for me, Lewis? Time. *Money*. I'll pay you back for the flights and everything but, at my current allowance, I'll be in debt till 2050.'

He hesitates, then smiles. 'Just call me a Good Samaritan. Or maybe I was terrible in a previous life and want to make up for it now.'

'But—'

'Ali. I hate to come over all big brother-ish but do you want to know something I've learned as an old fogey?'

I sigh. 'Not really, but I bet you're going to tell me anyway.'

'You don't have to question absolutely everything in life. Sometimes if nice stuff happens, you should just accept it for what it is.'

Lewis pulls out of the car park and I can see Cara waving from her balcony. As I wave back through the car window, I realise that's probably why my heart's beating so fast.

Nice things happen to me so rarely that when they do, I can't help feeling they won't last. That this is only happening to me to trick me into relaxing, before something else goes terribly wrong.

*

But nice things *keep* happening. At the airport, a uniformed chauffeur is already waiting to drive Lewis's car to a secure compound, while another guy takes our bags without being asked.

We follow him into the terminal and I'm ashamed of my shabby bag, which looks even shabbier next to the matt black trolley case Lewis has brought. Part of me is expecting a firm hand on my shoulder, a challenge from security. *You're not meant to be here, are you? Should you be travelling without your parents?*

At check-in, I hold my breath, waiting for them to make a fuss about my age. Lewis watches my face as the woman hands me the boarding pass. 'The privilege lounge is open now, on the first floor. Enjoy your flight, Miss Forster.'

I look down at the ticket. *'Business* class?'

He shrugs. 'I had some frequent flyer points going spare.'

'But doesn't business cost thousands and thousands?'

'Which part of *don't question absolutely everything* did you not understand, Alice? Besides, we need to arrive fighting fit, ready for whatever is at the other end. I can never sleep in economy.'

As we go through the VIP security line, I realise this is what life must always have been like for Danny – and what it could have been like for my sister, too, if she'd become the star she was destined to be. It makes me feel guilty that all this is happening because they died.

Yet I've hardly been unscathed. At least once I'm through security, I can stop worrying about Sahara for a while. Worrying about any of it, in fact. During the flight, I have to try to switch off.

I've done what I can for Danny, for now. I've decided if the letter I posted doesn't get through, I *will* write another and another, until one does.

The security guard hands me back my backpack. 'Have

a great flight, Miss Forster. The privilege lounge is to your right.'

I imagine Meggie's voice: 'Go for it, little sis. Make the most of this. I want to hear every detail afterwards.'

The lounge *is* amazing. Everything is cream or stone-coloured, so at first my still-sore eyes see it as a single blur. But then I notice the different textures: soft leather seats, cool marble floors and long glass counters loaded with treats and drinks.

Lewis hands me a fresh orange juice in a crystal tumbler. 'Best not to drink alcohol before a long-haul flight. Oh, I've put your name down for a neck and shoulder massage, Ali, but you could swap it for something girly like a manicure if you want.'

'No, a massage will be fine. More than fine.'

We find a snug corner with two round leather sofas – they're daybeds, Lewis says – facing the runway. You can't sit upright on them, they're too squidgy, so I stretch my legs out and wish I'd worn something smarter than this old linen skirt which is already creased.

I'm the youngest person in here. Lewis comes a close second. Everyone else is ten years older, at least. They're frowning at laptops or growling into their phones. You can't hear exactly what they're saying, but they sound angry. No one gazes dreamily out of the window or smiles when the staff bring them a cocktail or a glass of champagne.

'I don't want to be like them when I grow up, Alice,' Lewis whispers.

I laugh. He's already pretty grown-up: he has his own company, a car that makes people point in the street, a set of monogrammed luggage that probably cost the same as three years of fees if I ever make it to university. But I get what he means. They all look so bloody miserable, whereas Lewis doesn't mind showing that he's excited to be here, even though any kind of excitement is *unprofessional*.

He takes out his laptop. 'Everything's on schedule. We change planes in Bangkok, and should be in Phuket in approximately seventeen hours' time. Then we'll rest after the journey and head for the islands after that. It's possible . . .' he looks at me, '. . . that we could have the answer in less than twenty-four hours. Are you ready?'

Am I? Perhaps I won't know till it happens. The more terrifying thought is that *nothing* might happen, that the beach isn't *my* Beach. Even if it is, there might be no miracle, no sudden revelation.

It could all be over.

'As ready as I'll ever be. What do you think we're going to find, Lewis?'

He looks at me. 'I don't know. Maybe nothing. But at least that'll be an ending, of sorts, eh? Knowing you've done absolutely everything humanly possible.'

I smile, even though I know it's not enough just to try. I won't be able to rest until I've set my sister free, even if it takes the rest of my life.

However long or short my life might turn out to be.

31

We board first because we're flying business. There's even a special entrance, so we don't have to queue with the economy passengers. It feels unreal, especially after the best shoulder massage ever in the lounge.

I remember our last flight – back from Barcelona after Zoe was hurt. Moments before I got onto the plane, I'd realised the killer *had* to be Sahara. And when I got on board, she'd saved me a place. We were crammed together in those tiny seats. It was the longest two hours of my life.

'How the other half live.' Lewis smiles at me and helps me step into the plane. Perhaps he realises I'm afraid.

I smile back, but I'm actually thinking: what happens when the other half *die*?

This time, our seats are more like leather armchairs placed in pods opposite one another, with video screens and pillows. When we get on board, the Thai attendant gives us hot towels and offers Lewis champagne, but not me; I suppose because she already knows my age.

Lewis simply takes two glasses and then gives one to me and the attendant winks at us both.

'I thought we weren't supposed to drink before a flight!'

'Champagne doesn't count. Plus, it'd be good to get some sleep.'

He holds his glass up to mine, but I hesitate.

'What are we supposed to toast to?'

'Closure?' he suggests.

The bubbles are soft and cool in my mouth and the

excitement spreads through my bloodstream. I don't suppose I'll ever fly business class again. Plus I've never travelled further than Greece. Thailand is supposed to be one of the most beautiful places on earth – with the most beautiful women, judging from the flight attendant. She has the tiniest figure and incredibly delicate features, yet Lewis doesn't seem to have noticed her. He's doing his best to keep me entertained, showing me the movie guide and the menus for the three gourmet meals we'll be served between take-off and landing.

'Time to turn off your phones or other electronic devices, please, Miss Forster and Mr Tomlinson.'

Lewis pulls a face when she's moved on to the next passengers. 'It's like losing a limb.' But he switches off his iPhone and stows it in one of the many leather pockets that surround his recliner.

I take out my phone. There's a text from Cara: **Take care, best friend. Don't know what it is u have to do but come back safe. C xxxxx**

And just as I go to push the power button off, a new text pops up: **Hope u r having fun with Cara, sweetheart. Fun is what u deserve. C u tomorrow, luv mum**

My mum's sweet text language makes my breath catch in my throat. How could I lie to her like this? She'll be devastated when she finds out what I've done.

'Ali?'

Lewis reaches to take my phone and turns it off for me.

I make a silent promise that this trip is the last time I'll deceive her, so as the plane taxis to the runway, I'm planning to become the perfect daughter. I'll be obedient and loving and never complain – and I'll even go to Olav three times a week, until he has no choice but to admit I am the sanest, happiest person he's ever counselled.

OK, maybe not the happiest. That would mean forgetting Meggie.

But certainly the girl who makes the most of every second in her charmed life.

The flight puts me in a strange state of suspended animation. We do nothing for ourselves: food is cooked, movies are streamed, hot towels and even duvets are brought for us. I'm pretty sure the attendant would tuck me up and tell me a bedtime story if I hit the call button now.

But when the cabin lights dim and the world outside does too, it gives me too much time to think about that question: what happens if this fails?

Even stranger, what happens if this succeeds?

I do sleep, but never for long. I dream that I'm picked up by the wind and it's throwing me through the air, and I'm falling fast and hard, unrestrained.

Lewis catches me. He's holding a parachute, but the strings are all tangled and the chute isn't opening and someone is cutting through the cords—

I wake suddenly and realise the plane is bumping through pockets of cloud. I guess even business-class passengers aren't immune to turbulence.

In the luxurious gloom, I watch Lewis, close enough to see him despite my sore eyes. He's sleeping. His glasses are tucked into his shirt pocket and his lips are slightly parted as he breathes. Funny how I never used to realise why women fancied him; I see it now. He's handsome, just not in a conventional way. More so when he sleeps.

It's strange to be this close to him while he's somewhere else.

Sleeping with him.

I blush and look away. What a ridiculous thing to think.

And yet . . . we are spending the night together. I never thought my first night with a man I love would be quite like this.

Love?

How mad is that? I don't *love* Lewis – do I? Not in that way, anyway. He's done all these amazing things for me, so of course I have feelings for him. Without him, my life would be—

'Penny for them, Alice. . .'

I jump. 'How long have you been awake?'

Lewis smiles a faraway smile. His hair's standing on end against the pillow. 'Not long. But time's different up here, isn't it? Sometimes when I'm flying I'd like it to go on forever.'

'Why?'

'There's a freedom about being offline. No calls. No emails. Nothing to fix.'

'I can't believe *you'd* think that, Professor.'

'I'm absolutely serious. They're talking about letting people use their phones on planes. Can you imagine anything worse than being behind one of these guys shouting instructions at their PA for fourteen hours?'

I look round the cabin. It *is* pretty much all guys – the same ones who spent an hour in the business lounge being bad-tempered. Or even if they're not the same ones, they might as well be.

'Awful,' I agree.

'If that happens, I might have to book a one-way ticket to the moon. At least there's no 3G signal there yet.'

'But you make your whole living online.'

'Mmm. That's how I know how toxic it can be. Look at you. Without this Beach of yours, don't you think life would be better by now?'

'Better? I don't think I'd have got over Meggie any sooner, if that's what you mean.'

'No. I didn't mean that exactly. But if you hadn't spent hours and hours online worrying about other people's tragedies – that Triti girl, and the German kid who was kidnapped – you could have focused on your own grief. Found a way of coping.'

'No way. I'm going back to sleep,' I say, and turn away from him. He knows *nothing* about how it feels to lose someone.

Except, as I close my eyes, I realise he *is* right. There's a kind of liberation being thirty thousand feet above ground level, unable to consider going online or fixing someone else's problems.

Could this be a taste of how things will be when this is all over?

I open my eyes again and reach for Lewis's hand to say sorry for snapping. He squeezes back.

For the first time, I do actually allow myself to wonder about life *after* the Beach's version of the afterlife.

It might even be good.

'Good morning, Miss Forster, would you care for some breakfast?'

The voice is so soft that I think it's another dream – about angels this time, perhaps. But dreams don't generally come with the smell of hot coffee and fresh croissants.

I open my eyes. I'm on the plane. The sky outside is light now.

'You've been out for nearly seven hours, Ali. Good going!' Lewis is already tucking into a plate of noodles.

'We have a choice of Asian style or European,' the attendant says.

'European, thanks.'

She places the tray in front of me: fresh fruit, a basket of bread, jams, plus a dainty dish containing a doll-sized cooked breakfast.

'You know they breed extra-small chickens to lay eggs specially for aeroplane meals,' Lewis says.

'What?' It takes me a second too long to realise he's joking.

'Give me a break, Lewis, I'm not even properly awake yet. How much longer do we have to go?'

He points to his TV screen. It shows a world map with an out-of-proportion plane superimposed on top, at least as big as India. But I get the message. We're nearly there.

'Under two hours, I'd say. Then we change planes. Then, finally, we get to take our first steps in Thailand.' He pulls his lips apart with his fingers in a strange grin. 'Land of *smiles*.'

'I'm almost too nervous to eat.'

'I'll have yours, then—'

I stop him reaching over to grab my croissant. 'I said *almost*. It does feel weird, eating breakfast for the second time in twelve hours.'

'One of the jet-setter's secrets, Ali. The sooner you acclimatise to the new time zone, the more ready you are to hit the ground running.'

'Not sure that *hit the ground* is the best phrase to use when we're miles above the earth, Lewis.'

I'm in no hurry to land, I realise. I'm more chilled here than I have been in months. Good company. No Sahara. No internet. No pressure to fix the unfixable.

Once we do hit the ground, that's when the pressure starts again. But I'm ready. Excited, almost. A new continent. An old mystery.

My last chance.

32

Asia.

I didn't expect so much green. As we come in to land at Phuket Airport, sea turns into forest. No, *jungle.*

The word thrills me, and the view thrills me even more.

'You're smiling,' Lewis says, leaning over to check how close we are to the ground. We changed planes in a foggy Bangkok, going straight from air-conditioned plane to air-conditioned bridge and air-conditioned lounge. I felt removed from reality.

But now our final destination is only seconds away.

'Is that a nice way of saying I normally look miserable?'

'No. But you haven't had many reasons to smile lately, Ali. I hope this holiday will change that.'

Holiday sounds wrong, but I try not to let my smile fade. Lewis is doing something so wonderful for me. It's not his fault that the minute I begin to have fun, I feel guilty about my sister dying and about my failure to find out why.

Except . . . I'm not the one to blame.

The thought is so unexpected that it shocks me more than the impact as we touch down with a bump.

It's unexpected, yes, but it's also true. Someone else chose to take Meggie's life – and Tim's and Zoe's too. Then the police jumped to conclusions and refused to consider the possibility that Tim didn't do it.

None of that is my fault.

Is it time for me to forgive myself for something I didn't even do?

'Come on, daydreamer, another bonus of our business-class status – we get off the plane first!'

My right leg has gone to sleep and I let Lewis take my hand to help me up. He really would make someone a fantastic boyfriend.

Not me, though. Obviously. I have Danny.

Or, at least, I did.

The pain of not knowing whether our last meeting was the final goodbye should be enough to put me off relationships for a very long time. Far better that Lewis and I are close friends. And anyway, what would he see in me?

'Ready?' he asks.

I nod.

'Ladies first.'

At the top of the plane steps, I take my first breath of Thai air through the gap between the cabin door and the bridge.

I'm disappointed that it doesn't smell like a posh oriental spa. The strongest scent is kerosene.

But the air is warm, as welcoming as a tropical ocean.

A second later, we're back in the air-conditioned terminal and it leaves me longing for outside. We queue – the business-class ticket doesn't win us a smile from the border guard, whose suspicious eyes peek over the top of his surgical mask.

'Has no one told him this is the land of smiles?' Lewis whispers and I pull a face.

'Be careful. He could send us back home.'

It's only when the guard inspects Lewis's passport for what feels like ten minutes that it occurs to me. We might already be on the wanted list. If my parents happened to pop over to Cara's, then it's all over.

I try to stay calm. Would Interpol really get involved with a seventeen-year-old who does a bunk with her 'boyfriend' during her school holidays?

They might if her parents told them she was depressed, deluded, *mad*.

'Next. NEXT!'

I look up. The guard's eyes are blazing with anger because I dared to keep him waiting for a fraction of a second. I step forward, forcing myself to smile, as though I cross international borders every day of the week.

Out of the corner of my eye I spot Lewis waiting on the other side. His face is creased with tiredness and anxiety.

Yet again I wonder why the hell he's doing this for me.

Finally the guard throws the passport back at me with the stamped immigration form tucked inside. As I walk away from the booth, unable to believe I've got away with it, Lewis steps forward to take my hand. But this time, he pulls me along.

'Let's get out of here,' he says, and we make our way towards the luggage carousel, where his posh case is already waiting and looking much more pristine than either of us. He drags it off before it can make another revolution and we walk through Customs.

And into chaos.

People are shouting and waving signs at us, none with our names on them.

'Taxi, taxi!'

'Hotel, very nice! Special price for you! Very cheap! Cheapest in Phuket.'

They pronounce the Ph more like a B and their voices are insistent. The kerosene smell has gone, replaced by heat. I never knew heat had a smell till now but this is intense.

Voices, honking horns, the screech of brakes.

I *love* it.

'There should be a car waiting . . .' Lewis scans the exit. 'Over there. Off we go.'

I want to watch some more. After the luxuries of the last

twenty-odd hours, this unfiltered reality is intoxicating.

But I follow him anyway. Morning sunlight dazzles me for a moment, then I see a long black estate car . . . no, I think it is actually a proper limousine, with a gold lily flower logo on the door.

'Mr Tomlinson? Miss Forster?' The driver is wearing a high-collared jacket in soft gold silk. He lurches forward so suddenly that I think he's tripped, but then I realise he's desperate to relieve me of my shabby backpack before I can take another step. He opens the door and a new smell hits me: leather polish and sharp citrus aromatherapy oils.

Now this *does* smell like a posh health spa. There's chilled water and cool towels in a console between our seats. When I run the towel over my face it has the same scent as the fragranced air-conditioning.

'The journey will take only twenty minutes,' the driver says once we're inside. 'Welcome to Phuket. Now, please relax. Is the music all right for you?'

I hadn't noticed it till now – it's classical and soothing, and so completely at odds with the frenzied life beyond the smoked windows that it makes everything even more surreal. The engine is so quiet that you wouldn't know the car was moving if you closed your eyes.

But I'm not going to close my eyes, even though they're gritty from the flight – and still swollen from the fire. There's too much to take in; I don't want to miss a thing.

After we leave the airport, it's like driving through a film set. It must be rush hour because the whole of Phuket is on the move, sometimes three or four adults balanced on a single moped, weaving in between open trucks crammed full of animals or buses crammed full of people.

At junctions, the traffic lights are mounted high above street-level, like on American freeways in the movies. Jumbled stores line both sides of the road. One is built like the grandest of temples, in marble so white it glows like false teeth. But right next to it there's an open shack that's only being held up by the piles of tyres and random car parts it's selling. If they removed just one grimy engine, I'm pretty sure the entire terrace of shops would come crashing down.

And everywhere there are kids in school uniform, freshly laundered like a detergent advert, untouched by the dust and the heat.

I'd expected palms and sand and unbroken blue skies, but this . . . this is so incredible. If this is the world, I want to see every corner.

'It's so much more than I thought it would be,' I say to Lewis.

'Hmm?' He's checking his phone.

'Is everything OK?' I reach in my pocket for my own phone. I don't even know for sure if it'll work out here but I hold my breath as I switch it on. Will there be something from Cara? Or worse, from Mum and Dad?

The plan is that Cara will text and email us both when it all goes tits up and then I'll email my parents to tell them it's all right, that I'm safe and will explain everything soon. Of course, I won't tell them where I am. Every second counts.

No one has reported you missing yet! Be careful, C xxxxx

I'm relieved the phone works, but I try not to imagine the effect my trip is going to have on my parents. I have to be selfish. It's not Olav that I need, it's *this*. Closure.

A little girl is clinging to the back of her mum's motorbike. She's wearing a white dress with a sailor collar. She notices me watching her and waves so enthusiastically that I worry she'll fall off.

I wave back. Perhaps it's more than closure I need. It's new horizons, too. How strange if I come to find the Beach and end up discovering the world.

*

Exactly nineteen minutes after we leave the airport, the driver turns into what looks like a national park. Ahead, there's a lake surrounded by beach houses: not dilapidated huts, but pastel-painted three-storey buildings that would look just right in New England, or somewhere, but seem very out of place here. Our limo passes a bus painted in psychedelic patterns, the kind you'd expect hippies to have used on a trek through Asia in the sixties.

More greenery but still no sign of a beach. Finally, the car turns right and we drive up to wrought-iron gates so ornate that they could have been stolen from a royal palace. The guards here look even sterner than the guy at the border but, when they see us in the limo, they raise the barriers.

Lewis puts away his phone. 'Hope this place is going to be all right. At the last minute the choice was a bit limited.'

Trees jostle for position along the final stretch of drive, and to one side I can see people out playing golf on greens so bright they look radioactive.

'Oh, *wow!*' I gasp.

The hotel is like a giant pavilion. The second our car stops, both passenger doors are opened at the exact same moment by two porters.

'Welcome to the True Lily Hotel,' they chorus in sing-song voices. There are more cool, citrusy towels, and then garlands of white flowers are placed around our necks. Their perfume is thick, almost too intense.

Like the flowers Sahara sent.

I stumble as I enter the lobby. One more step and I'd have ended up in the water: the floor is made up of walkways suspended over huge pools full of fish and lilies.

The maze of paths makes me dizzy; I look up and feel dizzier still. The roof is *so* far away. Birds swoop and soar into the open eaves. Giant fans whirl but I can't feel any draught.

Then I realise the building has no back wall. Instead it's

open, with a view across another enormous lake. My eyes are still sore but everything's more in focus here, and more vivid.

Is that an *elephant* on the grass outside?

'Ali, shall we?'

Lewis touches me lightly on the arm and I take careful steps as we head across another pond towards a sofa area. Already a bamboo tray is set with a porcelain tea set.

Tea? I can't imagine drinking anything hot right now. Every step I take, I sweat even more. *Classy.*

I sit down opposite an elegant woman in a dress that reaches her ankles. What does she think of me, all dishevelled and over-heated? It's obvious I'm not used to this, that I don't belong.

But she smiles kindly, pours my tea.

'Miss Forster. Welcome to Thailand and to the True Lily Hotel.'

It'd be rude to refuse. I'll pretend to drink. But when I lift the cup to my lips, I almost drop it.

It's ice cold.

Meggie always used to laugh about my name. 'Little Alice in her own Wonderland. Nothing makes sense for Alice! Off with her head!'

I've never felt more like a character in someone else's topsy-turvy world. Even the Beach felt more familiar than this.

Beach? I haven't even seen the reason we came here yet.

' . . . the role of the concierge is to make your holiday truly memorable,' the lady is saying. 'We offer various trips to places around the island, including the setting for the Bond movie . . .'

I don't want to see where they filmed a Bond movie.

I want to see Soul Beach.

Lewis is nodding politely as the woman – her badge says

Guest Services – continues telling us about places we don't want to visit and restaurants where we will never eat.

This isn't a bloody holiday. I try to catch Lewis's eye. He looks funny with the blossom necklace against a white shirt that's crumpled from almost twenty-four hours of travelling. His face shows exhaustion, though he's still nodding.

Finally the woman finishes her monologue.

'I'm happy to answer any questions before we show you to your villa . . . the Tiger Lily, it's one of our most luxurious.'

Villa?

'I think you've told us everything we could possibly need to know,' Lewis says and, despite the tiredness, there's a twinkle in his eye as he looks at me. 'Alice? Anything else before we go to our *villa?*'

'Only one thing,' I say. 'Where's the beach?'

33

Of course, there's no way we honoured guests could be allowed to *walk* to the beach.

No, the woman summons a golf buggy and we rumble off, away from reception, over a bridge, past little landscaped gardens leading up to tiny front doors complete with letterboxes and numbers. Behind the doors I can just glimpse red-tiled roofs.

It's freakily similar to the neat estate I live in at home.

Until a group of sparrow-sized birds with bright yellow legs and even brighter yellow faces swoop by the side of the buggy.

And then the baby elephant blocks our path.

OK, maybe not quite like home.

The buggy driver brakes gently alongside and turns to the left. There's an opening and beyond it, mopeds and vans race by on a main road.

'In Thailand, beaches must not be owned. All are public, but we have outstanding facilities for our guests, of course,' the driver is telling us, as he helps us step down from the golf buggy. There's a fierce-faced man in khaki uniform at the gate. He steps into the road and halts the traffic to let Lewis and me cross.

This isn't right.

In the distance, I glimpse the sea. The colours are perfect, the lower half a deep turquoise, the heavens a clearer, brighter blue.

But the rest of it doesn't fit at all.

Lewis takes my hand and we head for the water. There's a paved walkway leading towards the beach, and either side there are stalls and shops. We pass an open-air massage place full of bored-looking Thai women, fanning themselves with newspapers. To the right, a tourist shop is selling hats and mats that wouldn't look out of place on Brighton beach. Another stall has cherry-red sarongs and emerald tie-dye dresses swinging in the sea breeze.

Ahead there are bleached-wood loungers with cushions deeper than my mattress at home and parasols woven from palm rushes. Finally the path stops and the sand starts. I take off my trainers and leave them on the paving stones.

As I step into the sand, it shifts under my feet. Warm. No, *hot,* so hot that I have to keep moving so I don't burn my soles.

To my left, a restaurant packed with holiday-makers eating lunch.

Wrong.

Reggae music blasts from a bar to my right.

Wrong.

No harsh rocks, no secluded bay, no jetty, no birds of paradise.

No beautiful teenagers.

No Danny.

No Meggie.

Wrong, wrong, WRONG!

'Beautiful, isn't it?' Lewis whispers.

I can't answer. It *is* beautiful. Possibly the most beautiful place I've ever visited in my life. Close up, the sea is as clear as air, and translucent crabs skitter across the sand like ghosts.

But it's *nothing* like Soul Beach. All this way, all this money, all the pain I'll be putting my parents through. *For nothing.*

'It's not supposed to be *here,* by the way, Alice.'

'What?'

'The place we're looking for. It's a good couple of hours away but there are no hotels over in that direction, not since the tsunami. This resort is just our base for the trip. Closest I could get accommodation that didn't look like a health hazard. No good coming this far to be laid low with dysentery or something.'

'Oh.'

'Let's see how we feel later, but my plan would be to recover today and then, tomorrow, we will go to find what you're looking for.'

The relief makes me light-headed. Or maybe it's the heat or the jet lag or that weird herbal tea. Whatever it might be, I begin to fall, until Lewis steps in front of me and catches me in his arms.

'Thank you,' I whisper.

He nods. 'You know I'd do anything for you, Ali.'

I smile, but I wish he hadn't said that. It makes me feel even more faint.

When I wake up, I have no idea where I am. Whether it's night or day.

Slowly, I *make* myself remember, dredging my tired brain for snippets of information.

Thailand. Daytime, I think, unless I've slept all the way into night. It is dark here, and I'm groggy, but my instinct tells me I've been out no more than an hour, two at most.

I'm certain about one thing: I need water. There's a tiny sliver of light to my left, enough for me to see a bedside table. I reach out and a carved stone lamp comes on as I touch it, giving off the gentlest of glows. There's a bottle of water in its own ice bucket. I lift it to my lips and drink.

And *drink*. Even once I've finished the bottle, I could drink another one, but it's enough for now.

The room – sorry, I'm remembering now, the *villa* – is huge. The bed on its own is larger than my entire bedroom at home. It's set on a platform: around me there are glass walls, and thick curtains keeping out most of the daylight. I have a vague memory of the manager mentioning a remote control and so I sit up properly and peer under the bedside table. Push one button – all the lights fade up. Push a second – classical music fills the room. Push the third . . .

The curtains draw back smoothly, like I'm in a theatre. Sunshine blinds me momentarily. But even now I can see, I can't make sense of what's in front of me. I sit up – still dressed in the t-shirt I wore for the flight, *ugh* – and glance through the floor-to-ceiling glass.

My room seems to be floating in the middle of a lily pond.

I climb out of bed, my legs rubbery, and the soles of my feet make contact with the cool white marble of the floor. I walk across the room. There are sliding doors in front of me and I pull them apart. Heat hits me. Glass steps lead down to . . . no, down *into* the pond. It's too tempting.

I dangle my right foot in the water. *Ah.* So much cooler than the air. I step down again and the water reaches to my knees. It's a delicious feeling.

The 'pond' isn't natural – it's tiled, for a start, and there are lights in the walls, the beams rippling in the water. But the whole pool is surrounded by trees and kept completely private by stone walls that are covered with greenery. The stone looks oddly familiar . . .

Of course. It's the same grey-black colour as the rocks on the Beach. My heart begins to pound.

No. Don't get your hopes up. Maybe that's pretty much the standard colour for stone across the whole of Asia.

'Mooo.'

The noise is so loud it makes me jump.

'MOOO!'

Again. Are we next to a farmyard? Whatever's making that noise must be enormous.

Except it seems to be coming from right next to me.

Lewis will know.

I wonder if he's up and about. I should find him, get the plan confirmed for visiting the *real* Beach. This isn't a holiday.

'Ow.'

I've stubbed my toe on something. A blue glass chair, set into the tiles, halfway under the water. It makes me smile and I sit down on it. This does feel like Wonderland. James Bond curtains. Underwater furniture.

'Moo!'

Farmyard sound effects.

Except this time it's clearer where the moo is coming from. Over in the corner of the water garden. I wade towards it.

A frog. Or, more of a toad, I guess. He'd only just fit in the palm of my hand. Except I wouldn't pick him up because he looks a bit . . . well, warty. His body is round and brown, with orangey stripes down his back.

'That wasn't really you, was it?' I say to the toad, who stares back with dark, challenging eyes. I guess he doesn't speak English.

But then he moos again. *So* loud that if I wasn't seeing it close-up, I wouldn't think it was possible. The expression in his face is defiant, as if to say, this is my country and my pond, I'll moo as much as I like.

I begin to giggle. Then it turns into a belly laugh. Maybe I've finally lost it. But at this moment, wading around in the privacy of my own water garden, thousands of miles from everything familiar, I feel lighter than I have for a whole year.

The Tiger Lily Villa gets more like Wonderland with every new discovery.

The shower has more controls than the space shuttle. I fill

the glass cubicle with citrus-scented steam before I manage to get any water to come out. When it does, it's like a monsoon. I'm completely baffled by which shower gel to try from the rainbow of potions in glass decanters, so I try a bit of each one.

There's even a choice of bathrobes. I pick one made from cool navy cotton.

Wherever I walk, the lights fade up automatically and music follows me too. A wood panelled corridor leads from the bedroom and bathroom to a heavy wooden door. When I open it, there's a huge dining and lounging area, with floaty white curtains and exotic flowers and plants along three walls . . .

And to my right, there's a glass wall: beyond it, a vast garden leading down to a lily-covered private lake.

In the garden, a figure sits under the parasol, reading a paper.

Lewis has changed into shorts and a t-shirt. He's not wearing glasses, and his hair's wet and drawn back from his face. His head is slightly bent as he reads. He's as still as the lake.

I've never watched him like this before. Suddenly he looks so different. Like this is his element. It makes sense – at home, in his flat, he surrounds himself with plants.

The concentration in his face draws me to him. All the frantic gestures he usually makes – running his hand through his mad hair, fiddling with his phone, downing another can of Diet Coke – are a distraction. But now I'm seeing a new Lewis, the person behind his running commentary of self-deprecating wisecracks.

A beautiful mind.

I don't know where that phrase comes from, but it's precisely right.

But it's not just his mind. His legs are pretty good too,

and his face, in profile, is classically handsome, like a Roman statue.

How have I not seen this before? His busy-ness has disguised who he really is. Now he's calm, I can finally see him clearly.

He dazzles me. Right now, it's like he's brighter than the sun.

And like the sun, he makes my skin burn.

Suddenly I'm all too aware of how thin this bathrobe is, and how my hair is dripping and my face is scrubbed clean with no make-up. I take a step backwards but he *had* to choose that moment to look up, didn't he?

'Ali! You've surfaced from the depths of sleep. Excellent!'

I check the tie around my waist is firmly knotted and walk towards him, holding my hand up to shield my eyes from the fierce sunlight. 'How long have I been out?'

'Couple of hours. Not very long. The theory goes that to fight jet lag you're supposed to stay up as long as you possibly can, but I grabbed an hour, too. Woke myself up in the pool.'

'Pool?'

'Um . . .' he points behind us. How did I *not* notice the long, narrow strip of pure blue that seems to project into the lake itself? Or the adjoining whirlpool that looks like a cube of jade crystal?

'I guess I can use jet lag as my excuse,' I say, knowing it's a poor excuse when he's already wide awake.

He smiles. 'Hungry? Let's have lunch.'

I look down at my dressing gown and my pale legs poking from underneath. My Soul Beach tan is only an illusion created when I go online – it doesn't travel into real life.

'Don't worry, Ali, we don't have to set foot outside the villa.'

Of course, the villa has its own kitchen, just inside the grand entrance.

'Don't suppose the guests ever come in here. It's probably strictly for their manservants or battalion of chefs,' Lewis says. The room is narrow and slightly tatty. There's no air-con, only a mesh across the mean window to keep the insects out. 'The kind of people who usually stay here don't do their own cooking. They probably don't even know how to turn on a tap.'

'Is the villa *very* expensive?'

'Reassuringly expensive, but I decided that as the chief executive and sole employee of my own company, I deserved a little bonus,' he says. 'Plus, they upgraded us. Which was nice of them, wasn't it?'

I nod. 'You know, Lewis, I'm not all that hungry.'

'I'll bear that in mind, but you should have *something*. Now, you just go and lay the table, and I'll rustle something up.' He hands me cutlery and glasses and I walk down the grand entrance hall back to the dining lobby. I can hear him chopping.

Lewis's room must be in the other 'wing' – and if that's the same size as my side, then this villa is bigger than my house. I'll have to take loads of photos to show Mum.

If she ever speaks to me again after she finds out what I've done.

While Lewis is busy, I go back to my room to change, and to check my phone for messages. Nothing more from Cara, but the worry takes a little of the shine off this dreamy place.

I pull on shorts and a t-shirt and turn my backpack upside down looking for make-up. All I find is some orangey concealer and a hairbrush. Worrying about what I looked like wasn't a concern when I packed my bag.

So why does it feel like it matters so much now?

I go back to the dining room and sit down, then stand up, then sit down again. I can't settle.

'Right, I hope this will perk us up.' Lewis is carrying a

large bamboo tray with a jug of iced water and lots of plates. He lays them out on the table in front of me.

'Miss Forster, a light lunch as requested. All fresh, to make up for the dehydration of spending way too long at thirty-four thousand feet. Here we have sliced papaya with lime quarters. Baby bananas with almonds. Mango with ice cream—'

There's a ping from the kitchen. He disappears again.

My mouth is watering – somehow he's managed to guess the only things I can imagine eating right now.

When he comes back, he's holding a white porcelain bowl. 'And hot chocolate dipping sauce.'

'How on earth have you done all this? The kitchen was empty.'

He shrugs. 'The chocolate was in my hand luggage for emergency snack attacks, so I just melted it. Plus there was ice cream in my mini-bar, and loads of tropical fruit in a bowl in the snug.'

'Snug?'

'You mean you don't have a *snug* in your wing?' He pulls a shocked face. 'Well, if you're very nice to me I might let you come and see mine.'

'You are the perfect man, aren't you?' I say it as a joke but it comes out wrong, sarcastic almost. 'No. Really.'

He raises his eyebrows. 'Bon appétit, Ali.'

I reach out, but my hand hovers over the plates. I'm unable to choose. 'They all look too delicious.' Finally I pick up a glistening slice of mango. It's so juicy that orange liquid runs down my finger. I hesitate before tasting it, bracing myself for disappointment. The last time I saw fruit as ripe as this was on the Beach, where perfection is never what it seems.

'Problem?' Lewis asks.

'No.' I bite into it. The mango dissolves on my tongue. A second later, the flavour hits my taste buds, an explosion of sweetness with a scent so strong it's almost like fresh flowers. Delicious.

'Nice?'

I nod. The taste is so intense that I don't want to speak.

Weird. Who knew you could be knocked sideways by a simple slice of fruit? It's almost like the first time I've ever tasted it.

And then I realise. It's because of Soul Beach. All these months I've been hanging out with the Guests, watching *them* eat and drink the delicious-looking things Sam has prepared for them. The only time I've tried to join in, they've tasted of ashes or of nothing. They've reminded me of everything that separates me from my sister and the boy I love.

Here, it's different.

This is how it tastes to be alive.

34

'Right. Enough lazing around. I think we should explore, don't you?'

Maybe it's all the sugar in the fruit, but I'm completely re-energised. I slap on a load of sunscreen before we leave. Getting burned is not going to help me find what I'm looking for.

Burned. I think of Zoe, at the fire run in Barcelona. No. Don't go there. I force myself to focus on right now. Like Lewis said, today is a recovery day then, tomorrow, we start afresh. The bigger issue – what I'm actually going to *do* if we find a doppelganger for Soul Beach – is something I don't want to think about. I've been focusing so hard on not getting my hopes up that I haven't considered what we'll do if it *does* exist.

The Tiger Lily Villa looks even bigger from the outside. It has the same pointy Thai-style roof as the hotel reception lobby. There are two gleaming gold bikes propped next to a tree.

'The resort's so huge, I think we should use these instead of going on foot,' Lewis says. 'The amount it costs to stay here, they're probably made of real gold.'

I pick the one with the slightly lower saddle. When I climb on, it's still too high and, though I wrestle with the clip, it won't budge.

Lewis looks round. 'Hang on, let me.'

I hold the bike steady while he unjams the post. So hot. But not just because of the sun. Being this close to him makes me feel self-conscious in a way I never have before.

'Fixed,' he says. 'Try that now.'

I do. 'Better.'

He grins. A bead of sweat is travelling down from his brow. I'm about to reach out to wipe it away, as I would have done before, but I stop. My cheeks redden.

I want to touch him, I realise. More than I've ever wanted anything.

No. It's the heat, the jet lag, the journey.

'We'll soon cool down once we get the wind on our faces,' Lewis says, and I feel myself blushing deeper. He's practical, a good mate. He's not interested in me like *that;* why would he be? We're friends.

And yet, my hand tingles where I almost touched his face. The wind won't do anything to cool down these new feelings for Lewis.

I climb onto the bike, looking anywhere but at him. Thank God he doesn't suspect anything. Nothing's changed for him even though *everything's* just changed for me.

'Chocks away, Alice!'

He takes off so confidently that I wouldn't be surprised to see him using the satnav app on his phone to find his way. But when I pull alongside him, I see an expression of wild pleasure on his face and realise he's just enjoying the freedom.

My Lewis.

We cross a bridge and almost collide with a golf buggy full of staff and laundry. They smile and say something in Thai as we sail past.

'Brilliant, isn't it?' he says.

'Yup.' I haven't ridden a bike for ages. The breeze *is* cooling my flushed face and the sun feels delicious on my arms and my neck, although it's making me sweat.

'You know what's even more brilliant?' he calls out.

'Nope.'

'I know no one is going to call me to demand I come over and sort out their shrivelled hard drive, because no one knows where we are!' He's laughing as we cross a bridge over another lake and then freewheel at high speed down the other side.

He doesn't have a clue how I feel but perhaps it's better that way. I laugh too.

But the laughter catches in my throat. Suddenly, things feel different.

What's wrong?

Even though the only other people I can see are hotel staff – tending the gardens, re-painting the outside of an already pristine-looking villa – that *darkness* has come back.

The feeling, no, *certainty*, that I'm being monitored. The same icy sensation I had in my sister's old bedroom, and with Sahara, and at the fire run just before Zoe was trampled . . .

The sun's still strong but I don't feel the warmth any more. Sweat trickles down my back and makes me shiver.

That's when I realise those dark feelings in the past *must* have been my overactive imagination. Like Lewis said, no one even knows we've left the country, never mind that we've travelled to Thailand. I'm not even on the same continent as the killer any more. I should be making the most of being safe, at last.

'Hey, watch out!' Lewis shouts, and I only just swerve in time to avoid a skinny black cat who clearly wasn't going to move. I wobble for a few seconds; it doesn't take much to knock me off balance.

'I reckon the beach was that way,' Lewis is pointing across to our right.

'I'll take your word for it.' Right now, I want to turn round and head back to the safety of our villa, but I realise I'm being irrational.

Breathe slowly. Calmer, calmer.

That's working. The bikes run so smoothly and the landscape is stunningly lush. I didn't know there were quite so many shades of green, from leaves so dark they're almost black, through to lime flowers so vividly neon they hurt my eyes. But actually, being here seems to be making my vision clearer: I see the difference now between our villa and these ones nearer the main lake. These are smaller and built much closer together. The bikes parked outside are a dull brown rather than gold. That makes me smile; even in paradise, there's a class system.

Ahead of us, a guard stands to attention when he hears us approach, then tips his hat and stops the traffic as we cross. I'm not sure I'd ever get used to that.

Now that I know the beach isn't going to look like *Soul Beach*, I appreciate it more. Our bikes go over the dip and suddenly the sea is there, and in the afternoon sun it *does* look the same turquoise as I remember from my online paradise, with the same starbursts as a breeze whips up tiny waves.

If I tune out the ever-present reggae and the high tones of the skinny masseurs gossiping as they pummel fat tourists, then I can almost imagine hearing Meggie's voice, exactly as I heard it when I first walked along Soul Beach. The hour I first *believed* . . .

'Ali, shall we park up? I've never tried cycling on sand but I can't imagine it's easy, especially with killer jet lag.' Lewis grins at me. I'm already halfway onto the beach, my front wheel kicking sand into our faces.

'Sorry, miles away.'

And he nods, and I know he understands exactly where I thought I was. 'Are you too jet-lagged to risk a beer, Ali?'

I follow him up a couple of rickety steps into a restaurant that's tantalisingly close to the shore. A beer might cool me down a little, though as long as I'm with him, I'm going to feel flustered. 'Was this whole coast affected by the tsunami, Lewis?'

'A lot of it, I think. I'm not sure if this actual beach took a hit. Scary thought, though. Thousands of tourists sitting with their beers, like us. Hundreds of thousands of locals going about their everyday lives. Then . . .'

He doesn't have to spell it out. We both saw the news footage.

The waiter brings us menus but Lewis shakes his head and orders local Singha beers instead: two brown bottles as big as skittles. We take our first sips in silence.

'So is there anything about this place that reminds you of Soul Beach?' he asks.

'I didn't think so earlier, but now, well . . .' I gaze out to sea. 'The colours are the same. If I half close my eyes, then maybe. What about you?'

He shakes his head. 'I only had the briefest glimpse. But those rock formations at the very end of the bay,' he points towards the coast beyond where the reggae café is, 'they seem similar. Then again, a rock is a rock is a rock, right?'

Except the rocks on the Beach acted as prison walls to the Guests until they all had no choice but to 'save' themselves.

All except Danny.

'So how far away is the beach you found online, Lewis?'

'A taxi ride, plus a speedboat trip. There's a whole group of little islands. Makes most sense to organise a private trip. I've already spoken to the all-singing, all-dancing concierge, and they can do it tomorrow. That's if you think you're ready.'

I want to say *no*, I'm not ready yet. How brilliant would it be to wake up in the morning with the Thai sun on my face? To hang out on *this* beach, where sand is sand and sea is sea and I don't have to look for the hidden messages all the time?

It'd be wonderful just to while away a few hours drinking beer with Lewis. To pretend to myself that we're on a date, that he likes me too, that everything is normal.

But that's not why I'm here – and we can't ignore the fact that the clock's ticking towards the moment when Mum and Dad find out I've gone and all hell breaks out.

'Tomorrow will be great,' I say.

I think I see a flicker of disappointment cross his face, but then he grins and I decide I was imagining it. Perhaps the reason he's doing all this for me is because he wants to end our high-maintenance friendship and, after this, at least he won't need to feel guilty if he never sees me again.

That thought makes everything seem dark, as though someone's pulled a thunder cloud across the sun.

'To Mission Implausible,' he says, knocking his bottle against mine.

'To friendship,' I toast back, wishing it could be so much more.

35

The light changes again before I can take my first sip of beer. I know I'm jet-lagged, but surely it's too early for sunset?

Then the rain starts. From sunshine to storm in less than five seconds.

We try to drink our beers as the water thumps down on the umbrella above us, but soon it's dripping through the fabric, onto our heads.

Lewis pays for the drinks – I'm embarrassed that I haven't bothered to get any Thai baht of my own – and by the time we make it back to the bikes, there are deep pools of water on the path and we're soaked.

'That'll be why everything round here is so lush and green,' Lewis says as we leap onto our bikes. I'm behind him and I try not to look at the way his t-shirt clings to the muscles on his back. We cross the road without waiting for the security guard to do his lollipop lady routine, and cycle back into the compound.

I mean, the hotel.

There are three different routes we could take. 'Which way, Professor?'

It feels important to make the right choice. Hundreds of bright strikes of lightning are now forking down from the sky to the earth, and the thunder that follows scutters through my bones. I suppose at least if I get hit, the bike's tyres will absorb the shock.

'Let's try this one. Not like we can get any wetter, is it?' And he sets off up the middle path.

After about ten minutes, we're no closer to anything that looks familiar, and so we stop a passing buggy driver, who insists on personally leading us back to the Tiger Lily Villa.

The whole complex seems deserted.

Yet that feeling of being watched has returned – which is completely illogical, because this has to be about the most remote, most secure place I've ever stayed at in my entire life.

Lewis unlocks the front door and, as we squelch along the entrance hall to the dining area, rainwater drips from our clothes onto the white marble.

'Hear that?' I ask Lewis. My toad's back, and it sounds as though he's brought all his mates round for a pond party. They're as loud as the thunder.

'What the hell?'

'Toads. I found one in the water earlier on.'

Lewis takes his phone out, taps away, then smiles. 'You were almost right. They're bullfrogs. Says here you can eat them. If they keep going into the night, they could well end up as a microwaved midnight snack.'

I laugh. 'Bullfrog burgers don't appeal, but I am getting hungry again. Which is a good sign, right?'

'Early dinner, then? I'll reserve their fusion restaurant, makes sense for us to be well-nourished before tomorrow's adventures.'

I look down at my sodden clothes, and run a hand through my hair. How could he *ever* see me as anything more than the tomboy kid sister he never had? 'I may need some time to get ready.'

'You always look great, Ali, even soaked to the skin, but I know you girls do like to dress up.' He's taking the piss, but gently. 'An hour give you enough time to dry out?'

I nod, turn towards my 'wing' of the villa. 'Hey, the door's locked.'

'The turndown lady must have been. Here, I forgot to give

you your key. Both wings are uber-secure – I think that's pretty important to the average Russian billionaire. They probably can't even trust their friends.'

The key card unlocks the door, then I close it behind me with a solid clunk. If billionaires feel safe here, then a seventeen-year-old schoolgirl should be fine.

The full-length mirror in the bathroom is unforgiving. 'Drowned rat' doesn't even begin to describe me. My backpack's still on the bed, where I turned it upside down before. Did I pack anything suitable for a posh restaurant? I had no idea Lewis was going to bring me anywhere as fancy as *this*.

Right at the bottom there's my go-anywhere dress in sky-blue, made from that silky, crinkly fabric that looks fine even if it's been scrunched in a ball. That'll do. But I have no shoes except the ones I'm wearing. I can't go to a restaurant in a swingy dress with soggy wet trainers on my feet. What was I thinking?

I wasn't thinking, though, was I? Yesterday, I didn't really care what I looked like in front of Lewis. He was a mate. Why would I?

But now . . .

When I look up at my bedraggled reflection again, I realise I've blushed bright crimson.

I've got it bad.

Lewis grins when I walk back into the lobby.

'Wow! You *shall* go to the ball, Miss Forster.'

I shrug it off, even though it's taken all my ingenuity and what I can remember of Meggie's sisterly beauty tips to achieve the transformation – not to mention the vast array of freebies in the villa bathroom. Plus the most welcome pair of complimentary flip-flops since Cinderella took delivery of her party shoes.

'Yeah, amazingly, my fairy godmother managed to locate me just in time.'

He laughs, then frowns. 'Have you heard from Cara yet? About whether your parents know what's going on?'

I'd been too busy blow-drying and eye-lining to remember. Not because I think I'll somehow convince him I'm beautiful or anything. I just don't want to show him up at the fancy restaurant. I take my phone out of my bag. Two messages: **The eagle has landed. Things getting hot here. Time to send that email to yr folks. Hope you're OK. Love, C xxxxx**

That one arrived . . . I do the calculations in my head . . . around the same time we got back to the villa. So, one hour ago. And the second one, only a few minutes ago: **Honey, for my sake as well as yrs, will u email yr mum? She's not happy. C xxxxx**

Lewis has opened up his laptop and I search for the email I've already typed out in my drafts folder. It says sorry in twenty different ways, but it doesn't tell her where I am. Lewis and I agreed it was the only way; if they have to track me down, it buys us more time.

But it does make tomorrow's trip all the more urgent.

I read the email, add yet another 'sorry' and a whole line of kisses, then press *send*, checking my sent items folder to make sure it's gone.

'I feel like crap for doing this to them,' I say to Lewis.

He puts his arm around me. 'Once they get the old Alice back, it'll be worth it.'

Then he lets go suddenly, as though my skin is hot to the touch.

The doorbell chimes: weird, it sounds exactly like a normal doorbell, which seems so wrong here in paradise.

'Your pumpkin carriage awaits,' Lewis announces. 'Actually, it's a golf buggy but if you close your eyes then you can imagine you're being drawn by liveried mice. And we can't risk cycling – it'd be a shame to get wet when you look so lovely.'

I head into the dimly lit hallway, glad he won't see me blush all over again. It's becoming a habit when Lewis is around.

The restaurant is amazing. The food is incredible. The service is six-star.

But I could be eating fish and chips on a wall round the back of the Tesco bins and it wouldn't matter, because it's Lewis that is making this so special.

'After this, Ali, what do you want?'

'I don't think I've got room for pudding.'

He laughs. 'Yeah, because that's *really* what I meant. What about the rest of your life?'

'I don't really think about that.'

'If it's not too cheeky of me, can I suggest that you *should* start thinking about it? You could have a brilliant future, Ali.'

'I don't think so. My sister was the one with the world at her feet, Lewis. A way more dazzling future than mine.'

'But you're not her, are you? Maybe she was all fireworks: brilliant, but gone in a moment. Your future might be more of a slow build-up to something incredible.'

'I'm not incredible.'

'*I* think you are.'

I stare at the dessert menu. I haven't read it, even though the waitress has been back twice to ask if we want anything else. '*Don't.*'

'Don't what?'

'Pretend. It's embarrassing. I respect you, Lewis, but I'll respect you less if you tell me white lies.'

Lewis shakes his head. He looks pretty incredible himself tonight, though I felt too shy to take the piss the way I normally would. He's caught the sun already, and his hair looks lighter too. The white shirt he's wearing smells of fresh air and he wears old-fashioned cufflinks shaped like black cabs.

I wonder how fiddly it is to undo them . . .

'Ali?'

I look up from the cufflinks and gulp. 'Sorry.'

'I was just saying that it's rude to ignore someone if they're paying you a compliment.'

'Sorry. It must be the jet lag, I didn't hear—'

'Let me tell you again, then. You're incredibly bright. Kind, almost to the point of doing *too* much for other people – though that's not a fault to be ashamed of. You make me laugh more than any girl I've ever met. Frankly, women aren't often funny, in my experience—'

'Sexist,' I say, glad to have a reason to interrupt because I'm getting more and more embarrassed.

'Is it also sexist of me to say . . .' he pauses, '. . . to say that you're also really, really beautiful?'

At first I think I misheard. Then I notice Lewis blushing, too, and my own cheeks burn hotter than ever.

Now he's the one hiding behind the menu. 'Damn. A thousand apologies, Ali. Blame the heat and the wine. Completely inappropriate. Sorry. We're friends. You don't see me that way. Blah blah. Put it behind us. Note to self, Lewis, you've made a fool of yourself – but what else can you expect from a geek who is brilliant at handling microchips but doesn't have a clue when it comes to girls?'

'Lewis?'

'Hmm.' He peeks over the menu, a grim expression on his face.

'Stop apologising.'

He nods. 'I'll sign for the bill and then let's get to bed— um, I mean, have an early night—'

I hold up my hand to shut him up. In the seconds that follow, I fast-forward in time.

If I ignore what he just said, we'll have an awkward end to the evening but tomorrow it'll all be simple again. Forgotten. Easily the best, most straightforward option.

If I agree with him about the heat of the moment, the jet lag, the drama of the situation and insist that, yes, we're friends and that's all it should ever be, then it saves his embarrassment and mine. Except . . . I will be lying.

The third option is the most dangerous. The kind of thing that Cara would do but I never could. A risk not worth taking. In my head, I run through the best way to change the subject . . .

But my hand is ignoring my brain. It's reaching forward, taking the menu from Lewis and then grabbing his hand.

'I . . . think you're pretty incredible too,' I tell him.

He tuts. 'Yeah. Well, whenever you have a hard disk that needs the kiss of life, I'm your man, but—'

Kiss.

Me.

'Now who won't take a compliment, Professor?'

He stares at me, and then down at my hand in his. He says nothing, but time slows as he leans in towards me.

He's going to kiss me.

Right here.

Lewis is going to kiss me.

And, oh! How much do I want him to.

But then he leans back, though his hand is still where it was. He raises his other hand just enough to attract the waitress's attention.

'The bill, please,' he says, then smiles at me. 'And a buggy back to the Tiger Lily Villa, as soon as you can.'

36

Rain hits the fabric cover on the buggy like the heavens are clapping us home.

The restaurant was so plush and padded that we could barely hear the storm, but out here it's still raging. Raw, but energising too. As we travel back, the resort goes dark, momentarily, so we can see nothing but the path that the buggy's dim lamps are lighting up.

'Power cut,' the driver says. 'But no worries. We have generator.'

And sure enough, within seconds, all the villas are glowing again, softly, like fireflies.

Lewis and I say nothing on the journey. We don't even touch. But my mind is working at a hundred times its normal speed as I try to work out what might happen when we get back to the villa. Will he kiss me? How will it feel? Will it be the best kiss ever – or the most embarrassing, terrible thing that could possibly happen?

I try to slow down my thoughts. What would Cara say to me right now?

Never mind what he might do, honey. What do you want?

I *want* him to kiss me. Possibly more than anything else I've ever wanted.

There's a warm light on outside the villa to welcome us home. The buggy driver holds up an umbrella so we don't get wet. Lewis tips him and the man disappears back into the night.

We walk down the central hallway, slightly apart. The

sculptures and plants are lit from underneath, casting strange shadows across the fine white curtains which are all that divide us from outside. The bullfrogs are mooing louder than ever.

In the dining area, I gaze out at the pool which is lit a brilliant blue. The lake beyond only appears when lightning bolts crack across the heavy red sky, though I can just make out a line of flaming torches bobbing on the surface of the rain-ringed water.

Still neither of us says anything. Until . . .

'Strange, isn't it?' Lewis says. 'From the first day I met you I've always felt so completely comfortable around you, but now . . .'

I nod. The gap between us isn't that big but it's like we don't know how to cross it.

'The snug,' he says. 'You haven't seen the snug.'

'Let's see the snug, then.'

He unlocks his door and the lights fade up gently as we step inside. I catch sight of myself in the mirror. Wow. I look . . . nice. But like myself, now, instead of like my sister. Funny, till tonight I thought that I could only be attractive when I looked like her.

Flattering lighting must be part of the deal when you pay this kind of money for a villa. But how much is it? Three hundred pounds a night? Five hundred? A thousand, even?

For that you're guaranteed to look almost as beautiful as your surroundings.

I don't know if this 'wing' is bigger, or just arranged differently, but the 'snug' is lovely. The sofa is more like a superking-sized bed made of soft leather and it takes up most of the room. On top there are vivid Thai cushions in oranges and reds, matching the torches we can see blazing on the lake opposite. The built-in bar has enough different spirits to keep even Cara happy, plus a satellite-dish sized fruit bowl piled high with goodies.

At the other end of the room there's a door. I catch a glimpse of Lewis's bedroom before he closes it.

'Drink, Ali?'

'I guess. Um. Wine, please. A very small glass. Water, too.' I perch on the end of the sofa. The bedroom has unnerved me. Lewis is older – not *much* older, the same age as my sister, but he might expect . . . *more*. Especially after all he's done for me.

When I was with Danny, we both knew that there was no future, so *more* was never an issue. And the boyfriends I had before weren't that serious, not even Robbie.

Lewis could be serious. Could be *right*. But even though I know him better than I've known anyone, I need time. At home, there are a thousand excuses to take it slow, not least my parents monitoring my every move. But here, with the bedroom just a few steps away . . .

He wasn't planning this, was he?

'How's that?' He holds out one crystal glass of wine and a tumbler of water with plenty of ice.

'Good.' I take both, but put the wine down on the table and gulp back the water. My throat is dry.

Of course he wouldn't have planned this. What's happened here this evening has happened naturally.

Lewis sits down, with a big enough space between us to make me feel reassured but impatient too. He hasn't poured himself a drink yet.

I can only just hear the bullfrogs now. Apart from that, there's nothing except the faintest hum of air-conditioning. No rain, no thunder. Sound-proofing must be important to billionaires.

The chambermaid has lit an aromatherapy burner and that familiar sharp citrus fragrance wafts through the room.

It's strange, the idea of giving a place a signature scent. But perhaps it's a nice thought, too. The bubble bath Meggie and me used as kids still reminds me of her more than pretty much anything else except her singing voice.

When I get home, I might smell *this* hotel smell and be transported back here instantly.

'Ali . . .'

I turn my head slightly and Lewis's face is close to mine.

Yes, I say in my head. *Now.*

He hears me.

His lips are on mine. Soft at first. Making sure this is OK.

But then when I begin to respond, the kiss is more urgent. More passionate.

The other boys I've kissed. They're all forgotten.

Time's stopped.

One hand traces down my cheekbone, the other is on my neck. I reach around to pull him closer, my arms on his back. Through the shirt, I feel the definition of his muscles. So right. Warm. Protective. Strong.

Have we both *always* known this was how it could be?

I am not plain Ali any more. Not some sixth-former with bad results and no clue what to do with my life.

I'm beautiful. That's what his kiss is telling me. It's overwhelming, the powerful pressure of his lips making me light-headed, more drunk than I actually am.

It's like the difference between the tropical fruits I could never taste on the Beach, and the ripe, *real* fruits we shared at lunchtime.

Have I ever felt this alive, this *wonderful*?

I don't know how long it is before he pulls back slightly. Minutes. An *hour*? His eyes are dark with excitement. Where did a geek learn to kiss like a film star?

Perhaps it's not about learning. Perhaps it's simply about finding the person you're *supposed* to kiss.

'We're two seriously bright people, Ali,' he whispers. 'Why the hell didn't we work this out sooner?'

I smile. 'Let's make up for lost time.'

Even though he kisses me confidently, I can tell he's going to let me set the pace. Except my body is responding to him in a way I never thought possible. I can't imagine wanting this to stop.

Ever.

And that's when everything goes dark.

37

We pull apart *so* reluctantly.

I can only just see him, in the tiny flame from the aromatherapy burner. His face looks even more handsome, all sharp angles and full lips.

'What's happened, Lewis?' Instinctively, I've grabbed his hand. Despite everything I've been through in the last year, the dark still has the power to make me afraid.

He looks around. 'Air-con's off, too, so probably another power cut.'

'Can you phone reception?' I whisper, as though a bogeyman might hear me if I speak any louder.

'Line's probably down.' He leans over to grab the phone with one arm, keeping hold of me with the other. He lifts the receiver, then replaces it with a sigh. 'Yeah. Dead.'

The word makes me cringe. 'I don't like this.'

'It's fine, Alice, really. There's bound to be a generator that'll kick in soon. But not too soon, I hope.'

He leans in to kiss me again.

It's even better than before, but I pull away after less than a minute. It's still dark, but now I notice there *are* lights on in the villas on the opposite side of the lake. 'Look,' I say, pointing over the water.

'Maybe it's just this villa,' Lewis says. 'A fuse or something.' He sighs. 'Much as I hate to tear myself away, the lights won't come back of their own accord if it *is* a blown fuse. What if I cycle to reception? You'll be OK here, won't you?'

'I'd rather come with you.'

'Look outside. It's still belting down. Only one of us needs to get soaked, eh? You've got the tea lights for the burner, and I'm pretty sure I saw a torch in the bathroom. I'll cycle as fast as I can. I don't want to be away any longer than I have to.'

He kisses me again, too briefly, and I cross my fingers, hoping the lights will come back on as we kiss so we don't have to separate. But . . . still darkness.

'Back in the blink of an eye,' Lewis says. When he opens the door, the bullfrogs are joining in as the thunder rumbles grumpily. I let the door close softly behind him.

Torch. I'm on a mission to find it. The more I concentrate on the search, the less I'm going to freak out in the dark. I'm seventeen, for God's sake. A power cut is no big deal unless you're a little kid.

I pick up the aromatherapy burner and gently tip the water and oil into my empty glass, so it won't drip onto the tea light and extinguish it. Then I lift the burner up to light my way and push open the door that leads to the bedroom and, I guess, a second bathroom too. The layout seems slightly different on this side. The tiny flame only lets me see about a metre ahead, so I take small, cautious steps. But I'm calm. Determined. Lewis will be proud of me.

The bathroom is to the left, bedroom to the right. Inside the bathroom, I think it's moonlight that shines through the frosted window, bright enough to help me make out a kind of walk-in wardrobe with towels and a safe, the same as on my side of the villa. This has to be where the torch is kept.

Something moved.

Behind me. I hear it scuttling across the tiles. A cockroach? A *rat*?

Stop panicking. It's only my imagination. I will my heart to slow down, take some deep breaths. The reception's only five minutes away by bike. Lewis won't be long.

'Argh!'

The *something* just ran over my foot.

I drop the burner and it hits the marble floor with a crash, followed by the musical ring of tiny splinters. Then, silence again.

Hold on. Where's the tea light?

Shit! It's landed on a pile of towels, still alight. I reach for it before the towels catch fire. Hot wax burns my hand but I manage to snuff out the flame.

Of course, now it's *seriously* dark, and there are sharp fragments of broken burner spread all over the floor, ready to cut the soles of my feet. Do I wait till Lewis comes back or try something else?

What about Lewis's phone? There's bound to be a torch on that, if not an app to generate enough power for the entire villa.

I tiptoe carefully out of the bathroom, lowering my feet slowly to feel for splinters. The bedroom's ahead. If the worst comes to the worst, I can lie down on his bed and wait. Beds are safe places: no splinters, no sharp edges, no naked flames.

In the far corner, I can see a ghostly blue light. A phone display.

Yes!

I cross the room, the marble floor smooth under my feet. There's a small table in the corner that Lewis has set up as a recharging station, with his laptop and iPad and phone. Of course, it's not charging now the power's off but the phone shows the time.

Just before ten. Weird, it feels so much later than that.

I pick up the phone to see if I can find the torch function.

Hmm. Lewis has a password. Of course he does. There's probably a NASA-level biometric security system, too. But there's just enough light from the time display to get me safely out of here and back to the snug. I might be ready for that wine he poured for me now.

I remove the phone from the charger and hold it up to illuminate my route. His bedroom's smaller than mine. Only half the room is underwater, and there are two limestone walls in place of the glass.

Lewis gave me the best room.

A warm feeling floods through me, and then an even warmer one when I think of the kiss. Any moment now, he'll be back and the power will be on and we can pick up where we left off.

On his bed, there's a small stack of paper. Typical Lewis. He can't forget work, even though he keeps saying how good it is to be away from all that. But that's OK. I like the idea of a boyfriend with ambition. Money doesn't matter but I want someone who will make the most of his talents, his precious time.

I laugh at myself. We've only kissed three times, so obviously it's completely over the top to be thinking he's my *boyfriend* already.

All the same, it feels right.

As I pass the bed, I notice one of the pages has slipped onto the floor. I pick it up and curiosity gets the better of me. What's *so important* that it can't wait? The dim phone screen gives me just enough light to read.

It's an email, I recognise the layout. Weird to print out emails, but Lewis is very aware of cyber-security, of what can go wrong when computers die. Maybe he prints stuff out as some kind of old-school back-up.

From: Tim
To: Zoe
Date: April 14 2010
Subject: Re: Strangeness

**No, I'm pretty sure she didn't tell me everything.
Well, I know she didn't.**

I'm suddenly aware of how fast my heart is beating.

This is weird. I haven't seen this email before, not in all the stuff that Lewis found on Zoe's two laptops. Maybe he's only just hacked into a new part of her hard drive and he hasn't shown me yet because . . . well, I don't know why. Maybe because today was my first day of normality in over a year and he didn't want to spoil it.

But it's so *Lewis* to be working behind the scenes to solve the mystery.

Another thing strikes me: the date. This was sent just a few days before Tim 'committed suicide'.

I move the phone further down the page.

> **This weird thing happened just before she died. She was getting really edgy, not like her at all. Paranoid, more like S. I thought maybe S had wound her up – you know how she was always full of conspiracy theories.**
>
> **M said someone was sending her presents. She thought they were from me at first, except I said – why would I send her presents when I could give them to her myself? She got fan mail forwarded all the time by the TV people, but this stuff came to the halls. And the presents weren't even posted. They were left for her. One was even left on her bed.**
>
> **It was girly stuff. A lipstick – expensive, she said. Then a bottle of nail varnish in a glittery pink shade. She liked the colour. But then they sent a silk scarf, in red, a colour she never wore, and she threw it out.**
>
> **Then they sent her another red scarf – or maybe it was even the same one. She thought it might be, even though that sounded strange to me at the time. Why would someone go through her rubbish?**

**Now, I guess, it doesn't sound quite so unlikely.
Anyhow, it totally freaked her out. That time, she
gave it to S to get rid of – though I reckon that was
M giving S a signal because she half-suspected S of
sending the stuff herself.**

**M tried to play it down but I could tell she was
upset. All TV stars have stalkers, I guess. But there's
one gift now that sticks in my mind. The last one.**

**It was a hairbrush. One of those old-fashioned ones,
black with soft pink bristles.**

A hairbrush?

My head is spinning. My sister's hair was brushed through
after she died. The police think it was the last thing the killer
did.

And they never found the hairbrush.

I drop the page on the bed. Now I can see from the layout
that all the printed pages are emails. I sit down, wondering
what else Lewis has found. It's too dark to read quickly but I
scan the tops of the pages, holding the phone next to each one.
There must be a dozen emails I've never seen, with subject
lines like *stalker* and *scarf* and *visitor*. All between Tim and Zoe.

One of those writers is now dead, the other in a persistent
vegetative state.

So why has Lewis brought these emails with him? They
must have been printed before we left.

It's OK. I can ask him when he gets back. Except . . .
perhaps I should wait and see. I bet he won't appreciate it if
he finds out I've been going through his things. He could be
back any second. Maybe I've got time just to read one more,
then I'll go back to the snug.

From: Meggie
To: Lewis

From Meggie? To *Lewis*? But they never knew each other!

What the hell? My sister never mentioned Lewis, and he's always said he'd never spoken to her, let alone emailed her. He recognised her, yeah, because they went to neighbouring schools. But whenever I've asked him, he's insisted she was just another pretty face in the crowd.

The rush of blood in my ears is deafening now. This makes no sense at all. Why would Lewis have lied to me about this? *And what else could he have lied to me about?*

Suddenly, I'm cold, *so* cold. My teeth are chattering and I have to dig my nails into my palms to stop myself shaking.

What could be the connection between Lewis and Meggie? *Think, Alice.*

Dread is slowing my brain right down. Lewis can't be *involved* in all this, can he? He's a good man. My closest male friend. He only investigated Meggie and Tim and Zoe as a favour, to help me.

Didn't he?

The alternative is too horrible to contemplate. But I know one thing – I can't let him catch me here. I have to act normal, buy myself time to work out what this could mean.

I try to put the papers back in the same order so Lewis won't know I've been here, but as I fumble in the dark, I touch something else. Not paper, nor the cool cotton of the bedclothes.

Satin?

I point the phone screen towards where my hand is, to see what I've found.

Not satin; silk.

It's a large, perfect square and it seems to shimmer in the dim light.

It's a scarf.

A red silk scarf.

The darkness inside me is like a year of nothing but night.

Being invisible is beyond unbearable. That's why it has to be tonight that I reveal myself.

Once we are honest with each other, Alice, and you know everything, then we can start over. There will be no more misunderstandings.

Secrets have kept us apart for so long. But here, things are different from at home. Everything is beautiful. Especially the truth.

So, listen, Alice. Let me explain.

Soon you will see me as clearly as I see you: in full sun.

38

My hand looks like a claw clutching the silk.

No.

This can't be happening. I'm wrong. I *have* to be wrong.

But what if I'm not? I open my mouth to scream.

Nothing comes out.

It must be a coincidence.

But how many coincidences will it take to make me admit the truth?

My sister was sent two red scarves days before she died.

Tim was found suffocated – with a red scarf securing the plastic bag around his neck.

And now I find a red scarf here, on Lewis's bed. Why has he brought this with him to Thailand?

My fingers fly to my own throat.

But I *know* Lewis. I've kissed him. He's the one person I trust completely.

Yet how has he repaid that trust? By denying he ever knew my sister, even though she was emailing him, begging him not to let her down. The harder I try to make sense of it, the harder it is to believe he's the man I thought he was.

And if he's not that man, then who the hell *is* he?

A liar.

A schemer.

A *killer?*

No. It's not possible.

This is Lewis. The friend who has never failed me. He came into my life at exactly the right time, just days after I had the first email about Soul Beach. He's been there for me, at my side, every step of the way.

Every step . . .

It's a coincidence.

It must be.

Except, of all the people I know, Lewis is the only one with the skills to build the Beach.

What if he's not my rescuer at all?

What if he's my sister's killer?

And not just my sister's killer, but the person who faked Tim's suicide, who pushed Zoe over the edge and then into the path of the dragon procession in Barcelona?

My heart thumps. I try to find reasons why it can't be him. *Not Lewis*.

OK. Focus, Alice. Take the Beach. Why would the killer be behind the Beach? All the time I've been going there, my sister and Sam have been urging me to look for the murderer. If Lewis had killed Meggie then why would he have set up a site that convinced me justice had to be done?

Unless it's all been a game for him? A sick, voyeuristic way to play with my emotions and get close to me.

Till I began getting too close to the answers and he had to change tactics, even close the Beach down.

But what now? Why would he bring me here?

To be his girlfriend – or his *final victim*? Bile rises in my throat. It's all I can do not to throw up. I can't bear the thought, am trying not to believe it. *Not Lewis*. But what other explanation is there?

I want to curl up in a ball, but instinct forces me to move, to plan. If I'm right, then I am in more danger than I've ever been in before. My *heart* tells me Lewis is a good person. But my head – and every single piece of evidence – is saying the exact opposite.

I must stop thinking, start acting. Before it's too late.

I lay the scarf back where it was, with the papers on top. My hands tremble, making the paper rustle, and it sounds incredibly loud. I tiptoe into the snug, and deliberately knock my wine glass over onto the sofa and my dress, then make a bad attempt to mop it up with cocktail napkins from the mini-bar. I need an excuse to get changed, back on my side of the villa.

Behind that security-proof door.

Outside, I hear a buggy pulling up. At least that means there's someone else coming back with Lewis – buying me time to get back to the safety of my own room?

Shit.

I've still got Lewis's phone.

I run into the bedroom, plug it back in, then race out, hitting my knee hard against the bed head.

I have to clamp my teeth together so I don't cry out.

Lewis is in the hallway, talking about fuses. He sounds exactly the same as he did fifteen minutes ago, but now I want to throw up out of fear. And betrayal.

You can freak out later, I tell myself. Right this moment, I must focus on survival.

I feel my way along the snug wall, towards the dining lobby. 'Lewis?' I call into the darkness. I've said his name thousands of times.

Now it sticks in my throat like a shard of glass.

'It's OK, Ali.'

He's closer than I realised. Close enough to reach out and grip my hand.

Just minutes ago, I'd have found the gesture so comforting. Exciting, even.

Stupid girl.

Now it feels as though he's taking possession: as though he's never going to let me go.

'The engineer is just checking the electrics, he thinks it'll be a simple—'

The lights come back on again, blinding me for a moment.

'—enough job,' Lewis finishes, laughing. He lets go of my hand and heads back up the hallway to thank the engineer. I see him putting a tip in the man's hand and sending him off.

'A tripped circuit,' Lewis says, coming back towards me, smiling broadly. 'Now, where were we?'

'Actually . . . I know my timing sucks, Lewis, but I don't feel great. The jet lag, maybe, and the wine. I dozed off and spilled wine all over myself, so I need to clean up. And then I'm going straight to bed.' Fear makes me gabble.

Lewis frowns. 'Oh. Of course. That's fine.' He puts his arm back round my waist. 'It's all right, isn't it? What we just did?'

'It was lovely,' I say. It's not a lie. It *was* lovely. Which makes what I'm thinking now *unbearable.*

He touches my face with his other hand.

'You're really cold, Ali. Listen, why don't you sleep with me tonight?' He blushes. 'I-I don't mean like that, obviously. I just mean in the same bed. I don't want to be apart from you . . . and I promise I won't, you know—'

Try to kill me in my sleep?

'No. I thrash around like crazy when I'm sleeping. I'll only keep you awake. I'll be OK.' My voice is higher pitched than it should be.

For a few seconds he says nothing. Has he realised?

But then he nods to himself. 'Cool. Yeah, you're probably right. Take it slow. Your friendship means more than anything to me, Ali.'

I try to smile. I hope he's reading my awkwardness as a reaction to what happened earlier. I turn to go, but he keeps hold of my waist.

If I scream now, will the guy in the buggy be too far away to hear it?

No, I mustn't let Lewis know that I know. Once I'm behind a locked door, I'll be safe. I can call home. Or reception. I only have to make it as far as my own bedroom.

Lewis leans into me and kisses me softly on my forehead. Despite everything, my body responds almost as strongly it did before I knew.

But a flash of red appears when I close my eyes.

That scarf is as incriminating as bloody fingerprints.

'The speedboat company is sending a driver first thing in the morning for our trip. Tomorrow could be the day you finally get the answers you want. In the meantime, sweet dreams, Miss Forster.'

I close my eyes so he can't see the fear in them. 'You too, Mr Tomlinson.'

I don't breathe properly till the door of my room shuts behind me with a heavy thud. There are three huge bolts and I pull them into place slowly, so Lewis won't hear me. I can hear him moving around in the lobby area. What is he doing?

I have to hope I was convincing. That he hasn't guessed that I *know*.

On the bathroom wall there's a lighting master switch for the whole wing and I turn it up to maximum. It hurts my eyes, but at least there will be nowhere for Lewis to hide.

In the bedroom, the bulbs blaze inside and outside. The bullfrogs are silent finally. Perhaps they don't like being floodlit. I don't get undressed, even though my dress smells of wine; I want to be able to run for it, if I have to.

Even though I know the only way someone's getting in here is with a battering ram.

I pick up the phone on the bedside table to call Cara. Or my parents.

It's still dead.

But shouldn't it be working again now the power's back on?

I look for my mobile: on the bed, under the bedclothes, by the table, beneath the bed.

Nothing.

A sick feeling overtakes me as I realise I must have left my bag outside in the lobby. I could race out there, but I can still hear Lewis's footsteps on the marble, the sound of a relaxation CD playing. If he's already suspicious, at least I'm secure in here. I must wait till he's gone to bed, then get out and *get help*.

Now I've made my plan I should feel better. But I don't. Instead, the truth spreads through me like poison.

Lewis killed my sister. Suffocated Tim and made it look like suicide. Pushed Zoe into the path of the fire run procession, just after she'd promised to tell me what she knew – and what she suspected – about both their deaths.

I collapse onto the bed. My brain is on fire but jet lag is hitting my body like a steam-roller. I'm still fighting to think of an alternative explanation – any reason to believe it's not Lewis – but the evidence seems overwhelming.

Why, Lewis?

Every single thing he's ever said and done must have been a lie. Almost a year of getting to know me, making me feel I was special, heaping suspicion onto Sahara, listening to me when I didn't feel I could confide in anyone else on earth.

Yet he knew *everything* already.

Tears come, even though I try to stop them. Was everything leading up to *this* moment? Did he always plan to get me here, as far from my friends and family as possible and then – a shiver passes through my body – murder me like he did the others?

Will the last breath I ever take be thousands of miles from home?

My last breath . . . I thought it couldn't get any worse, but then I remember – all three of Lewis's victims were deprived of oxygen. For Tim and my sister, that was enough to kill them. In Zoe's case, she might as well have died.

I gasp for air. Perhaps he's planning to kill me and then make it look like an accident, as he did with Zoe. Or suicide, as he did with Tim. Mum and Dad are already convinced I've lost my grip on reality, so how suspicious will they be if he makes it look like I travelled here on a romantic trip and then ended my own life?

They'd never survive losing me as well as Meggie.

'You bastard, Lewis. You total *bastard*!'

My voice bounces back at me off the glass walls. *Too loud.* Right now everything I do carries a risk.

And there's no bigger risk than falling asleep when I need to listen out for Lewis going to bed. I grab my iPod and jam the bud into one ear, playing music as loud as I can to keep myself awake. I keep the other ear free to hear what Lewis is doing.

I want to cry, but I won't. I must focus on getting out of this alive, not focus on the lies Lewis has told for eleven long months.

He made one mistake. When he invented the Beach – and how obsessed must he have been to do that? – he didn't realise that it would change me as a person. I'm scared, yes. More scared than I ever have been in my life.

Yet I know this won't defeat me. What happened to Meggie and what I learned on Soul Beach, even if it was fake, has made me grow up fast. Too fast, maybe, but now I know I'm strong.

I won't let him win.

All those lies, all those times you pretended you liked me, even that kiss. It didn't work! You never fooled me for a minute.

Except that's not true. I lie down under the bright lights,

forcing my eyes to stay open even though they're so sore and gritty from exhaustion. Actually, Lewis fooled me completely. And I realise something that's even worse.

All that time, I believed there was finally someone who liked me for myself, not because of who my sister was. Someone who never knew Meggie, never worshipped her voice, her laugh, her beauty. Someone who saw me as Alice alone: a person in her own right.

Wrong.

That stings like crazy. Yet again I'm the understudy sister, and yet again I'm a horrible disappointment.

If I was enough, then Lewis would have been prepared to let me live.

39

I wake gradually. My body is splayed out on the soft mattress and cool cotton sheets. I'm disorientated, but calmed by sleep. Except . . .

I remember. *Lewis. Oh, God, Lewis.*

In the darkness, I begin a replay of those awful realisations and—

In the darkness?

But I left all the lights blazing to keep myself awake.

I blink. My eyelids are still heavy and swollen. No, not heavy.

There's something pressing against them, blocking out the light. It feels soft, like fabric, but heavier than a sheet.

I go to grab whatever it is. But my arms don't move.

I try again. Too heavy. And then I feel tightness against my wrists.

Someone has tied me up, and put a blindfold over my eyes. *Someone . . .*

'LEWIS! Lewis, let me go!'

But he doesn't answer. And I realise something else.

He's brushing my hair.

I thought I knew how fear felt, but this is different to anything I've ever experienced. A furious energy courses through me, like electrocution. Except electrocution would be over almost instantly, whereas this is endless torture – the fear making my body convulse, over and over and over . . .

I feel the hairbrush passing from root to tip.

It makes my scalp burn, even though the movement is soft, the rhythm slow.

I'm back in my bedroom, aged six, maybe seven. Mum is brushing my hair before bed, holding on to the hair above any knots, so I can't feel anything as she teases them out. Soothing.

She finishes and moves onto Meggie, who squirms and protests that she's too old to have someone else brush her hair, that it's hurting, that she'll shave all her hair off and wear a wig. And then, when Mum stops, my sister grabs the brush and holds it up to her mouth like it's a microphone. She poses in the mirror, all smiles again.

Ready for her close-up.

Am I seeing the past because this is the end of my life? Or to give me hope that there is still a way out?

But there isn't a way out of this. There should have been no way *into* my room either, but . . .

'Please, Lewis. Tell me what you want.'

Silence, except for the tug of the bristles and the crackle of static as the brush passes through my hair again and again and again.

'No one needs to know. I can keep secrets. Look at how long it took me to tell you about the Beach.'

Even though he knew everything about it all along.

I can hear him breathing. It sounds unfamiliar. Sinister. Could it still be Sahara? No, that's not the sound a woman makes when she breathes. The air catches in his throat, with a low, ragged hoarseness. It's a man – the same man whose powerful, perfect kisses made me feel drunk.

I won't beg.

I won't grovel.

I think of Zoe pushing open the door to my sister's bedroom and seeing Meggie, her cheeks blush-pink, her hair spread out on the pillow like a halo of golden light.

The killer brushed Meggie's hair after she'd died: it can't

have been before, or she'd have found a way to tell me so on the Beach. What does it mean that he's brushing mine now, while I'm still alive?

But then I realise I'm clutching at straws – because the Meggie I've been talking to for so long on my visits to Soul Beach, the Meggie who told me she remembered *nothing* and didn't suffer before death, was an invention.

Lewis must have put the words in her mouth. And he was so convincing. He must have understood her completely.

'Did you love her? I always thought that the person who shared Meggie's last moments must have loved her so much. Do you want to know why?'

He doesn't speak but perhaps his breathing has slowed. Could *this* be a way to get through to him?

'It was because you left her so beautiful. That's what Zoe told everyone. I think that smothering must be like a deep, deep sleep. Not an act of violence at all.'

Shit. Am I trying to write my own death warrant? Yet this tactic – of convincing him that I'm on his side, that he is a gentle soul at heart – is the only idea I have right now. I must keep going, however fake it sounds to me.

'But what I've never understood is why someone who loved her would have cut her life short. She had so much to do. And she wasn't a selfish person. She might have shared the good times with you, if you'd found a way of talking to her, a way of explaining how important it was to you. How much she mattered.'

Why isn't he saying anything?

'You could have made her understand, Lewis. Just as you made *me* understand, tonight. You made me feel so special. So why did you . . .'

I pause. The strain is making my voice sound wrong – which is dangerous. He has to believe that everything's OK. The moment he realises it's not, then . . .

But tears are beginning to soak into my blindfold. He'll see them, bleeding through the fabric. He'll realise everything is lost. And then it *will* be over.

My arms are numb from the ties. I try to test them, but I daren't struggle because he must be able to see every move I make.

His breathing has quickened again. The brushing is less rhythmic and it hurts because he's pulling harder, as though there's a tangle he can't get out.

'ALICE!'

For a second I wonder why he's shouting when he's so close he could simply lean down and whisper in my ear.

'ALICE! Open the door! It's really important. ALICE, please!'

It's Lewis.

Shouting. No, *screaming*, his voice high and shrill with urgency. Instantly recognisable.

Yet his words are muffled.

He's calling from some distance away.

Not from this room.

And even as he continues to call out, the breathing in my ear continues. Close. Loud.

Faster and faster.

NO!

I open my mouth to call out to Lewis, even though nothing's making sense.

And then a hand comes down over my face, pinning me onto the bed and forcing the fist into my mouth so I can't call out.

As fear passes through me again like a shockwave, I try to understand.

Lewis is outside.

I am inside.

So who the hell is locked in here with me?

40

'ALICE, *please wake up!*'

Lewis sounds desperate. But he's too late.

'It's really urgent. It's about Sahara.'

Sahara! Of course.

The fist is driven further into my mouth, stretching my lips so much that it feels like the skin is tearing. The brutality of it is more shocking than the pain. How could she do this to another woman?

Except perhaps she's barely human at all and only exists now on cunning and base instincts. Even her breathing sounds like an animal's. But it was enough to fool me into thinking the killer could have been Lewis, when I was right all along.

Lewis. Oh, Lewis.

He's innocent. Despite my terror, there is the tiniest comfort in knowing I wasn't wrong about him. That the kisses were real.

Something cold touches my throat. I know instantly what it is, even though the blade is not pressing hard enough to break the skin. I nod carefully, to tell her I understand. I won't move. I even try to slow my breathing, though it's so difficult to do that while I am fighting the panic that makes my heart feel like it's about to burst out of my chest.

'Alice . . .'

But Lewis's voice is flatter now, as though he's already accepted I'm fast asleep and his news will have to wait till I wake.

NO! I scream inside my head. *Break the door down. Find a way in. There must be a way in, otherwise how did she get past the deadlock and the bolts?*

And then I realise: Sahara didn't break in. She was in here waiting for me all the time. I bet she even hid my mobile.

After she disconnected the power *and* the phone line.

She is a true psychopath. I'd always hoped that her crimes were crimes of love, of passion. It didn't justify them, but at least I could try to make sense of the terrible things she'd done by imagining she'd acted out of some warped desire to protect my sister.

Yet it takes ruthless planning, not passion, to follow me all the way to Thailand and lay this trap. The power, the silk scarf on Lewis's bed, the fear she made me feel – and the need to barricade myself in.

With a serial killer.

'I'll come back in the morning,' he calls out.

Hope leaves my body, like blood draining into the gutter.

Please, Lewis. If you really are the person I thought you were when we kissed, then you must realise I'm not asleep. You must realise something's not right.

But it's useless.

I'm on my own.

Though I won't give up. Maybe I can appeal to her feelings for Meggie. She did care about my sister, in her own freakish way.

'Sahara, I know Meggie meant the world to you. Of the many people she met at uni, you were the first, weren't you? She was so excited to be your neighbour. Told me about you way before she mentioned Tim or anyone else.'

It's true. Though Sahara and I both know what came later: the bickering, the possessiveness, the accusations of stalking.

'Living next door to her like that must have been fun. Like

boarding school books I used to read when I was a kid. Did you read those books, Sahara?'

I know nothing about her childhood, except I think she comes from money. What must have happened to turn her into *this*? Or perhaps she was simply born this way. . .

'Meggie changed so much in those first few months, you know, Sahara. She grew in confidence. You supported her through *Sing for Your Supper*, which was more stressful than most of her friends realised. Even though she'd dreamed of being a star, the reality was tougher than she'd imagined.'

Sahara says nothing but her breathing has calmed. And then the knife leaves my throat. Have I got through to her?

Except now she begins to brush my hair again. Goosebumps spread across my body. But if this soothes her, at least it buys me time.

Time for what? No one is coming for me. Not till morning and, by then, surely, this will be over.

'My sister . . . she was too casual, sometimes. Didn't always say what should have been said – like how grateful she was to you, Sahara. And I know from my own experiences how caring you can be. After Meggie died, people were wary of approaching me, as though I'd done something shameful. You reached out to me.'

Of course, now I know why. The suffocating sympathy, the fake distress, the need to lay her claim on my grieving.

And all the time *she* was the one who took away Meggie's breath. The bitch.

What will Lewis find when he returns? Will I be prettier in death than in life? A weirdly calm part of me is glad I'm wearing this dress, that I hadn't changed into a crappy t-shirt for bed. I might make quite a glamorous corpse.

No. As long as he's in the villa, there *is* hope that I can make it out alive. I have to keep her talking. No one but Sahara knows why she killed my sister. She must want to explain, otherwise why would she have stayed in touch?

'Sahara, the burden of not being able to talk to someone must be terrible. Would it help to explain why to me? It's not like I can tell anyone else now.'

Silence. Have I gone too far? Everything I say risks aggravating her. If she thinks I've accepted I'm going to die, perhaps she'll kill me now.

Hold on. I can hear something else. Harsher breathing. No, *whimpering*.

Something wet falls onto my face. Drop, drop, drop. Tears. She's crying.

'Please, Sahara. Talk to me. Make me understand. Surely you can't feel any worse than you already do?'

The sobbing gets louder. It's a low growl, like an animal caught in a snare.

'Sahara . . .'

'*Shut up!*' The whisper in my ear is angry. She doesn't sound like herself any more. Perhaps this is what happens before she . . . does what she has to do. She enters another state, a trance or—

The cold tears are splashing onto me, faster and faster.

I decide to try one final time. There's nothing to lose.

'Please, tell me. I might understand.'

The sobs switch instantly to horrible, bitter laughter.

'Understand. *Understand?*'

Her whisper sounds all wrong. I am trying to work out why when it comes again, louder.

'How can you possibly understand when you don't even know who I am, Alice? How could you not know me? I love you. I love you so much.'

The voice isn't Sahara's at all. It belongs to a man.

Even before he tears the scarf away from my face, I realise who it is. And I wonder how I could have been so blind for so long.

41

'Ade?'

He half smiles, though the tears are still running down his ghostly face. 'Finally.'

Finally. Fifteen months of not knowing telescopes into no time at all as I see the face of the man who killed my sister and her soul mate.

A face I've seen many times before, of course, but I don't think I've ever looked at it properly. Ade was always the straight man to Sahara's freak show, the fixer who so generously arranged for me to talk to Tim before he died. The go-between.

What a horribly effective disguise.

He lies down on the bed next to me, then turns his body so we're face-to-face. With my arms tied, I have two options: close my swollen eyes or look into his. I look, trying to see what I should have seen so long ago. The mark of a killer.

I can't explain why, but I am calmer than before he took off my blindfold. Have I accepted my fate?

Gradually, he comes into focus. He was always too beautiful for Sahara, with her plain, masculine features. In this strange light – Ade must have dimmed the lights inside the bedroom, leaving only the underwater ones in the pool that ripple as the rain continues to fall – his skin has a disturbing blue shade. His skull is so close to the surface it seems to shows through, his cheekbones and forehead glowing bone-white.

He's wearing black leather gloves.

'I am hurt you didn't realise who I was sooner,' he says, as though he's talking about a mystery gift sent on my birthday.

Or flowers sent on driving-test day.

Yet underneath the casual comment, I sense darkness. He's only just under control. Anything could make the rage surface and then . . .

'I thought you were smarter. You guessed the wrong person twice, though I suppose you got some of it right, my little Alice in Wonderland.'

When Ade smiles, his eyes don't move – as though he's learned his smiling technique from a correspondence course but hasn't quite mastered it.

'*What* did I get right?' My voice sounds childish.

'The love. Of course I loved your sister and that's why her life had to end when it did. And how it did. I *was* gentle. I knew *you'd* understand. You saw the hangers-on, the parasitic pond-life that circled her from that first TV appearance.'

I don't remember them being that bad. And anyway, my sister kept them at arm's length. Me, my parents, Tim: we were the ones who helped her stay grounded.

'She was changing, Alice. Spoiling. Like a beautiful peach in a fruit bowl. One side absolutely flawless yet, when you turn it over, the other side is infested by blackfly, the skin slack and broken, the smell rotten.'

It takes everything I have to hide my disgust for him.

He tuts. 'It was hard for me, Alice, but I had to do it before the sickness spread. She was so perfect it would have been a sin to let her fester.'

Fester? My sister never had a chance to fester. She died aged nineteen. She wasn't a saint – she could be grumpy and self-centred – but there was nothing spoiled about her. He makes her sound contagious.

'And Tim? Your best friend? Did he have to die too?'

'He always saw more to our friendship than there really was.' There's not a trace of regret in Ade's face. If anything, he looks proud of himself. 'Though, of course, I did support him emotionally after Meggie's death, at no small cost to myself. Living with a murder suspect really restricts your social life, you know.'

The arrogance shocks me. Tim was suspected of a killing Ade himself carried out, yet Ade is moaning about his social life. 'It doesn't explain why you killed him.'

'Alice, he was so unhappy without his beloved Meggie. Like a walking corpse. The only energy he had was reserved for inventing more and more bizarre plots to clear his name. Mostly dead ends, of course, but there was a risk he might have got close by accident.'

'You're lying. I saw emails where he wrote that he was feeling better.' Maybe I shouldn't have said that, but it's so hard to listen to this warped view of everything that happened.

'Oh, bless you, you're loyal. I think that's an excellent quality in a girl. But the truth is, if I hadn't faked his suicide, he would have done it himself in the end.'

Ade's voice changes with every sentence: kind, mocking, cold, humorous. Each time, it sounds quite genuine. Except when you put them all together, it jars. He's nothing but an impersonator. He mimics being human without understanding how far away from it he really is.

My right wrist begins to throb as the tie tightens. Maybe my skin is swelling. A hopelessness passes through me. What is he going to do? You don't follow someone to another continent unless you know how you want it all to end.

He hasn't noticed that I'm in pain. 'I suppose you'd like to know about Zoe, too?' He sounds like a parent offering a child their favourite bedtime story. 'She was smarter than Tim. Clearly it affected her, seeing Meggie a few moments after she died. I did take a lot of care to make your sister beautiful, but even so . . . the juxtaposition of perfection and death is one that could have an unsettling effect.'

Ade sighs. 'For a while, I hoped the fear would be enough to keep Zoe safe. If she'd had a proper breakdown, and perhaps some intensive drug treatment to banish bad thoughts, then I wouldn't have needed to wipe the slate clean, as it were.

'But she was more determined. I don't know if she suspected me exactly. There was a time when she'd lined up your geeky friend Lewis as chief suspect. He was the perfect distraction, so thank you for introducing him into the mix, Alice.

'But alas, Zoe was too dogged. She had too inquiring a mind. I couldn't take the risk.'

The casual way he talks about what he's done is heart-stopping. 'Don't you feel any guilt?'

Doubt crosses his face. 'I've never been *cruel*, Alice. Or done anything that wasn't one hundred per cent necessary. I'm hurt you could think otherwise. Almost everything I've done since Meggie died was about protecting *you*, you know.'

Anger is rising within me. The way he says Meggie 'died' without acknowledging that it's him who killed her. The fact he's justified it to himself by deciding he's my *protector*.

I try to swallow the anger. My only chance of survival is to keep him talking, to pretend to be grateful to him for his *kindness*.

But I'm kidding myself. He won't let me out of this room alive, will he? Ade doesn't seem to have a conscience, so it's a waste of time trying to think of a way to appeal to his better nature.

Yet time is my only weapon. The longer I can distract him, the more chance there is that I will be discovered. Ade's favourite subject is easy to guess: himself.

'Thank you. For protecting me.' The words taste bitter and unconvincing, but his face relaxes and he nods as if to say, *You're welcome, it's what any gentlemanly serial killer would do.* 'But who looks after *you*, Ade?'

He scowls. Perhaps I have gone too far now. Even an egomaniac like Ade will detect the irony behind my fake sympathy.

'Sahara did,' he says, eventually. His face is hard to read.

'She knows?'

He sighs. 'I cannot be sure how much she had worked out for herself. She was never the most inquiring girlfriend. People struggled to understand why we stayed together, I know that. She wasn't all that pretty, but she was passive, unquestioning. My ideal woman.'

Passive is the last word I'd use to describe Sahara, but perhaps he's revealing more than he intends to about their relationship. If she does know, and has known all along, then it could explain her nervy, dramatic behaviour. Perhaps, in her own way, she was a victim – and was trying to protect me by hovering around.

But she should have done more. She could have prevented Tim's death, Zoe's accident. *And* what is about to happen to me.

'Have you told her, or did she guess?'

His eyes are translucent as he tries to remember. 'I think she had her suspicions that something wasn't right, though people are always excellent at refusing to face the truth when it doesn't suit them. But I've explained it all to her now.'

Again, the coolness chills me. 'Does she understand?'

He sighs. 'I doubt it. She was always quite self-centred, Sahara, don't you think? Though I suppose that will be written out of history now. People only say nice things about the dead. Yet those who are left behind suffer more.'

I realise something even more chilling. *He's talking about his girlfriend in the past tense.*

And then I remember Lewis calling out: *it's really urgent. It's about Sahara!*

'Did you . . . I mean, is she . . .' I let the question hang in the air, afraid to remind him of the dreadful things he's done to the others – and what he still might be planning to do to *me*.

Ade smiles sadly. 'She was never going to be one of life's contented people, Alice. There would always have been some drama or other. This way she did finally get to be centre-stage in her own little story. Almost a happy ending.'

42

Oh, God. He's killed again.

'What did you do to her?'

'It wasn't painful. I'm not deviant, or a monster.'

That's exactly what he is. 'Did she have to die?'

'Everyone has to die when their time is right.'

'But that's not your decision.'

'She was warned enough times.'

Warned? What did he do to her? I judged her harshly, but perhaps I should have tried harder to understand. 'Couldn't you have just split up, rather than killing her?'

He sighs again. 'This obsession you have with death, Alice, it's really not very seemly in a young woman. It could take over your life, you know.'

Death *has* dominated my life for so long, yet I failed to consider Ade.

Someone close to Meggie.

Someone with the opportunity.

Someone with the motive . . .

'Ade, was there . . . more than friendship between you and my sister?'

He scowls. 'I didn't want to *date* her, Alice. My feelings for her weren't grubby or sexual. She was a kindred spirit, with the potential to be great.'

Until you took that potential away.

'But she's nothing compared to you, Alice. You are a gem. Bright. Increasingly beautiful. And as we've said, loyal. You must promise never to underestimate yourself.'

Is that a hint that he might let me live?

'Ade, what about your family? Do they understand you . . . what you are?'

'I have little in common with them. A surname. Oh, and skin that burns the second it comes into contact with sun.' He sits up, but keeps his back to me. He's holding something. The knife?

'I almost didn't follow you here, Alice. Thailand, with my complexion? You might as well have led me down to hell. Still, the nights are cooler. I've always been more of a night owl.'

I don't feel cool. My skin is burning, especially where he's tied me up. I shift my head slightly to see how he's done it. Then I gulp.

I am held in place by four red silk scarves.

'At least, after this, my parents might understand what they did.'

I try not to let myself think about what that could mean. 'Do you have brothers or sisters?'

'None. You and Meggie had no idea how lucky you were. Siblings are to be cherished. The same genes, yet different. Nature's throw of the dice.'

'An only child?'

'The apple of my mother's eye. Perhaps I wouldn't have liked to share her affections. Or, more importantly, her money.'

'They're rich?'

He turns back and smiles at me. 'Obviously, money does come in handy – for things like last-minute plane tickets! But I'm not an ostentatious person. Not like *Lewis*. I don't see what you see in him at all, Alice.'

'He's a friend,' I say, hoping Ade won't realise the significance of the things I said when I thought he was Lewis.

Ade considers this. 'Yes. Separate bedrooms – handily for me.'

I say nothing. He must surely realise that Lewis will try to wake me again, that the danger will increase with every hour he lets me live.

Yet he seems in no hurry as he talks about his childhood, about realising he was different – or, as he puts it, *special*. The longer he goes on, the less aware of my presence he seems, as he lists a teacher who failed to spot his potential, the classmates who bullied him because they envied him.

I don't know how much more of his self-pity I can stand. 'And all of that means what you did is OK, does it?'

'Don't you realise I'm *ill*, Alice? A tragic waste of a brilliant mind. I'm no ordinary *criminal*. If the police ever catch up with me – which is hardly likely, with their track record so far – then they'll find me a nice cosy secure hospital, full of very smart psychiatrists asking me endless questions about why I did what I did and wanting to know absolutely everything about my appalling childhood.

'You know, after so long not being able to talk to anyone, I think I'd quite like the chance to discuss myself endlessly. But not enough to risk being caught.'

He *is* going to kill me. 'Why do you hate the rest of the world so much?'

Ade frowns. 'Alice, that's below the belt. I was driven by love, not hatred. Apart from anything else, if I didn't love *you*, you wouldn't be alive. There have been so many opportunities.'

'Like the fire at the lab?'

He winces. 'A little close for comfort, I admit. I only wanted to get you out of that place. I do so hate being excluded. And I also thought a near-death experience might put you off your tedious geek friend. I hadn't counted on him whisking you away on a romantic tropical holiday to get into your pants.'

I want to scream back at him that not everyone is as devious as he is. 'He was helping me.'

'So sweet. But what humans dress up as altruism is nothing but a façade. A means to an end. You scratch my back, and so on . . .'

'It's not like that for other people, Ade. You must realise that. With treatment you might be able to—'

'*Treatment?*' he scoffs. 'What I have in mind is more romantic. We could go now, you and I. Walk away from the humdrum. You're too special to waste your life.'

'What?'

Gradually, I become aware of something else.

Noises.

Outside.

It could be a cockroach or a cat. Or maybe it's the building cooling down, now we've reached the coldest part of the night.

But it's enough to make me wonder. *Hope.* I scan the room, take in all the positions of objects, furniture, Ade.

He's still talking. 'There's no need to be coy, Alice. You know there's something between us. Not a grubby thing, but something powerful.'

Oh, God. He really is mad. He smiles. Does he think I'm playing a game with him? *Flirting?*

The noise has stopped. I think it came from the bathroom side of the villa. Ade hasn't noticed, he's too preoccupied with this 'connection' he thinks we share.

Another noise. A footstep?

Please, let it be a footstep.

'I don't understand, Ade,' I say, desperate to keep him talking. 'Tell me what you mean by "something powerful".' My heart is pumping, as though I'm sprinting for my life, not lying on a bed with my movement restricted to a few centimetres. I watch Ade's face, trying to keep his attention focused on me.

He smiles. Those bland features were his best disguise, because no one expects a psychopath to look like a male model. Yet he has all the traits: everything revolves around Ade. No one deserves sympathy except Ade. Even those he killed conspire against him because people *miss* and mourn his victims. *How dare they?*

'You're playing with me now, Alice. Flirting.'

Crash!

I see the alarm in his face. Then, a second crash, even louder! Behind us, someone is throwing their full body weight at the bedroom door. I can't twist round to see but . . .

Lewis! Who else could it be?

Ade's face shows a real emotion at last: fury. A flash of light bounces off the glass walls as he thrusts the knife out in front of him.

'Coming to get me, now, Lewis? I'm ready for you!'

There's a third strike against the door.

The crunch of wood being torn from metal. Then a blast of air as the door finally bursts open behind me.

Ade leaps over the bed.

I sense Lewis in the room now, so close I could touch him. But also too close to danger.

'Lewis! He's got a knife!' I scream.

43

Suddenly all my fear is gone.

Only anger remains.

I'm struggling against the scarves that bind me to the bed.

Behind me, I hear Lewis calling out, 'You bastard! What the hell have you *done* to her?'

Ade grunts as he launches himself at the man I love.

Love?

They're fighting like dogs behind me, growling and panting. The ties dig into my wrists and ankles as I move. Sweat runs from my forehead into my eyes, making them sting. I can't wipe it away.

'Lewis! Run for help!'

But he's not running. Maybe he can't even if he wanted to. The sounds are primal. I can't tell one voice from the other any more.

I can't tell who is winning.

Silk is stronger than it looks, and crueller too. I can feel the knots rubbing my skin raw but I don't feel any pain. All that matters is getting free.

The fabric around my left wrist seems to be stretching. I throw all my effort into pulling at that arm. *Now* there's pain, a fieriness as the skin and fabric both tear.

For a few moments, I'm scared the fabric will hold and my wrist will break.

But then . . .

I don't cry out when the tie finally gives way. Ade mustn't realise. I twist my body over onto my arm, so that if he happens to look up now he won't see I'm half free.

As the numbed fingers of my left hand work on the knots round my right, I dare to glance over my shoulder.

Ade is on top of Lewis. I can't see what he's doing but Lewis is making a horrible rasping noise.

The rage begins in the centre of my chest and spreads instantly, like acid burning through flesh.

You won't kill him, too.

Blood is soaking into the bed sheets from my right wrist.

There's no time.

I take a deep breath and pull as hard as I can, biting my lip so I don't cry out as the scarf digs deeper into my flesh.

With a groan, the fabric breaks away from the bedhead – so suddenly that my arm slaps against the bed like a dead weight. I lean forwards and the ankle ties release much more easily with two hands.

What do I do?

I look to my right and then I know.

I have to use both arms to lift the lamp base. As I turn it, I realise it's shaped like a Buddha. Wise eyes bore into mine. The base is even heavier than it looks and I'm weakened by heat and thirst and the numbness of my limbs.

Lewis groans.

Strength passes through me like an electric current.

Now.

As I lift the base above my head, Ade twists round and I see his gloved hands gripping Lewis's throat.

Time slows. There's hurt in Ade's eyes when he sees me looming above him, and realises what I'm holding. It makes me think of an injured animal who was expecting help but realises he's about to be put out of his misery.

'Alice, not you too.'

'Then let go of him!'

But he shakes his head. 'So you two can live happily ever after? Not a chance. Bitch!'

Can I do this?

Lewis's chest has stopped moving. He makes an awful gurgling noise.

I must.

'Not again, Ade. I won't let you do it again!'

Gravity does most of the work. As I bring the lamp down Ade instinctively turns his face and body away, but I'm too fast for him. In the split second before impact, I wonder whether it will be enough to finish this.

I want him dead.

The base hits the back of his head and neck with a loathsome thud. Then, as it makes contact with the marble floor, there's an explosive sound and shards of bloodied stone splinter outwards. One hits me in the face. Others scatter onto the surface with a strangely musical ring. But there's no sound at all from Ade.

He doesn't move, or relax his grip on Lewis. *Is he superhuman?*

But now Ade's slumping forwards and though his hands are still around Lewis's neck, they're loosening. There is no sound except for the rustle of his clothes as he falls face down, his cheek brushing Lewis's jaw as though I've caught them in the middle of some sick embrace.

Lewis isn't moving.

'Lewis? Lewis!' I crouch down at his side. His skin has turned china blue. I can't hear him breathing or see any movement.

'No! NO!'

Drool is dripping onto his face from Ade's mouth. The smell is musky. Repulsive.

I push Ade off. I can't think about what I've just done, not now, not yet. As his slim frame flops onto the white marble, I feel an awful certainty that he is no threat to either of us any more.

Lewis is all I care about. I kneel over him, touching his cheeks. They're still warm but apart from that there's no sign of life.

'Lewis. Can you hear me?'

I catch sight of Ade's knife, lying on the floor above Lewis's head. No! Don't let Ade have stabbed him. When I look down, there's blood on my fingers.

'*Please*,' I whisper, as I check Lewis's clothes for signs of stab wounds. There's nothing – and the blade of the knife shines silver, no redness on its sharp tip.

Then I feel something dripping down my cheek and, when I touch it, there's fresh blood from where I was cut by the shard of stone from the lamp. But I'm too wired to feel any pain.

'Lewis, please. Wake up.'

I slap his cheek, harder, *harder*, wanting it to sting him back to life. It hurts my hand but I don't stop.

No response.

Not Lewis. Not now.

'I won't lose you, too, Lewis. I *won't*.'

I try to remember the talk about resuscitation we had at school, leaning down towards his mouth, listening for breath. I'm close to his lips.

Ready to kiss him, but not the way we kissed before. I lean in, hoping I can bring him back to life with my own breath. A kiss a million times more important than the kisses before, because this time it could mean the difference between . . .

My lips are so close now that I can feel the warmth from his, and it gives me hope. But before we make contact, he opens his eyes.

They're blank for a fraction of a second. And then he remembers.

'Lewis! Thank God! I thought . . .'

He coughs, a painful catch where he's been throttled. 'Alice. Are you hurt?' His voice is a ragged whisper and his hand is reaching up towards where I've been cut.

'No! Not really. But you? I was so scared—'

'I'm . . . fine. Honestly. Help me up.'

I grab his hands and realise that I'm shaking so hard he can't quite hold them still.

He flinches as he stands up, yet despite that he seems so strong and alive. There's no sound at all from behind us, where Ade is lying motionless.

'Lewis, I can't look. Is Ade dead . . . have I *killed* him?'

44

Lewis squeezes my hand. 'I'll look, but before I do, Ali, you did the right thing. It was the only way.'

'Yes, but—'

'No buts. He was trying to kill us. And he would have. Me first, then you. He had no conscience.'

Had. Lewis thinks I've killed Ade too.

I reach behind me to feel for the bed and sit down on the very edge. Through the glass walls that were my prison, the sky is still inky blue but the rain has stopped and the bullfrogs have begun to moo again. What sounded funny before is chilling now, like they're groaning in despair.

My thoughts and heart race, as though I've just woken from the most terrifying nightmare.

Ade was the killer.

Sahara is dead.

I might be a murderer myself.

He deserves to die.

My own bloodthirstiness shocks me. I'm one of the good guys, aren't I? All I've ever wanted is justice, not revenge.

Except is that really true? When I lifted that lamp base high in the air, I *knew* what it could do, something so heavy and solid. I didn't hesitate. I wanted him dead.

My sore wrists throb now, and the blood coursing through my body feels red hot. I'm aware of Lewis moving behind me, a soft thud as he shifts Ade – or is it Ade's body – around to check him over.

What if he *is* alive? I remember what he said about

hospitals and shrinks devoting months, even years, to the study of what makes Ade tick. A perfect future for him, all that attention will be almost flattering.

While my sister has nothing. *Is* nothing.

'Ali?'

Lewis's voice is soft, *kind*. He's left Ade's side and is sitting next to me on the bed. I know what that means.

'He's dead, isn't he?'

I feel Lewis's hand take mine and he squeezes it, and doesn't let go. 'There's nothing we can do for him any more. Well, I don't think there ever was anything we could have done to change the person he was. Right now, we have to focus on the living.'

I can't find any words to reply.

'Ali, it was self-defence. You know that, don't you?'

I hesitate. 'What if it wasn't?'

He turns my face towards his. 'He wasn't going to stop until I was dead.'

'No, but the way I felt about him . . . well, it sickens me. I wanted him to die, Lewis. That makes me a murderer, doesn't it? As bad as him.'

Lewis shakes his head. 'Please. Don't waste any more time thinking about that *bastard*. He's not even the same species as far as I'm concerned. The thought of what he did to you . . . what he could have done. Well, put it this way, I don't think a single blow was good enough for him. I wish he'd *suffered*.'

The anger in his voice surprises me.

'You're a human being, Ali. After what happened to your sister, it's natural you'd want this to end. When you stop having feelings, when you're as numb and selfish as he was, that's when you need to worry. OK?'

'OK,' I say.

'Good. In a moment, when you're ready, I will call reception and ask them to call the police. But you must promise me first that you won't blame yourself for what happened here. There's only one person who is responsible, and now he'll never be able to ruin any more lives.'

Lewis rests his other arm around my shoulder. His breathing is laboured and I pull him towards me so he's leaning against my chest. I close my eyes and, after a few seconds, we're breathing in and out in the same rhythm.

And I can no longer tell who is leaning on whom.

45

After Lewis makes the call, everything moves so fast.

Within minutes, people fill the bedroom. Hotel staff, first. Someone with a medical kit. Then policemen with high-pitched voices in unfamiliar tones.

Lewis and I allow ourselves to be escorted out of the bedroom into the dining lobby. There's a hint of lightness in the sky, splashing the smooth lake water with red reflections, even though it's not even three a.m. I wonder how the police are going to begin to make sense of this: a Westerner's body on the floor and a guy with red marks around his throat who won't let go of a girl whose wrists are bleeding.

The officer in charge seems to have decided that we're guilty of something and is firing relentless questions at us in Thai. Fortunately, the fierce hotel duty manager gives as good as she gets and is refusing to allow him to get close. I suspect she's more concerned about her hotel's reputation than the two of us, but it doesn't really matter.

'First, hospital,' she says. 'The police will want to accompany you but there is no obligation to say anything. Certainly not when there is a risk of confusion after a head injury.'

'Head injury?' For an awful, surreal moment, I think she's talking about Ade: that he's come back from the dead. Then I become aware of a slow dripping sound.

'Lewis, you're bleeding!' There are tiny circular splashes of red against the white marble tiles. I stand up and see a bloody mess on the back of his head. 'Oh, God. He needs help.'

'It's OK, Ali,' he says, but his voice sounds weaker. 'I think I fell quite heavily when Ade first came for me. Funny, it doesn't really hurt. It's more that I am really rubbish when it comes to the sight of blood.'

The manager is calling out to a minion, who unwraps the first aid kit and applies a dressing to the base of Lewis's skull. He winces and seems to be turning paler by the second.

'You do have insurance, right?' the manager asks as we hear a siren outside.

Lewis nods.

'That's good. We have ordered a private ambulance to take you to the clinic all the expats use.'

And then she switches to shouting at the policeman as a couple of paramedics bustle the two of us into the back of the ambulance. Lewis insists on walking, but has to be helped up the steps and agrees to lie on the stretcher.

As the ambulance moves off with us inside, I see the blue lights of a police car flashing through the smoked glass behind us. They're following closely. I try not to think about the future, not to wonder what the penalty is for murder here in Thailand.

Ade killed my sister, killed Tim, tried to kill Zoe and Lewis and me.

And I have killed him.

It doesn't seem real yet.

'You OK?' I ask Lewis.

He gives me a weak thumbs-up. 'No worse than an average migraine. But it's better if I close my eyes and hold your hand.'

There's a paramedic in the back with us, but she's checked his pulse and then settled down to send texts on her phone, so I guess he's going to be OK.

Unlike Ade.

As the siren of our police escort shrieks relentlessly, I replay the events of the last two hours – and then the last thirteen months. Enormous chunks of it make no sense. I'm gripping Lewis's hand but as I look down at his face, eyes closed, neck red and swollen, it occurs to me: all the parts that don't add up involve *him*.

How did Meggie know Lewis?

Why was she emailing him asking for help – and did he see her before she died?

What possible reason could he have had to lie to me for so long?

My throat is dry and my cheek stings. *Stay calm, Alice.* Focus on the important thing: I know he's not the killer. I know he kissed me like I was the only girl on earth. He thinks I'm something special.

Unless . . . he is only with me because I'm the closest substitute for Meggie now she's gone?

I feel him staring at me.

'Ali, I have to explain,' he murmurs.

'No. Don't try to talk now—'

'I must,' he says, pushing himself up slightly onto his elbows. His skin is white-green, and he's having trouble focusing. But as the paramedic hovers, he forces a smile and she goes back to her phone.

'You want to know about me and Meggie, right?' he whispers.

Me and Meggie.

I've never felt so excluded. If we hadn't kissed, maybe it would have been easier . . .

Except, I've been lying to myself about how I feel about him for a long time, since way before this. I was so loyal to Danny that I managed to kid myself into believing I only wanted Lewis as a friend.

I force myself to look at Lewis. 'Right.'

'First of all,' he says, 'there was no *me and Meggie*. Not as far as I was concerned, anyway.'

I look up. 'What's that supposed to mean?'

'Meggie was a friend of my mate's girlfriend. That's how we met.'

'Even though you've always told me that you never met? That you only half recognised her?'

He sighs. 'Just listen, please, Ali. Like I always have when you've told me impossible stories. It's a hard enough thing to explain, even without a head injury.'

I suppose he has a point. 'Go on.'

'We met at a party when we were in Year Twelve. In the Easter holidays. We chatted for a bit. I thought she was averagely pretty, I suppose. Ali, you look like you're about to interrupt . . .'

I was about to tell him that no one ever dared call my sister *averagely* pretty, but I stay silent.

'So, yes, Meggie was pretty. But we had nothing in common. She was chatting away about her auditions, how she was going to college but really wanted to be a singer. I know it's not very charitable of me but I thought she was an airhead. A wannabe. And that was fine because I thought she'd probably write me off as a geek and everyone would be happy.

'Except when we got back to school, my mate kept telling me that I had a secret admirer. I mean, me? I thought he was taking the piss but then we went to the pub one night and there she was. Meggie. A cosy foursome. My mate and his girlfriend made some excuse and then it was an even cosier twosome.

'It was . . . well, a hell of a surprise. I was flattered, sure. I saw the looks we were getting in the bar. Other men wondering how come I was with someone so out of my league.

'But even though I knew I'd be the envy of my mates,

I couldn't make myself like her, Ali. She was interested in everything I wasn't and vice versa. I could never have told her about hackers or my job. Her eyes would glaze over and . . .'

'You thought she was a dumb blonde?'

Lewis smiles sadly. 'Maybe it was reverse snobbery. But I could never have talked to her the way I talk to you – about life and ideas and whatever comes into my head. I always know you'll be interested because you're interested in me and what I think. Whereas Meggie . . .'

The ambulance turns a corner and we sway to the right. We're hurrying. Maybe the driver thinks Lewis is in a worse way than he looks.

'Ali, the only reason she was interested is because I wasn't bewitched by her, unlike ninety-nine per cent of guys. Have you noticed how cats always find the one person in the room that doesn't like them and pester them? It felt like that. She wasn't interested in me, but in the challenge.'

I shake my head. 'No, because the person she fell in love with at uni was nothing like her, either. Tim was quiet and maybe a bit geeky.'

Lewis nods. 'OK. I'm a judgemental prick. But I promised you the truth and this is it. I bought her the one drink and then told her I had revision to do. It was the lamest excuse in the book, especially because I'd already decided I wasn't going to college so did no work whatsoever for my exams.'

Of all the things I was expecting, it wasn't this awkward blind date – my sister unable to believe that someone wasn't falling for her charms, Lewis trying to find a way to give her the brush-off.

And then there's the stuff he said just now about how the two of *us* talk. It makes me feel less hollowed out.

'Should have been the end of it. But your sister was quite . . . determined. I'd see her at parties, or she'd turn up at the pub with another guy. Or she'd be doing this twirly thing with her hair or she'd stare at me a bit too long.' He pulls a face. 'It was embarrassing. And it had nothing to do with me, really. It was her little game.'

'And then?'

'And then it was autumn and everyone went to college except me, and that was fine because the business was making money, I got a car, I could do what I wanted. I forgot about your sister. Even better, she forgot about me.'

I want to leave it here, but I can't. 'Except it's not the end of the story, is it, Lewis? I found an email from her on your bed. She sounded desperate to talk to you.'

The ambulance is slowing down, now, and the police siren has been turned off. Through the dark glass window I can see an illuminated H sign.

'I'd printed it off to show you. I kept waiting for the right time, but I'm a coward.'

I think of the Lewis who fought so hard against Ade. I wouldn't call him a coward. '*This* is the right time, Lewis. But hurry.'

'It was April, a few weeks before she died. I got a voicemail message. Some texts. Casual at first, but they got more intense. So weird. I knew she'd been on that TV show. She was all over the papers. Wasn't she too famous for me now? Plus I'd seen a picture of her in the paper with some boyfriend.

'One day I got so pissed off that I answered instead of letting it go to voicemail. I was about to tell her to get lost when I realised she was crying down the phone.'

He looks away. The ambulance is braking.

'What was wrong?'

'She said she was being followed and her email had been hacked. She suspected her college friend but she wasn't sure. There was no one she could trust. She wanted me to come to Greenwich, see if there was anything I could find out, but I . . .'

'What?'

'I thought she was crying wolf, Alice – that this damsel in distress act was just to play me off against some other boyfriend. I said no.'

The implications of what he's said hit me. My sister needed help. He turned his back on her. 'You could have—'

He sighs. 'I *know*, Ali. There isn't a day I don't regret it. If I hadn't said no. If I'd listened to her. If I'd visited Greenwich. . .' His voice is no more than a whisper now. 'When I heard the news that she'd been killed, I was devastated. I couldn't see how I could ever put it right.

'But then your ex's brother came to me, told me that Meggie's sister was getting hassly emails. I thought . . . here's a way to redeem myself. More than that, protect *you*. I thought it'd almost be like a punishment for me to spend time with Meggie's sister, because I thought you'd be like her – sweet but silly. We'd have nothing in common.'

The ambulance doors open, and I'm blinded by the bright lights from the lobby of the emergency department.

'I had to lie about knowing Meggie. You'd never have trusted me if I'd explained what happened. And then you'd have been in danger. Ade would . . .'

The paramedic is talking over our heads to an orderly who's taking one end of the stretcher. She touches my arm and points outside, wanting me out of the way while they move Lewis.

I don't move.

'You should have told me, Lewis. Like I told you about the Beach.'

He nods. 'I was going to. I hated lying. But then something else happened.'

'What?'

Lewis takes a deep breath, then his hands fly to his throat. He must be bruised, or worse, from when Ade tried to strangle him. 'I realised I was falling in love with you, Ali. I was falling for you because you're nothing like your sister: not silly or irritating or lightweight or pretty.'

Not pretty. I don't know whether to laugh or cry. The paramedic is getting more insistent, tugging on my arm.

'Not pretty. *Beautiful*, Ali. You're the last person I should have fallen for, but also the first girl I've ever loved. So now do you see why I couldn't tell you? Why it would have ruined absolutely everything?'

I stare at him.

'I knew that the minute I told you the truth you'd hate me. And with good reason. Because clever clogs Lewis Tomlinson failed when it really mattered. I let your sister down. How could you ever trust me not to do the same to you?'

46

I back out of the ambulance, tripping on the last step.

And I run.

Into the lobby, through the glaring white reception. I see a sign for the toilet, race inside and lock myself in a cubicle. Then I throw up so hard it's like all the anger and fear and guilt are spilling out of me.

Though, if that were the case, I'd feel better now it's over. But I really, really don't.

When I let myself out of the cubicle, there's an embarrassed-looking Thai policeman standing guard. I'm a suspect, after all. No, worse than that. A killer.

I can't deny it.

'Can I wash my face?' I say to the man. He doesn't reply – I guess he doesn't speak English. I go ahead anyway. The cold tap dispenses hot water that makes my skin even redder.

I stare at my reflection, the flushed cheeks, the cut that's started bleeding again. And my eyes – the windows of the soul, supposedly.

Tonight, my soul darkened forever when I ended a man's life.

Can you tell just by looking at me?

No. I couldn't tell Ade was a murderer by looking in *his* eyes. I imagine his face, dead pale eyes staring ahead, full of fury at being denied more time to kill.

Am I the same as Ade, now? We've both taken a life.

'OK, I'm done,' I say to the officer, even though I know he can't understand me. 'Let's go.'

He opens the door and ushers me through, his face set in a mask of mild disgust. I bet I stink of blood and sweat.

The hospital reception could be anywhere in the world, with signs in English. There's no sign of Lewis. He's probably being examined.

I feel totally alone. What is going to happen to me?

The policeman weaves in between the padded blue chairs, past an empty water cooler, and shows me into a small office with a desk and a filing cabinet but no windows. Another policeman is standing guard outside, and inside a Thai woman dressed in a white tunic and trousers tells me to sit down. As I do, my legs go wobbly and I half fall into the black leather chair.

The woman and the policeman stay standing.

'I am one of the emergency doctors here,' the woman says in American-accented English. 'Your friend is being examined in another part of the hospital. This is a detective from the local police who is anxious to question you. However, it is my responsibility to ensure you are well enough for that. First, do you believe yourself to have been injured during whatever has taken place?'

'No.' Then I look down at my wrists. I can't feel any pain but the skin is red, with open sores that ooze blood where Ade tied me down. Tears prick at my eyes as I remember how that felt: not physically but *inside*. 'Except there.'

Both of them lean in to peer at my arms. Maybe it's my imagination but the detective's expression softens a little.

'I will send a nurse in to have them dressed,' the doctor says.

The detective says something in Thai to the doctor.

'Oh, and the officer will take some photographs as possible evidence. In a short while, some of his colleagues and an interpreter will arrive to take a statement. I trust you are prepared to co-operate.'

'Yes. Yes.' Saying no doesn't sound like an option.

The doctor leans in. 'Am I correct in understanding that you are not yet eighteen?'

'I'm seventeen.'

'In which case the detectives will need the written permission of your parents to conduct an interview. We can do this by fax.'

My parents. The thought of what they're going through is the final straw: tears fall rapidly down my cheeks. 'Do they know I'm OK?'

'I understand the message has been passed to them via the police forces here and in the UK. However, they wish to speak to you urgently.'

'Yes. Please. They've gone through a lot.' Perhaps I should explain some more, to stop the detective judging me, but where would I start? 'I need to hear their voices. And they need to hear mine.'

'Mum?'

The delay on the line seems to last for hours but then I hear a sob. No, I hear *sobs*. Mum and Dad, crying together.

I imagine them at home, on the sofa, the phone in Mum's lap in loudspeaker mode.

I've put them through *so much.*

'Alice. Oh, Alice. It *is* you.'

The relief in my father's voice hits me like a tidal wave and I realise how close I came to dying again. What if Ade had killed me, then staged my suicide?

It would have broken their hearts.

'I'm so sorry,' I say, my own voice beginning to break. 'I was so desperate for justice that I lost sight of how dangerous it was. Of what was at stake.'

'But you're all right?' Dad says. 'That bastard didn't harm you?'

I look at my wrists, now wrapped in bandages. They smart like acid but I'll live. 'I'm absolutely fine.'

'Thank God,' Mum says.

Have they told them everything? The police here are playing it by the book, not questioning me till I've had a rest, though a female officer is now with me in the office, keeping guard. Mum and Dad must know Ade is dead but surely they can't know how.

You did the right thing, Ali. It was the only way.

Lewis was right. Perhaps now I can stop apologising and always feeling guilty over so many things that were caused by *Ade's* choices, *Ade's* crimes.

Not mine. Not Lewis's either.

For a few seconds, I do nothing but listen to my parents' breathing. Over the last year, I've grown away from them, isolated by the secrets I've had to keep. Now that Ade has gone, we can grow close again.

'I . . . want to apologise, Alice,' Mum says. 'For doubting you. For thinking you were crazy to keep fighting for justice. Without you, maybe we'd never have known it was Adrian. And there could have been other girls. Other victims.'

I picture his victims. My sister, Tim, Zoe. Now Sahara. 'What did he do to Sahara?'

'A car,' my father says. 'Carbon monoxide.'

I should be sad, and I am, in a way. Another pointless death. Yet if only Sahara had acted on her suspicions. Ade himself said he thought she knew something was wrong. If she'd spoken out sooner . . .

'It was a million-to-one chance that someone heard the engine running,' Mum is saying. 'The lock-up garages are normally deserted. She was incredibly lucky.'

'She's *alive*?'

'Oh, Alice,' Mum whispers. 'You thought he'd killed her too?'

'Because *he* thought he had,' I say. 'He told me so.' Despite my doubts about Sahara, I'm relieved. Maybe Ade was the one who exploited her emotions, moulded her into the strange person she became.

'Did he tell you about the letter?' Dad says.

'What letter?'

'Glen, it can wait.'

'No. Tell me. Please,' I insist.

Dad continues. 'He left a letter with her in the car. That's how the police realised you were in danger. Once Cara understood we needed to know where you were, she told us everything and we called Lewis. The local Thai police were on their way, too, but there wasn't much time. Ade could have done anything . . .'

I see Ade when I close my eyes. Remember how close I came, how lucky I've been.

'The letter was to his own parents,' Dad says. The police read parts of it to us down the phone, though we won't be allowed to see it. It's evidence for the inquiry.'

The murder inquiry. Will I be prosecuted?

'The note was rambling,' Dad says. 'Part justification of all the things he's done. Part blaming his parents for making him want to do bad things. But mainly it sounded *boastful*. He was gloating about how clever he'd been – right down to ordering those flowers the day you passed your test.'

Mum begins to speak. 'We should have known—'

'It sounds like a confession,' I say before she can speak. 'Which must mean he'd already decided . . .'

'To kill himself.' Dad's voice is low with anger. 'I don't think that bastard ever planned to come back from Thailand, sweetheart. I think it was always going to end with him and you. He wanted to take *both* my daughters from me.'

So Ade lied when he said the two of us could go off together.

286

What was it he said? *'Walk away from the humdrum.'* But all the time, he knew he could never let me escape. Of course, I suspected that, but knowing it for certain makes me so dizzy that I'm glad I'm sitting down. Without Lewis, it would have ended the way Ade intended.

Without Lewis, I wouldn't be here. He protected me as he couldn't protect Meggie. He put things right.

'And how is Lewis?' Dad asks.

I look at the office door, wishing Lewis would walk through it right now. 'I haven't seen him since we were brought here but the doctor told me his head injury doesn't seem too severe.'

'We were so angry when we realised he'd taken you away,' Mum says. 'Put you in danger.'

'I made him do it,' I say. 'And Cara, too. I wouldn't take no for an answer.'

'Even so, Alice. He's a grown man. He should have—'

'Alice can be very determined,' Dad reminds her. 'And Lewis did make a difference when it mattered, Bea. I don't think she would have been any safer from that animal at home.'

'No, well, we'll never know, but we want you home on the next flight, Alice, OK?' Mum says. 'No arguments. We'll book the ticket and there's a consular official on his way. He'll get you to the airport and—'

'No. The police want to talk to me,' I say.

'They've already spoken to the British police. They won't hold you.'

Relief floods through me, but it doesn't change my mind. 'I'm waiting for Lewis.'

I hear Mum take a deep breath, about to argue, but instead I hear my father say, 'Let her wait for him, Bea. They've been through so much already. I'd actually be happier to have them travel together.'

I smile. 'We'll look after each other, Mum, I promise. And I won't do anything dangerous ever again.'

'Ah, Alice, you're seventeen. You're going to do a lot to scare me over the next few years. But if you could try to stick to all-night parties and dyeing your hair strange colours, we'd be very, very grateful.'

And we all laugh, because it is funny. But also because, despite the distance between us, we're strong together.

A family. Not the same without Meggie at the centre of it, but still a place I can feel safe.

47

When the police finally come to talk to me, just before five in the morning, they seem much less interested than they were.

Someone senior here has spoken to someone senior in London and they realise this is a case that has nothing to do with Thailand. The only thing they seem fixated by is how I lifted the lamp so high and brought it down with such force when I hardly seem able to lift a glass of water to my lips now.

'Because I knew it was us or him,' I say. 'Because it was the only option.'

Eventually, I sign a statement that I can't read because it's written in Thai, and they allow me to wait for Lewis in the office. On my own, at last. A nurse brings me a pillow and a sheet and I've cobbled together a bed for myself by moving the two leather chairs together. Lewis must stay under observation for one more hour till they're sure he's OK to leave.

I need to get some rest first, so I can be strong for both of us. Get us home.

But even though I am exhausted, I can't sleep. How could I, with everything I've discovered in the last few hours?

It's the end. Or at least, the beginning of the end.

I get up, pace the tiny office.

A kind of justice has been done. Tonight, Meggie must be leaving the Beach – or wherever she fled to after the storm came. And Danny? I wonder whether I will still be able to visit the Beach once my sister has gone. Whether I can go back and say one long, last goodbye.

But then I remember. I can't do that. The invitation had disappeared last time. Expired.

I try to imagine what's left of the Beach, if anything. Is Danny still there? Perhaps it's better I can't go back, because I'd have to tell him about Lewis.

My thoughts drift back to the perfect evening with Lewis before everything went murderously wrong: to the dinner and the rainy journey back to the villa and the kisses. My skin tingles at the memory, but I'm afraid he'll always remind me of my sister, and I'll always remind him of how he failed her.

And yet . . . hasn't everything that happened with Danny taught me about the importance of letting go of the things you can't change?

There's a clock on the wall: five fifty-five a.m. Less than half an hour before Lewis is ready to leave.

Is Meggie on *her* last journey yet, now that justice has been done? Will she find a sense of complete peace and rest, in contrast to the endless partying on the Beach? Or a reunion with relatives she hardly knew?

Or is it simply a letting go?

I can't bear it.

A burst of energy comes from nowhere. I have to try to say goodbye one final time. I'm in the most high-tech hospital I've ever seen. There must be a thousand places to get online. I'll start in here.

The desktop is clear except for a phone, but there's a power lead that looks like it should connect to a laptop. There's a drawer in the desk and, sure enough, behind a lipstick, a box of headache pills and a collection of uncapped pens, there's a small, prehistoric-looking black laptop.

I open it, press the power button and it starts. The familiar Windows tune is faint but the lights flash and then, finally, the desktop appears, the green hospital logo in the centre and an IE icon among lots I don't recognise. I lean over the keyboard, my heart beating fast but my hands surprisingly steady.

I can't mess this up.

The connection is faster than I expected. I enter my password into my email program and I wait. *Hoping*, even though I have no real reason to hope. The Management aren't exactly known for their compassion.

As my inbox loads, I scan for messages in bold. *New* messages.

I ignore the spam ones, the money-off-free-next-day-delivery-buy-new-stuff-now messages that clog up my account.

There's one that stands out – sent yesterday, and pushed right to the top of the priority list, with a red exclamation mark next to it to make sure I don't miss it.

> **Subject:** For the attention of Miss Alice Forster regarding Daniel Cross
> **Sender:** Vincent Cross [personal]

Danny's father.

He must have read my letter. Why else would he email? Did he believe me?

I'm about to open the message when I see the one immediately below. Sent at two a.m. today: that must be in Thai time, because in England it's still yesterday.

> **Subject:** Exclusive Invitation to Soul Beach [expires 06:19 TST]

48

I'm racing back in time, to the moment the first email from my sister arrived.

It was the morning of her funeral and the email was blank. A hoax; it had to be. A week later, when everything that made my life seem certain and bright had been buried too, the invitation arrived.

> **Subject:** Meggie Forster wants to see you on the Beach

Despite everything, I *believed*. The love I felt for Meggie was strong enough to make me hope, and that extra eleven months with her has been reward enough. But perhaps this invitation is my bonus for pushing and challenging in her memory. For getting justice.

The time on the computer reads 06:03. I only just made it online in time. What if I hadn't logged in till later – would this email still have been here?

I lean across to lock the office door from the inside. Then I double-click:

> **Dear ALICE,**
>
> **As you may be aware, your access to Soul Beach, the web's most exclusive 'resort based' social networking site, is coming to an end.**
>
> **However, we have considered your contribution to the growth of the site, and are granting you a**

window of access to give you the opportunity to complete any necessary admin prior to the closure of your account. Please enter via this link.

This access will be revoked at 06:19 Thai Standard Time.

Thank you for your co-operation.

The Management, Soul Beach
Where every day is as beautiful as the last.

I click on the link, trying to collect my thoughts: the messages I want Danny to pass on to my sister, if he ever sees her again, and the words of comfort I can offer him.

06:05.

The screen goes dark, as though the system is about to crash. I hold my breath.

Danny's words to me drift into my mind:

The only good choice now is for you to walk away. And stay away.

But that was before I found Meggie's killer. I deserve to see her again. It should be my reward. Except when has the Beach ever granted me what I want, without adding some kind of horrible twist?

Forces like these are unpredictable. Nothing comes without consequences.

Javier said that to me. I close my eyes and summon up a clear picture in my mind of him playing cards with Gretchen in the shade of a palm tree, gambling with piles of tiny pink and white shells.

Javier smiles up at me, fire and defiance reflected in his dark eyes.

And then I remember Triti, her face turned up to the heavens on a sultry Soul Beach night, her shiny earrings jangling in the breeze as she watched the most incredible fireworks display I'd ever seen.

I open my eyes again, lean into the screen.

I'm on the Beach. It's still wrecked, the sand a dirty brown, the sea covered in oil that reflects back a moody grey sky. It's hard to tell what time it is on the Beach but, if Lewis is right about the location, it must be the same time zone as here.

This has been my longest night.

The shore appears empty, but I know Danny should be here, suffering an eternal sentence in solitary confinement, regretting the things he did. I shiver. No one deserves that.

No one except Ade.

And then I hear something. The same sounds – the same *words* – I heard that very first time. A melody as familiar as the contours of the rocks.

'*Amazing Grace, how sweet the sound . . .*'

'Meggie? Megan London Forster, is that you?'

'*That saved a wretch like me.*'

Her voice is closer now.

'*I once was lost but now am found,*'

I spin round.

'*Was blind, but now, I see.*'

She's there, standing amongst the timber and metal remains of Sam's bar.

'Yes, Alice Florence Forster. It *is* me.'

My sister holds her arms out wide and I run to her. She feels so solid, so real, but something is different when we hug this time.

No flashback. No vision of black leather gloves. Just contentment so deep it almost makes me sleepy.

'You did it, Florrie.'

I smile at the nickname that made me so cross when I was small.

'I did.' I don't ask how she knows. 'Do you want me to tell you—'

Meggie shakes her head. 'No. Don't. Whoever it was, they weren't important. What's important is that *you* did it, and you're safe. Aren't you?'

I nod. 'Yes. I'm safe.' I'm surprised, but she's right to stop me. I don't want her to go wherever it is she goes next with her head full of what was done to her. What matters is here, and now. 'Justice has been done.'

'I knew it would be, baby sister. You're like that. Determined. I always wanted to be like you, you know. Clever. Sharp. Unlike me – a butterfly – pretty enough but too busy fluttering to achieve anything much.'

It makes me think of what Lewis said about her – and what he said about me. 'You achieved a lot, Meggie. You brought music into people's lives. You made them *feel* something they wouldn't have felt otherwise.'

Only after I've said it do I realise I'm talking in the past tense. 'I mean – you *make* them feel like that.' My mistake hangs in the thick air between us.

'It's OK. I know it's my time. I'm fine with it. It was getting a bit dull around here, you know? Same old people. Same old beach.' She laughs.

'I don't see anyone else.'

'Tim's waiting for me. I came back down because I hoped you'd be here, though Danny's gone.'

'Gone?'

'I scrambled down the rocks expecting to find him but there was no sign. Might something have changed in your world? Something *you* did?'

I shake my head. 'His is the only story I know that can't be made right, Meggie. Unless,' I think of the email from his father, 'well. Maybe it has.'

'I hope so, baby sister.'

I squeeze her tighter, before I ask a question that could have me banished if anyone from the Management is still listening. 'What's it like? Beyond the Beach?'

She squeezes back. I'm still in her arms.

'It's kind of . . . nothingness. But nice. Like the time between being awake and being asleep. Do you remember how it was when we were kids and shared a room? When I used to let you climb into my top bunk because neither of us could sleep on the night before a holiday or Christmas or something? And then once we were snuggled up together, we'd be out within minutes.'

'Except I'm not with you, am I? Not really.'

'You are. Just like I am always with you, Florrie. Not in a creepy way. I won't be hanging round, wailing, in a white sheet. But I'll be there when you need me. And don't you dare worry about me. I wish Tim hadn't died, but the selfish bit of me is glad he's with me.'

'I'm glad too,' I whisper. 'But don't tell him.'

'You've got someone with *you* too, haven't you?'

I wriggle out of the hug so I can see her face. I blush. How could she know?

'Older sisters always know. It's in their job description. I think he'll be good for you, you know. And you'll be good for him.'

'But—'

'I was never right for him. He needs an equal. Though any boy will struggle to be *your* equal, Florrie. You're special. Don't ever forget that.'

She looks so beautiful right now, with her soft blue eyes and her wild beach-babe hair. Ade tried to turn her into something she never was, a perfect angel with a halo of blonde hair brushed smooth as silk.

She was too strong to be turned into a *mannequin*.

I'm aware of sunlight shining into her eyes, making the colour even more intense.

'Dawn,' she says.

'Yes.' I know what it means but I won't cry. I have to be brave for both of us.

'Hold me, little sister.'

I do what she asks, my arms wrapped tight around her back, my face buried in her hair. She smells of sea-spray. I close my eyes.

I feel her chest expand. Breath being pulled into her lungs, a soft vibration in her throat as that song – *her* song – surrounds me like warm seawater. Her voice is as sweet and pure as it ever was.

'T'was Grace that taught my heart to fear.'

'Don't be afraid, Meggie, I'm with you now,' I whisper. 'You're not scared, are you?'

I sense her shaking her head as she sings, more stridently, *'And Grace, my fears relieved.'*

'No, of course you're not. You were always my wonderful, fearless big sister. I've learned so much from you.'

Her voice is fading, carried away on a breeze.

'How precious did that Grace appear . . .'

I try to cling on but it's no good.

'The hour I first believed.'

I sense a change in the air, like the first chill September morning after a summer that seemed to go on forever.

'You were the best sister, Meggie. The best. I've been the luckiest sister alive.'

'I once was lost but now am found,'

There's space where she was. Coolness. But I can still *just* hear her voice, though it's fading faster than I want it to, as the end of the song nears . . .

'Was blind, but now, I see.'

She's gone.

49

When I open my eyes, the screen is blank. The computer time reads 06.20.

And when I click back into my email account, the invitation email has gone, too. But the one from Danny's father is still there.

I rub my eyes and cheeks with the backs of my hands, getting rid of the tears I didn't want Meggie to see. I need a moment before I open that email, a moment to accept what just happened.

Come on, sis. No time to waste.

It's not really her voice, I *know* that. But I sense Meggie with me. Not a shroud in a white sheet, but her vitality, her brightness, her impatience. Before, I felt a responsibility to live her life as well as mine, and that was a burden.

Now it's like I have twice the confidence and twice the urgency. I open the email.

PRIVATE AND CONFIDENTIAL

Dear Miss Forster,

I write in response to your letter, which I was surprised to receive. Though we travelled extensively in Europe, as far as I am aware, my son never met an English female with your name, and certainly never had the kind of intimate relationship that your correspondence implies.

The letter's formality makes me uncomfortable but I read on. Surely he wouldn't have replied simply to tell me *that*?

I have had thousands of letters from cranks and from bounty-hunters who believe I'll pay up for 'information'. Mostly I don't read them – my correspondence team screens them – and I certainly never reply. It was a decision I reached a long time ago for my own sanity. But your letter was passed on to me because of certain facts you shared that it's not possible for some English schoolgirl to know. So here I am, replying. Maybe I no longer have a grip on that sanity.

You said you can't tell me how you know what you know. And I sure as hell cannot see how you'd know any of it, either. The private security operatives I have had working for me since the beginning are one hundred per cent trustworthy. But, you know, you're right: the 'accident' was no accident.

Maybe it was a lucky guess on your part, but I had my guys follow it up. We already had our suspicions regarding what the US and Mexican authorities had so conveniently concluded about Danny's supposed recklessness; sure, my boy could be stubborn, like me, but I knew he wasn't dumb enough to take the controls of a plane mid-flight over that terrain.

The mystery was why the plane was there in the first place, way off-course. Your letter provided a plausible explanation, though not one any father ever wants to read of his son. This was the information we needed, however, and my operatives are just through briefing me on the follow-up I ordered right after reading your letter.

Miss Forster, you were right and you were wrong. My son Daniel was foolish, but not evil. My pilot was both, it transpires.

The pilot? But the pilot died, how can Mr Cross blame him for—

The pilot was ahead of my boy. Way ahead. He set up the little 'deal' for Daniel, to make him feel like a big shot. But the *real* deal wasn't narcotics. It was kidnapping. Why settle for a minor drugs deal when you could get millions for holding the son of a billionaire?

My pilot had been security-screened, of course, but that had been years previously and he'd got greedy since. Greedy and over-confident. The plan was to make it look like he'd been kidnapped too, then share the profits after he and Daniel were released when I'd paid a suitably large ransom.

Except he talked too much. Another gang heard about the plans and thought they'd take a slice of the action. While the pilot's gang waited on the ground, another tried to intercept the plane. The pilot freaked, took evasive action and we can only assume that's why he crashed.

And so no one got the prize.

I gulp for air.

Poor Danny. To die because of a stupid mistake, and then to face an eternity of guilt when it wasn't even his fault.

Danny's death wasn't going to be resolved by the pilot's family forgiving him; it was about his own father discovering the truth.

Yet I feel an awful dread as I scroll down the email. The pilot's young daughters lost their father. Now they might lose the support I know Danny's father has been providing since the crash – after all, why would he pay when the pilot conspired to put Danny in danger?

Justice is important – but could I have done more harm than good in setting Danny free?

Of course, knowing the truth and proving it are two different things, Miss Forster. You can't prove you knew my son, yet I sense that you did somehow. And what my operatives found seems like the missing piece from the jigsaw – but how to prove it in a court of law?

There are other ways to get justice, ways that I don't want to explain to a nice schoolgirl in England. But there's a final point in your letter I will address: what happens to the pilot's family.

I thought that Daniel dying would turn me vengeful, but now I realise that's not the case. My wife says I'm a softie these days, but I have been providing for the pilot's family since he died and I won't change that. The people who killed my son will pay, but the next generation, the girls who had no knowledge of how their father behaved, they shouldn't have to suffer.

So, there you go, Miss Forster. I don't know why I wrote, except that you must care, for your own reasons, and I wanted the story to have an ending. Not a happy one, but a just one.

I don't want to hear from you again, but I thought that you deserved to know.

Sincerely,
Vincent Cross
CEO, Cross Enterprises

I close the email. Yes, I did deserve to know. I fear the justice that Danny's father's 'operatives' will mete out isn't what I would have chosen but, of all people, I know that grief affects every one of us differently. And it's hard to feel too much sympathy for the men who caused the death of my first love.

'Ali?' It's Lewis, outside.

The office door handle turns but the door doesn't move.

'Are you in there?'

I shut down my email, close the laptop lid and open the door.

Lewis has a fresh white dressing attached to his head and a shaved patch circling it, making the rest of his hair look even crazier.

'Is everything OK?' His face is less deathly, but he looks more anxious than he did in the ambulance – anxious about what I think of him, whether I forgive him. But I don't think there's anything to forgive.

I don't say a word. Instead I take a step forward and put my arms around him, hugging as hard as I hugged my sister. I feel his body relax and he rests his hands on my back.

Safe. Strong. Right.

'Everything is OK, Professor. Now, I think we need some sleep.'

50

A limo driver takes us back to the hotel, after checking that Lewis is not going to bleed on his upholstery. We don't speak on the way back, but don't let go of each other, either. The roads are quiet, the sky a pale blue shot through with pink.

It's a beautiful morning, all the more so because I might not have lived to see it.

When we get back, the duty manager explains that we can't go back to our old villa because the Thai police are collecting evidence for their British colleagues. I feel goosebumps form on my skin and Lewis holds me tighter. Instead, the manager shows us to a 'cottage' room. It's not nearly as private. As she lets us in, I can hear a child playing in the villa next door.

Outside, there's a small terrace with a Jacuzzi and inside, the décor is all dark wood, slightly worn. There's one double bed on a raised platform with steps leading down to a small wicker sofa and coffee table. There's a fruit bowl, but it's a third the size of the one in the billionaire's villa and the tiny bananas are bruised.

'We are fully booked,' the manager says apologetically.

'It's perfect,' I tell her.

And it is. I like that it's so different from the crazy luxury we had before. The only reminder is that smell, the hotel's signature scent of sharp citrus fruits. It makes me think of Ade's face, of his self-obsessed excuses and of what I had to do. As soon as the manager leaves, I throw open the wooden doors to the terrace to let the signature perfume out. Lewis lets me shower first and I change into the cotton kimono that comes with the room. Our stuff is inaccessible till the police have finished.

After Lewis has showered, he comes into the room wearing the other kimono. He frowns. 'Not sure it's my style, exactly. Especially with the dressing and brand new bald patch.'

'It's fine.' I feel awkward, now, sitting on the bed.

'I'll sleep on the couch, Ali.'

'Don't be silly. After everything we've both been through, I want you there when I fall asleep. And when I wake up – though that might not be for days, I'm so tired.'

Lewis nods and sits down alongside me on the cool cotton sheet. 'If you're sure.'

And I remember what Meggie said, about how the two of us used to snuggle up at night when we were small, how comfortable it made us feel, how much less lonely we were when we lay close enough to hear each other's hearts.

Lewis is different. His body is different. The feelings are different. But they're every bit as intense.

The phone rings, shrill and unexpected.

I open my eyes and look into Lewis's. For a second or two I don't know where I am and I don't think he does, either. That sleep was the deepest I've had in I don't know how long . . .

It comes back. *Ade. Danny. My sister.*

Lewis keeps one arm around my shoulder as he answers the phone.

'Hello? Yes, Mr Tomlinson speaking . . . Oh, yes, we did. But that was before . . . that's fine to forfeit the full cost but . . .'

He puts his hand over the receiver. 'It's reception. The driver I booked has arrived, the one who was going to take us to the beach I thought was Soul Beach. Obviously, after what's happened I'll cancel but we can go tomorrow if you still want to?'

I check my watch. Just before nine. We've been asleep for a couple of hours, no more. If anything, I feel even worse than I did when we got back from the hospital. 'I don't think staying tomorrow is an option. Mum and Dad want me home as soon as you're fit to fly.'

Lewis nods. 'You're not looking too great yourself. Beautiful, obviously, but wrecked as well. I think you need to rest more than you need reminding of everything that's happened.'

Except this will probably be my one chance to go there. My final opportunity to make sense of the gap between the Beach and my new reality.

'Rest is for the old, Lewis. Let's go now! But are *you* well enough?'

He smiles. 'I'd go to the ends of the earth with you, Ali. In fact, I already have.' He uncovers the receiver. 'We'll be in reception in ten minutes.'

I remember something. 'We've got no clothes!'

'The hotel will rustle something up. That's what five-star is for.'

No limo this time. We're in the back of a boxy taxi which has the roughest suspension ever. Each time we go over a pothole, the car groans and we're catapulted into the front seats.

But the driver is determined to get us there some time *yesterday*. I focus on the road ahead and the people I see through the window. Anything to stop me thinking about what we might find – or *not* find – once we arrive.

After twenty minutes, we turn right through a ramshackle gateway – and suddenly we're in the middle of a traffic jam of minibuses and tourists and dogs. There's a pier to the left, with boats jostling for the best position to attract passengers. On the right, cafés and ticket booths are surrounded by long, snaking queues.

'We're not in the True Lily Hotel any more, are we, Toto?' Lewis says, and I love that he can reference the *Wizard of Oz* despite carsickness. This place freaks me out. Still, if I can do what I had to do in the last twenty-four hours, then surely I can queue for boat tickets.

'You are here,' says the driver and, as I step out, my legs feel unsteady.

I'm trying to choose the shortest queue, when a Thai boatman, tanned the same dark colour as the pier, steps forward and holds out his hand to shake Lewis's. 'Mr Tomleeson. We am your private charter. OK, OK, OK . . .'

We follow the *OK*s through the crowd until we reach a small white boat at the far end of the row. There's a gangplank linking the shingle beach to the boat and I stumble as I step onto it. Lewis steadies me.

'I am Alfred, driver is Bo. Put on life-jackets. To big island first, right, then leetle ones?' the boatman says.

Lewis doesn't have time to reply before the engine roars into life, making the boat and my bones shudder.

'Ever been in a speedboat, Ali?' Lewis shouts.

'No.'

'It's, um, speedy. So hold on tight.'

He wasn't kidding. In films, speedboats seem to slice effortlessly through the water. But this one thumps up and down so hard it feels like we're smashing into concrete, not the sea.

The shore behind us is getting smaller. I notice that alongside the busy transit port we've just left, there's a second harbour. Lots of people must live there as there are dozens of houses with pitched wooden roofs and flags fluttering in the breeze.

Except I suddenly realise: they're not houses. They're boats too.

Alfred sees me staring. 'Sea gypsies. Born, live, die, all on boats. They see tsunami coming before it happens. On land, here, so many die. But the sea gypsies survive OK.'

'This part of the world was hit?'

Alfred nods. 'Very, very bad. All Andaman Sea. Everything you see, OK? New.'

Suddenly the chaos we've just behind left feels very different to me. Hopeful, even joyful.

We're heading towards a large island up ahead. I can't wait for this relentless thumping to end, but even from this distance I can tell this isn't the Beach. The island is too big and too open to the sea, and every metre of sand seems to be crammed with parasols or sun loungers or little shacks.

Lewis looks at me. I shake my head.

The engine cuts out and we drift towards the shallow bay.

'We won't want to stay very long,' Lewis tells Alfred.

'Look at feeshes,' he says and points towards the far edge of the tiny island.

I step straight off the boat into the warm, clear water and a zebra-striped fish nudges my foot. The sun is so intense I can almost feel my skin blistering already, so I pull my hotel-branded t-shirt out of my hotel-branded bag and pull it over the life-jacket and my hotel-branded swimsuit. Even the flip-flops on my feet have the lily flower logo. Only my sunglasses are my own.

We walk ashore. It's even busier here than it was at the little port. A group of Chinese tourists have arrived just ahead of us and are handing out coins for loungers, split coconuts, Singha beers. Everywhere is bright and breezy, crowded with multi-coloured wooden signs offering massages for two hundred baht, or four different flavours of Pringles.

I try to look beyond the clutter and the people. Maybe the rocks *are* the same shape with the same merciless crags. And the sand might be the same blond-white. But then isn't most sand that colour when it's been dried by the sun?

Lewis buys us a bottle of water each and we gulp it down. The Chinese tour group are being led towards a shallow area of rock pools, so we walk behind them and as soon as my feet touch the water, I feel fish circling. I look down and there are hundreds of them this time, doing a wild rainbow dance between people's legs. It tickles and it makes me giggle too.

I catch Lewis's eye and he smiles back, but cautiously, as though he can't quite believe I've forgiven him for everything.

I lean forward in the water and kiss him briefly on the lips. His skin still smells slightly of hospital antiseptic.

Alfred is smoking a cigarette and watching us. 'OK?' he calls out.

'Very OK,' Lewis whispers. 'But the Beach isn't here, is it?'

I shake my head. 'Close, but no cigar.'

We return to the boat, dodging hawkers. Alfred hops aboard and Bo starts the engine.

I try to guess which of the smaller islands we're heading for. There must be hundreds, popping out of the pale turquoise water like floating sea creatures.

The boat judders and the horizon stretches ahead of us like a silk ribbon, shimmering on the water.

That colour, that horizon, is so familiar that I feel an ache deep inside me. A longing.

The engine cuts out again, some distance from any of the islets.

'You swim,' says Alfred. 'We have snorkels. Fleepers. Or you just,' he shrugs, 'float with life-jackets to where you like. We here all afternoon. But watch out for sea urchin. Spiny. Very painful. OK?'

Lewis looks at me. 'Snorkelling or floating?'

'Floating,' I say. But as he heads for the ladder at the side of the boat, I realise I'd forgotten Lewis's head injury. He took the dressing off before we left, but the shaved patch and the red cut look so brutal. 'I don't think you should swim.'

He laughs. 'It's a graze. I only got them to put on this big a bandage so you'd take pity on me. And it worked.'

He's already climbing down the side before I can do anything to stop him.

I follow. There's a gap between where the rope ladder ends and the sea begins. I let myself fall gently into the water, which seems to welcome me in. It's weird, being kept afloat by the life-jacket. No effort, like when you fly in a dream.

'Where to, boss?' Lewis asks.

I turn through a hundred and eighty degrees. It all looks so different from sea level, especially once I can't see the boat any more.

To our right there's an island. From this low down, all I can see is the deep green shrubbery that scours the top of the rocks, but something is drawing me in.

This is it, my body is telling me.

'This way,' I say.

As I swim, I catch glimpses of life under the clear water: rippling plants, black-needled urchins, glistening scales of fish in coral, violet and jade. Maybe one day I'll return so I can learn to dive and immerse myself in the incredible underwater world. But right now I must focus on what's above it.

I sense Lewis behind me. Watching my back. The island is further than it looks and the salt water is making the grazes on my wrists sting badly. I try to control my impatience, to swim steadily, take it easy.

But impatience wins.

Finally, I glimpse the strip of sand ahead.

Sea, shore, rocks. They look like a flag of turquoise, white-gold and black. There's no sense of scale. It could be as long as Bournemouth beach, or as short as one of the rock pools we saw on the big island.

But it looks *right*.

My heart is pumping, my skin tingling.

Don't be too disappointed if it's wrong. None of this is important any more. Not really.

I'm not fooling myself.

My shin hits something under the water. A sea urchin?

I look down and the water's so clear that I can see almost all the way down. My leg has just hit the shattered wooden foundations of a small jetty.

Lewis has caught up with me. 'Is it here?'

I blink, look up again, as the gentlest of currents seems to reel us in towards the island.

'I think it might be.'

The bay is bottoming out. I reach out with my foot and feel soft sand give slightly under my sole. I begin to walk.

A memory flashes through my brain: Tim arriving on Soul Beach, blinking at the unexpected sight in front of him. The bar, the beach huts, the Guests.

It's not like that now.

Sun-bleached flotsam litters the shoreline. Timber and metal lie in sorry piles, too big to move by hand. There must have been people living here once, but not now. Tiny green shoots push up through the sand. Saplings-to-be, to replace the ones the tsunami must have uprooted.

I wade ashore. Lewis is holding back.

It is *almost* the same, but not quite. It takes me a few seconds to work out why.

Then I get it: the landscape is the same as when Danny said goodbye to me, but the weather's what's different. Then, it was stormy. Now, despite the devastation, it's beautifully serene. I drink in the sharp blackness of the rocks, the pattern the lapping waves make against the sand. To the left as I face the island, I see the tiny archway that leads to a marble-smooth piece of rock, where Danny and I found just enough privacy to be ourselves; to fall in love.

The Alice who did that seems very different from the Alice I am now. Naïve, I suppose. To think that love was all happiness, sunshine, butterflies. I thought love could work miracles.

Lewis takes my hand.

I look up into his face. Maybe I was right about love. How else could I have found my sister, found Lewis, found this place?

'This is it,' I tell him. 'You found the Beach.'

'*We* found it,' he corrects me. 'What a team!'

I smile. His hand in mine feels warmer than the sun.

I think he'll be good for you, you know.

My wild, mercurial sister wasn't right about everything, not by a long way. But I'm pretty sure she's right about this.

'It's exactly what I thought paradise would look like,' Lewis murmurs.

I turn and kiss him very softly on the lips, before whispering,

'And *this* is how paradise feels.'